Athena

the Newport Ladies Book Club

Athena

a novel

HEATHER B. MOORE

Covenant Communications, Inc.

Cover images: *Life's a Beach* © Alex Bramwell, iStockphotography.com; and *Umbrella Icon* © O-che, iStockphotography.com

Cover design copyright © 2012 by Covenant Communications, Inc.

Published by Covenant Communications, Inc.
American Fork, Utah

Printed in the United States of America
First Printing: November 2012

18 17 16 15 14 13 12   10 9 8 7 6 5 4 3 2 1

ISBN: 978-1-60861-944-3

To my daughter, Dana,
whose love for reading nearly matches my own.

Acknowledgments

IN WINTER 2009, ANNETTE LYON, Josi Kilpack, Julie Wright, and I met over an early-morning breakfast of omelets and hot chocolate to discuss writing a series together. Eighteen months later, our first ideas of characters matured into full stories of women who develop strong friendships with other very different women.

I'd like to first thank Annette, Josi, and Julie for their friendship and, second, for their dedication to making this series possible.

Writing about a Greek Orthodox woman may or may not have stemmed from the first time I met my grandfather-in-law, Jon Brown, a Greek Orthodox. We got to know each other over feta cheese and crackers. I know that if he were still alive, I might be able to persuade him to read this book.

Others on the road to publication who need to be thanked include Lu Ann Staheli, Sarah Eden, Michele Holmes, Jeff Savage, and Rob Wells—all members of my critique group whom I look up to in many ways.

A huge thanks to my supportive publisher, Covenant Communications, and the dedicated staff, including my editor, Samantha Van Walraven; managing editor, Kathy Jenkins Gordon; and cover designer, Christina Marcano.

And as always, outside the arena of writing, I do have another life—filled with family members and friends whom I greatly appreciate because of all of their love and support.

Other books in this series

DAISY—by Josi S. Kilpack
PAIGE—by Annette Lyon
OLIVIA—by Julie Wright

For ideas on hosting your own book club, suggestions for books, and recipes, or information on how you can guest-write about your book club on our blog, please visit us at http://thenewportladiesbookclub.blogspot.com.

Chapter 1

"THREE! FOUR! FIVE! SIX!" MY class chanted in unison, but it sounded more like we were all just grunting.

I smiled and delivered a sharp jab into the plastic dummy in front of me, even though sweat poured off me like the overflowing banks of the Santa Ana River. The kickboxing instructor took my smile as a sign to increase her intensity. I stifled a groan and forced myself to keep moving. Three months of this class, and I finally felt like I could keep up. Who said that Athena Di Jasper couldn't rise to the challenge?

The workout slowed, and we started the cooldown. My favorite part. The sense of accomplishment zinged through me. I felt strong, relaxed, and in control. The perfect end to a productive day. I'd even skillfully avoided my mother's advice about men earlier when she'd called me on the way to the gym. Most single men my age were either divorced with a couple of whiney latchkey kids or had some complicated issues that prevented them from maintaining a decent relationship or were gay. Around Newport Beach, the margin of normalcy for men in my age bracket had shrunk in the last few years. It only took me until my thirtieth birthday to realize that. Two years ago.

Wiping my face with the club towel, I made my way to the locker room, waving good-bye to a few of the women. I hesitated at my locker, debating whether it was more disgusting to take a shower in the commune stall or to drive home in my sweat-drenched clothes. Out of habit, I reached for my cell phone in my gym bag while trying to decide.

Three texts.

Everyone knew the best way to get my response was to text. Well, everyone but my mother. She insisted on calling—every day. My dad remained silent for the most part, in his own world of fading memories.

Text 1: *Put it on your calendar*
Put what on my calendar?
I scrolled to the third text and read in the order they were sent—all from Karl: *In town, can I see you tonight?*
Text 2: *8:30? I'll pick you up.*
Now *Put it on your calendar* made better sense. Karl liked to tease me about my inability to make one move without scheduling it on my calendar. Speaking of calendars, I switched to my phone calendar and saw two things—first, it was 8:05 p.m., and second, I had nothing scheduled that made a good excuse not to see my boyfriend. Yes, he was my boyfriend but not in the traditional sense of "we date three to six months then move to the next level."

He was just a guy I had dinner with when he came into town.

And my mother hated him.

"He's the only man you've dated for the past year. Are you or are you not going to get married?" A question Mother often asked when she used up her other interfering questions.

Karl was a nice guy. Okay. He was quite good-looking, charming in that rugged, younger-version-of-Clint-Eastwood way, and could probably date a lot more interesting and romantic women—but for some reason, he liked *me*. Probably because I was safe. I didn't make demands. I left him at the doorstep with nothing more than a kiss good night—a very chaste kiss, by the way. Surprisingly, he hadn't complained, or else I'd have reduced our twelve months of dating to a week. I remained mysterious. I was low-maintenance. I didn't complain when he was gone for weeks at a time on assignment. I didn't mind if he forgot to call (which hadn't happened yet). And . . . I paid him.

He was one of my photographers for the online magazine I launched ten years ago during my last semester at UCLA. A senior project that took off—or backfired, depending on how one looked at it—*Newport Travel* had brought in a steady income since then, even if it hadn't exploded into the vision I had for it when I started. At least my mother approved of the income.

What she didn't approve of was a man who traveled around the country snapping photos and then came back home for a few days and dated her daughter.

"You need someone who will settle down, be a family man, and hold down a job that lets him afford a place of his own. Maybe you should date a Greek."

Karl, who lived in a beachside apartment with three other men, didn't rank high on my mother's list of potential husband material. At least he didn't live with his parents like my last boyfriend, who *was* Greek (and dating him only lasted about eight days). But I couldn't always choose Greek, even though I was technically one myself, so I tried to keep my options open as much as possible.

Although that was getting harder and harder at the age of thirty-two.

So with no other option, and half dreading another night at home alone, I texted back. *8:45?*

Chapter 2

KARL KNOCKED—MORE LIKE RAPPED—a tune on the door. *He must be in a good mood*, I thought as I spritzed one more squirt of Japanese Gardenia onto my neck. I'd taken a two-minute shower, and I hoped the spritz would make up for the rest. As I walked to the door, I pushed my short hair behind my ears out of habit and glanced in the hallway mirror. The red-gold highlights lightened my nearly black hair. But no matter what style or haircut I chose, the hair went behind the ears.

Swinging open the door, I barely had time to appraise the long-absent Karl before he grabbed me into a bear hug. It was with more enthusiasm than usual, and as he squeezed the life out of me, I tried to remember exactly how long he'd been gone. Less than a month, I was sure. So why the overenthusiastic hug?

Finally, after I released a loud gasp, he let go, laughing. Before I could ask him if he'd found a new miracle fruit in the jungles of the Amazon that significantly altered moods, he planted a full kiss on my lips. For a second, I froze. Then I responded, cautious yet a little pleased. My stomach actually flipped, or maybe flopped, but it was definitely movement.

The kiss grew deeper and then too intense—intense because of the aforementioned tame kisses we'd shared previously—so I became a little self-conscious. It seemed he was pouring a bit more than a greeting through his lips. My heart sped up, and my cheeks burned, which bothered me even more.

Athena Di Jasper had only blushed once in her life. And this moment wasn't going to be the second time.

I pushed against his shoulder, gently, and Karl released me, but his face remained close, and his eyes had a lazy-slash-intent look in them.

"Are you drunk?" I asked, hoping my voice didn't sound too breathless or like the kiss had affected me in any way.

"Not yet," he said, leaning in for seconds.

I pushed harder this time. "You've been . . . drinking? Really?"

"I don't drink anymore," Karl said. "You know that." His eyes glimmered though. "It's great to see you, Athena."

"Did you have a near-death experience or something?"

He laughed, pulling me against him. This time with no kissing, so I relaxed into the hug, grateful it wasn't quite as tight as before and extremely grateful I'd added that extra spritz of perfume.

"Okay. Dinner?" I said.

"Mmmm." Karl released me, his hands lingering at my waist. This was not the Karl I remembered.

"Athena, you look great."

I guess he knew who I was after all. "You too." It was the truth. Now that he was in front of me instead of practically on top of me, I found myself appreciating his healthy tan. He wore a dark blue T-shirt that nearly matched his eyes in a noncliché fashion. His sandy-blond hair was shorter than usual, and his normally scruffy chin was shaved, making me wonder if he'd cleaned up especially for me.

I took a tiny step back. "Let me just lock the door."

He waited, remaining close, then took my hand once I'd pulled the door closed and tested the knob.

He continued to hold my hand in the car and even when we found our seats at the restaurant about a mile down the Pacific Coast Highway. The Thai place was small and nearly empty. In Newport, 9:00 was late for dinner.

We ordered, and Karl caught me up on the Amazon jungle trip—no, I wasn't being flippant earlier; he really had gone to the Amazon. And no, he didn't find any miracle fruit or nearly die at the hands of a rabid howler monkey. "I have incredible pictures," he said, his blue eyes almost black in the dim light. "I'll send them over in the morning." He paused, his hand on mine again. "Or maybe I'll come to your place so I can tell you about them while you look them over."

A small bell went off somewhere—in my head—but I don't believe in proverbial bells, so I ignored it. "Sure, after eleven in the morning though. I have to finish editing the feature article first thing in the morning, then I have a conference call at ten with a potential investor."

He arched a brow, his fingers absently stroking mine. "Does that mean I get a raise?"

"Hardly." I laughed.

The waitress appeared with two bowls of steaming soup.

"Hot one?" she asked.

"Right here," Karl said, releasing my hand and moving back to allow her to put the soup down.

"I have the mild one," I said. No matter how "mild" I requested, after only a few bites of anything with curry in it, my tongue was too numb to taste much else.

After a couple minutes of eating in silence, and by the time my tongue had undergone the stages of yummy, warm, hot, burning, numb, and no taste at all, Karl said, "You should hire another editor."

"It's too much work."

"Exactly."

"No, I mean I don't have time to post on job websites, read résumés, interview, and then hope the new one doesn't leave over a misplaced modifier disagreement."

Karl lowered the spoon that was midway to his mouth. "Misplaced modifier? Are you serious? Is that what happened to the last one?"

I waved my hand, having given up on the soup already. "That and a few other things. We just didn't mesh, and she didn't like taking direction."

He shook his head and took another spoonful. I sipped my ice water gratefully, hoping I could taste again by morning. "So until I magically have extra hours in the day, I'm the editor."

"Athena—you're thinking completely backward. If you just took a couple of hours tomorrow and put the effort into finding an editor, you'd have much more time in the long run."

I smiled, indulging him. I noticed he was almost done with his soup, which meant in about twenty minutes, I could be safely in my condo catching up on e-mails. Several had come through my phone during dinner, ones that required more than a quick reply. I also—

"Are you listening?"

I snapped my eyes back to Karl's. "What?"

"I said that I really want to spend more time together."

A small knot of panic tightened in my chest. "We do spend a lot of time together."

"More than once a month."

The knot of panic traveled to my stomach. "You're only around once a month."

Karl's eyes seemed to darken as he pushed his bowl away. "I'm staying around here for a while. *The Chronicle* wants me to be the key photographer for the upcoming election."

"But you hate that kind of stuff. Your talents are—"

"I know, but I thought it'd be nice to be grounded for a change." His hand was on mine again. "Traveling the world isn't like it used to be. Over the last few weeks, I've missed being home more than ever." His voice was lower. "And I've missed you . . ."

Oh no. Don't say it. Moisture broke out under my arms, and I fought to breathe normally.

"I want us to try dating like a normal couple." His smile was hopeful.

I let out a breath. *Okay. That might be all right.* But I couldn't smile back, couldn't meet his pleading, sincere gaze. It was like a cloud had formed between us and I couldn't quite see through the haze. "*Haven't* we been dating?" I asked.

"I want to see you every day, not once a month," Karl said; his voice had an exasperated edge to it.

Once a month had been perfect. *For me.* "I . . . I work a lot of hours. But I'm sure at least once a week we could—"

"Once a *week?*" His fingers were no longer stroking mine. He stared at me.

I looked down at the table; the haze was back.

His hand released mine, and I felt cold all of a sudden. When I looked up, his arms were folded across his chest, and he was focusing on something behind me.

"I don't want to promise time I can't give." Even as I spoke, I was aware how weak my argument sounded. "I don't want to let you down."

His gaze came back to mine, but the warmth was gone out of his eyes. "You just did."

My stomach twisted into a full-blown knot, bordering on nausea. This was not the carefree Karl I knew, the one who came in and out of my life, bringing moments of happiness but never the commitment I feared.

"Okay, can we just try once a week for now," I said, my voice shaky. I'd do anything to avoid what was becoming a public confrontation. Well, anything but give Karl the wrong impression of what I wanted in a relationship right now.

"Try?" Karl said with dangerously increasing volume. He shook his head. "It's not supposed to be an experiment. Relationships should be more spontaneous."

Exactly! I wanted to shout. That's what I loved about our relationship—it was the ultimate in spontaneity, and now he didn't want that?

He picked up the bill the waitress had unobtrusively left at the corner of the table sometime during my haze moments.

"Everything with you is scheduled, Athena," he said in a clipped voice. "When's the last time you did something without planning or checking your calendar?" His gaze bore into me. "When's the last time you turned off the computer and watched a sitcom? Or sat down and read a book?"

I opened my mouth to reply, but honestly, I couldn't think of an answer to any of his questions. I was sure there were plenty of unscheduled things I did every day. I just couldn't come up with any under so much pressure.

Karl pulled out a twenty and put it on top of the bill. Then he stood.

I followed him out of the restaurant. I was sure there were several very black pairs of eyes that watched us leave, having heard everything. I hurried after Karl, who decided to use his long legs to their fullest capacity to reach the car. The brief ride back to my place was dead silent. As he turned onto my street, I felt like I would burst from the tension between us. I had to defend myself somehow. The night couldn't end like this. Until just a few minutes ago, he'd been my idea of the perfect boyfriend—no serious commitment, lots of breathing room.

"I read all the time," I said.

Karl's eyes stayed on the road. "Magazines—*competitor's* magazines."

"No, I read other things." My mind whirled, trying to come up with something— anything I'd read recently besides online articles.

"When's the last time you watched a sitcom?"

My thoughts raced. *Aha.* "I watched *I Love Lucy* reruns this summer."

"When you had the flu." His voice was deadpan. "Do you ever watch anything regularly, other than the news?"

I had no answer.

"That's what I thought." He gave me no mercy. "Name one novel you've read in the past year," he demanded, his voice tight as he pulled into the parking lot.

"Novels? I haven't read those since English lit in college. Who has the time?" Heat and indignation coursed through me. Who was he comparing me to? "What novels have *you* read lately?"

"I just finished *The Hotel on the Corner of Bitter and Sweet*."

"Oh," I said, chagrined. I'd read a review—a bestseller from a debut author. "Was it good?"

Karl laughed, but it was harsh sounding. "Go read the book."

I swallowed, my throat feeling tight. Chances of reading the actual book were minimal with my schedule. He knew I'd never do it.

Karl put the car in park and sat there with the engine idling. "Look, Athena, you're a great woman. But I can't want more than you do. I don't work that way."

I looked at him, risking that he'd see the moisture in my eyes, but he kept his gaze forward. I waited for him to look at me. *Just tell him you want to date—seriously—and if it doesn't work, it doesn't work, but at least you tried.* Those words wouldn't come, no matter how I tried to talk myself into it. After a long moment of silence, I said, "I'm sorry."

Then slowly, half hoping he'd stop me, grab me into a hug, even kiss me again, I climbed out of the car. I hesitated for a second, giving him one more chance, giving *myself* one more chance to say the words, but almost involuntarily, I stepped away from the car and shut the door.

Chapter 3

MY EYES HAD JUST CLOSED when the mocking bird started up outside. Usually, I was well on my way through the morning when it opened its mouth to sing. But as luck—or fate—would have it, I'd just settled into a deep sleep after a night of constant battling. It was as if the mocking bird jabbered, "Stu-pid. Stu-pid."

Karl was great. Handsome. Kind. Affectionate. Charming. Funny. I didn't know what was wrong with me. I turned in my bed, pulling my pillow and its 800-thread-count Egyptian cotton pillowcase over my head. If there was one thing I was picky about, it was thread count. But even the almost-silk feel wasn't soothing. I'd been a brat last night—uncaring and unfeeling. Karl had put his heart out there, and I'd trampled it. No. Even worse, I had ignored it, turned it down, not even shown interest. And why? Because I had a job that never ended. I was always working, and yes, that was the price of owning my own business, but did I have to be so involved in every little step? Couldn't I trust an editor? Couldn't I let someone else take the reins once in a while?

It wasn't that I loved to work—I thrived on it, yes, but I did value other aspects of life. At least I thought I did until now.

My cell phone rang, and for once, I didn't care who was calling. Mother (she would call back). Rich investor (I would call back). Best friend (don't have one). Karl! I reached for the phone and blinked against the morning light to see the screen.

Unknown caller.

I plopped back into bed with a groan.

Then unexpectedly, tears pricked my eyes.

I smooshed the pillow against my face again, willing the burning to go away. *I'm not in love with him*, I told myself. *He's been great, but isn't the fact that I couldn't make a better effort an indicator that I'm not in love with him?*

The cell on the nightstand buzzed with a text message alert—probably from whomever's call I hadn't answered. I took a deep breath and sat up. Reading the text message quickly pulled me out of my self-pity mire. It was from the investor. *Need to change call to 9.*

I looked at the clock. 7:12. Good. I had time for a short run to clear my head for the meeting. Wallowing over Karl would not put me in the frame of mind I needed to be in.

I texted back: *Sounds great.*

I pulled on my running clothes, and my mind focused more and more on the upcoming call. It didn't take long to refocus on work—my salvation in more than one case. Work was like therapy for me, as I supposed going on a vacation or reading a book was for other people. When I was immersed in my business, the Karls faded into the background, Mother's persistent voice went mute, and I could almost believe my father wasn't suffering from Alzheimer's. I controlled my own destiny, and I loved that.

The California weather was deliciously predictable. The rising sun promised a hot day, but for now, the air felt salty and cool. I walked through the parking lot, warming up, then out of habit started to the left to follow my usual route. I paused. Turning, I decided to prove I *could* do something different, and it started now. I went right then turned left at the next block, away from the ocean.

I ran past the usual beach-style houses that were small and crammed together. The farther I moved from the ocean, the more grass appeared on the lawns. At the next corner, I turned into a short strip mall and sprinted across the parking lot. The smell of egg burritos at the Carl's Jr. replaced the salty sea air. My stomach grumbled, and I slowed to a walk, briefly considering buying a wrap to go, but it would be greasy and cold by the time I reached home. I was starting to sweat, so I moved onto the shaded sidewalk and slowed to a walk as I passed the stores. A man carrying a large box crossed in front of me, and I let him pass.

He flashed a smile then stopped at the nearest door, balancing the box with one hand while holding keys in the other.

The box slipped from his hand.

I moved to catch the box, but it was too late. The box smacked the pavement before I could reach it.

"Whoops," we both said at once.

I laughed then backed up a step. There was no telling what my breath was like.

The thirty-something man smiled absentmindedly, as if he was only barely aware of my giant leap to rescue his box. Apparently, there was nothing very valuable in it since there had been no sound of breaking glass. He unlocked the door then propped it open before reaching for the box.

I'd just started moving away when he straightened and said, "Are you coming in?"

I met his gaze. He was definitely noticing me now, or was I just more self-conscious sans make-up?

"No, I'm out for a run," I said, motioning to my attire as if he wouldn't have noticed the obvious signs without my demonstration, though I hadn't actually been running when we crossed paths.

He nodded, his eyes staying on me. Then he leaned against the door-frame as if he had all the time in the world. "Read any good books lately?" If my mouth wasn't dry before, it was now. Was this guy Jiminy Cricket? Or a friend of Karl's who knew all about our fight last night?

How random could this be? Then I looked at the sign on the shop: *Grey's Used & Rare Books.*

"You . . . sell books?" Now I felt embarrassed. This wasn't a con man sent by Karl to torture me. He worked at a bookstore, and like a good employee, he was making his first sale of the day.

I folded my arms and tilted my head, waiting. Not that I was interested in buying a book, but how long had it been since I'd even been inside a bookstore, used *or* rare? Although I didn't have time to read a book, maybe buying one would mean something to Karl, assuming I'd get the chance to tell him. I could mention it casually in the next e-mail exchange. He *was* still one of my freelancers.

The man grinned, and it was hard not to smile back. He had one of those contagious smiles, and the combination of his brown eyes and his slightly messy hair falling across his forehead made me feel self-conscious. He took a couple of steps forward, holding out his hand. "I'm Grey."

I took his hand, trying not to wince at the sweatiness of mine that he was sure to notice. "Athena."

Something flickered in his eyes, but he'd let go of my hand and stepped back too quickly for me to be sure. Maybe he'd caught a whiff of my unshowered self.

"What do you like to read?" he asked.

Did he always make small talk with sweaty joggers who just happened by at 7:30 in the morning? I peered to the side to confirm that the other stores weren't open yet. Only Carl's Jr. seemed to be operating this early in the morning.

"I read magazines, mostly."

He nodded as if he understood perfectly, and I thought his eyes glazed over a little, but maybe it was just the increasing vividness of the sun coming up behind me.

"Not much time for reading since college," I said with a short laugh.

He smiled but didn't seem to accept my excuse. Then he hefted the box up on his hip. "Got a new shipment in. You might find something you like."

I slid my cell phone from the pocket of my running shorts and assessed the time: 7:45. "Are you open already?"

"Not 'til 9:00, but I didn't sleep much last night, so I decided to get an early start." He was already turning away.

Me neither.

"Come on in," he called over his shoulder.

I watched him walk into the store and wondered if he was a creep. *Would he still be in business if he were?* He said his name was Grey, so that meant he owned the place, which probably indicated he wasn't a serial killer on the side. But then again, even serial killers likely had a day job. Another car pulled up in the parking lot, and three tiny Vietnamese women hopped out. I stood for a few seconds, watching them enter a nail salon two doors down. If the women he likely saw every day were alive and well, that probably meant Grey wasn't killing anyone, at least in this neighborhood. Besides, I was *spontaneous*, right?

I had stopped sweating, and I decided I could stay at the front of the store and browse for a few minutes. I'd cut my run short and head straight back afterward. It wasn't like I needed to really prepare for the conference call. I knew my business plan inside and out and had already decided the maximum ownership I was willing to part with.

The propped door beckoned to me, so I stepped into the cool interior. The lights were on, and two fans already buzzed. Bookshelves lined the walls from floor to ceiling, and tables stationed throughout the store were neatly stacked with books.

Grey stood at the register counter, pulling the books out of the box. He didn't even acknowledge me as I entered. Just as well. I hoped to find a book quickly then get out.

I turned over a book on the table closest to the door, staring at it in confusion for a second before I realized it was French. Relieved I wasn't losing my mind, I put it back and picked up another book—this time in English. *The Witch of Blackbird Pond.*

"A classic," Grey said.

I looked up, startled to see him standing right next to me. I hadn't heard him walking toward me. I fought the urge to back away, knowing I smelled and the fans weren't helping.

"Did you read it in middle school?" he asked.

I noticed that he smelled quite nice, not like he'd doused cologne or anything but like he was freshly showered and shaved. I avoided his gaze. "Yes, but the cover was different."

"It's been printed in dozens of languages and probably has more covers than that."

I leafed through it, wondering how long he'd stand there. He was taller than I'd realized at first, and I could easily wear heels and not be eye level, not that I was making any type of notation.

"I've got her other books too and a first edition of that one if you're interested," he said in that mellow voice of his.

Perhaps I was interested. I remembered staying up late when I was about twelve years old reading it. It looked like a quick read, and if I read it again, I could prove to Karl that I wasn't all about the schedule. "How much?"

When Grey didn't respond, I looked up. He grinned when we made eye contact, as if he'd been waiting for me to look at him. "How about I give it to you?"

I frowned. This was getting creepy. I waited for the warning signals to go off in my head, but there was nothing. In fact, I felt relaxed—more so now than I had in a long time—standing in a bookstore with a stranger.

"Why would you give it to me? Don't you have to stay in business?"

"Yes, but I also value my sanity."

He looked perfectly serious, so I asked, "Does the witch in the book haunt you or something?"

"No." He leaned across the stacked books, suddenly close to me. "But Mrs. Crenshaw does."

Before I could ask if Mrs. Crenshaw was a character I'd forgotten about in the book, he straightened, walked to the door, and pulled it shut.

I let out a small sigh of relief when he didn't lock it. I could still escape. He crossed to the register and held up a piece of blue paper. "If you'll call this woman and agree to join her book club"—he looked down at the paper—"the Newport Ladies Book Club, I'll give you my first edition copy of *The Witch of Blackbird Pond*, which is in better condition than one listed on Ebay with a high bid of $125."

I stared at him, stunned, not only about the bidding price of the book but also about the fact that I was actually considering the book club. It was a much bigger step than just reading a book. Karl would be impressed, I was certain.

"How often do they meet?" I asked.

Grey was at my side in a few strides, handing over the flier. "Once a month." Hope shone in his eyes, and it was hard to think of letting him down. "If you join the club, I can tell her I sent a referral, and she'll leave me in peace."

I looked at the flier, not really seeing the description of the book club but, more importantly, trying to avoid Grey's earnest gaze that made me feel sweaty again.

"I—I'll look into it." I knew I'd spent too much time in the store already, and normally, my anxiety would be sky-high from staying away from work for so long. But for some reason, I wanted to stay. So for that exact reason, I turned from Grey. "Thanks. I'll let you know."

"I'll be here. With the book."

I cast a fleeting glance at him as I pushed through the door. He wore a half smile, watching me calmly as if he had no worries that I'd be back.

Chapter 4

Looking for serious readers to join the Newport Ladies Book Club.
Women only! Eating and good conversation!
Space limited. Call Ruby Crenshaw ASAP.

I GLANCED AT THE DETAILS as I jogged back home, feeling the rising sun warm my back. I'd never really considered myself a serious *book* reader, but I'd read plenty in high school, even if I couldn't remember most of them.

After a cool shower and a review of my business plan once again, I waited for the investor to call. At 9:02, my phone rang. Jeffrey Adair. Practically right on time.

"Athena Di Jasper here," I answered, straightening my notes on my polished black desk.

I'd known the investor was from Texas, but it was obvious from the first sentence. His slow drawl took a few minutes to get used to but was no indicator of his fast business style. Within twenty minutes, we'd made a verbal agreement. Twenty percent for a $50,000 investment. I felt the trade-off was good.

Almost as if on cue, and before I could really digest that I had an actual investor for my company and that I didn't need to take out a bank loan, my mother called.

"How's Dad?" I asked before she could dive in. One thing about my mother was that she was easily distracted. If I could just keep the conversation off of me and my dating life, which had just been officially downgraded to "nonexistent," the day would go better for both of us.

"Dad's quiet today. We have an eye appointment this afternoon to renew his prescription."

A minijolt went through my heart as I pictured one of my visits home from college to find my father sitting on the back veranda reading a thick book, his reading glasses nestled against his nose. I hadn't seen him read anything thicker than a magazine for months.

"When's his next appointment with his regular doctor?" I asked, rising from my desk and walking to the office room window that overlooked the condo pool.

"Tomorrow," my mother said. "Do you want to have dinner with us tonight, Bee?"

"Uh . . ." The use of my childhood nickname got on my nerves. No matter how many times I told my mother to call me by my good *orthodox* name, she didn't seem to hear me.

"Jackie's coming with her kids. You know how they love their auntie."

My older sister and her brood of three kids should have been enough to keep my mother grandkid happy, but a Greek mother is never satisfied with just one daughter married. Jackie was only two years older than me, and it seemed with every year, she outshined me with the accomplishments of this kid or that kid. To be fair, they were adorable. Andy was eight years old, Maria was six, and cherubic Eleni, four.

I was about to offer the excuse of a date with Karl but then remembered . . .

"What time?" I asked, turning from the view of the pool I hadn't used in months.

The pleasure in my mother's voice oozed through the phone, making me feel guilty. "Six sharp. You know how your father needs to stay on a schedule."

I smiled painfully. My father didn't even keep track of the time anymore, but by having the meal at 6:00, my mother could be assured of everyone sticking around for a couple of hours.

My smile stilled when my mother added, "Andrew is bringing a friend from his office."

I stopped listening as my hands went numb. She was doing it again, and this time she had my brother-in-law involved. How my mother talked Andrew into bringing an available bachelor to a family dinner wasn't hard to guess. It seemed they all plotted behind my back. I should have been used to it, but I kept waiting for them to accept my life the way it was. When would they stop interfering? *Never.*

When my mother finally realized I wasn't responding to her high praises about Damion-Somebody, she said, "He's a nice Greek man, Athena. There aren't many of those left." She let out an exaggerated sigh.

"Mother," I interrupted her pout, since I should have been the one pouting anyway, "I've got another call coming in. I'll see you tonight."

Before she could complain that she hadn't heard the call-waiting click, I hung up. I was locked into the dinner for sure. It would be frightfully rude to back out on poor Damion, and I hoped he'd be a good sport about it and realize he'd been caught in my mother's snare.

I returned to my desk just as an e-mail popped into my inbox, and my breath stalled. *Karl.* I clicked on the message, still holding my breath, scanning for an apology, an invitation to dinner, anything. But there was no personal message. Just "FYI" and a zip file of attached pictures. I let out the breath I'd been holding and closed the e-mail before I was tempted to respond with a friendly question to break the ice.

What would happen if I invited Karl over to talk? My stomach tightened at the thought of giving him false hope. He'd told me what he wanted. What did *I* want? My gaze slid to the window, the leafy greenery, the clear sky of Newport, and I still didn't know—though I did know I'd be in my office until 5:30 at least, working as always and missing the life outside. A life I felt more and more reluctant to take a part in.

I had to make a change, and I knew it. My mother reminded me of that every day, and Karl had put it in neon lights last night.

I reached for the flier from the bookstore and reread the words. Joining a book club would be a start, and I could be a serious reader. I didn't know if I'd provide good conversation, but if I read the book of the month, I could certainly contribute.

I'm ready for a change, I thought as I dialed Ruby's number.

Two minutes later, I hung up, wondering what I'd gotten myself into. After clarifying that my social life wasn't too busy to commit to a Saturday evening book club once a month, Ruby seemed pleased but only after she'd sufficiently grilled me about my age, marital status, and favorite kinds of books.

I had stumbled but hoped I'd come across as an intelligent reader.

Ten seconds later, I'd scheduled the book club and Ruby's address into my BlackBerry. Thirty seconds after that, I was closing down my computer.

My hand hovered above the keyboard. It was only 11:00 a.m., and I was leaving the office?

Before I could talk myself out of it, I grabbed my keys and headed out of the condo into the sunlight. Energy pulsed through me as I thought about running such a spontaneous errand.

It wasn't until I pulled into the parking lot of *Grey's Used & Rare Books* that I started to doubt myself. I glanced at the time again, thinking that maybe he was gone. Surely he had employees that filled different shifts, but by the look of the parking lot, I wondered how much business the bookstore actually received. A jumble of cars filled the area in front of the nail spa, but the rest of the parking lot was sparse.

I suddenly felt nervous and checked my hair and make-up in the mirror. I looked much better than the first time he'd seen me—at least I wasn't wearing sweaty exercise clothing. Before I could change my mind, I forced myself out of the car and walked to the bookstore.

As I opened the door, the cool air rushed out. Grey was at the register ringing up a stack of books for an older woman. He looked very businesslike, wearing a pair of glasses—I guessed them to be for reading, since he wasn't wearing them when I first met him. I started browsing, staying busy until the woman left. Once she was out the door, I turned to face Grey.

"Well?" he asked, taking off the glasses and leaning against the counter.

I wondered if he was older than my previous estimate of midthirties, since he seemed to need reading glasses. Forcing myself to look away, I picked up a book and turned it over. "I called Ruby Crenshaw."

"And?"

I heard the smile in his voice. "I'll be attending her book club on Saturday."

"Nice!"

I looked up as he came out from behind the counter, holding a book wrapped in plastic.

We sort of gravitated toward each other. "This first edition is yours," he said.

I shook my head. "Thanks, but I'd rather you help me with something else."

"Anything."

For some reason, I felt there was real sincerity behind his words.

I hesitated for just a second, wondering if I was ready to take the plunge. I'd already committed to Ruby, so I needed to be prepared. "I thought you could find me something I could read before the book club. Ruby said to bring recommendations, and I haven't read a book in a while."

His dark eyes studied me. "Sure. I can show you a couple of books. Or would you rather take a list home?"

"Maybe both."

He laughed, and my heart seemed to expand.

"Mrs. Crenshaw can be a bit intimidating—but she's a nice lady," he said. "Wait 'til you meet her."

"I'll give you a full report," I said before I realized what that might entail.

He paused as if he were a little surprised as well. "I'd like that."

Before I could retract anything, he started combing through a stack of books, talking about an author named Barbara Kingsolver. I knew she was a bestseller, and I'd probably read some reviews on her work.

"Here," he said, holding up a thick brownish-yellow book. "A great book for discussion."

I took the paperback and read aloud, "*The Poisonwood Bible.*"

"An excellent study of human nature," he said in a serious tone, but amusement flashed in his eyes.

"It's pretty hefty," I said. "Is it good for a book club?"

"It's very popular from what I've heard," he said, his gaze casually looking me up and down. "You can read a few chapters and decide for yourself."

"Maybe I will."

A short nod, and he was on to the next stack, sorting through more books.

Thirty minutes later, I was out the door with four books in my arms and a list of other "must-reads," according to Grey. Jumping into my car, I felt as if I had armed myself somehow for whatever might happen at the family dinner that night. I was doing something besides working. I pulled out my cell and was about to text the news to Karl when I remembered we weren't talking, or texting. So for now, Grey and the book club would be my secret.

* * *

Six came way too soon, and as I pulled up at my parents' home, I saw that I was the last to arrive—unusual since I was ten minutes early. The dark blue sedan parked at the curb told me that even Andrew's friend was here. Great. Greek-Damion was a nice man with a nice car, a combination that would seal the deal for my mother.

Inside, Jackie and my mother kissed me in the entryway, gigantic smiles on their faces. My sister and mother could be twins. Each had perfectly coiffed hair, necklaces that matched their earrings, and dark red lipstick that set off their olive coloring. My mother still wore her red apron, which meant that there were finishing touches to be done in the kitchen.

The kids were nowhere to be seen; apparently they'd been shooed to the backyard for the *big* introduction. I didn't have to wait long. My mother guided me into the living room, where my father sat in his shroud of silence. Andrew and his friend stood by the window. Had they watched me walk up to the door?

When the men saw us, Andrew crossed to me and kissed my cheek, then turned to his friend.

"Damion, I'd like you to meet Jackie's sister, Athena."

I hated formal introductions laden with expectation. Why couldn't a man and a woman meet under natural circumstances (not that I was thinking of Grey at this moment)?

Right away, I saw that Damion was the dictionary definition of "nice." But that was the death of men in my opinion. Behind that niceness was blandness. His hairline had significantly receded—which I certainly didn't hold against him, but it reminded me all too much of my own age and how I would be considered a spinster in another era. Well, even in this era.

His voice was deep as he said, "Great to meet you, Athena," which was followed by a ready laugh, a bit too loud. He was also an inch shorter than me.

It's said that the longer a woman (or a man) waits to get married, the more impossible their expectations become. What did height really matter? An inch here or there; I could adjust and wear flats the rest of my life. He did have nice greenish-hazel eyes, and his fingernails were well cared for. Okay. When I had to drag out an attribute like clean nails, I knew I should just admit it. There was no attraction here. No matter how good of a job he had or how available he was or how much my mother seemed to love him or how he was already good friends with my brother-in-law.

"Nice to meet you as well," I said, delivering my most generous smile to Damion, when in reality, I wanted to smack Andrew—because he was the closest-standing relative. I immediately felt guilty. Andrew was just being the concerned brother-in-law, no doubt encouraged by my sister and mother. I didn't know a single soul who stood a chance against those two women when they put their minds together.

Please let Damion realize I'm not his type and we'd be terrible together, I thought through dinner as Jackie and Mother centered the conversation on my apparently fabulous accomplishments. All that lacked in making me truly perfect was a wedding ring.

He asked me the usual questions about my work and hobbies (which, of course, were work related). And my answers in reply to Damion's questions that were meant to be perfectly normal and serious made him boom out with laughter. My mother's laughter invariably followed, and at one point, I thought I saw her dab at a tear in the corner of her eye. Perhaps I had turned Karl away a bit too soon.

In an effort to steer the conversation away from myself, I turned to Jackie's kids. "Andy, what are you going to be for Halloween this year?" His eyes rounded with excitement, but before he could talk, Maria and Eleni jumped in.

"I'm going to be a Barbie princess fairy," Maria said.

"Me too!" Eleni shouted.

Damion laughed at Maria, who glowered at her sister. I smiled and looked back to Andy. "What about you?"

"Jack Sparrow," he said, lifting his chin.

"You'll make a fine Jack," Damion said.

"Mom said I could be the Barbie princess fairy first." Maria's attention was still on Eleni. "You can't copy me."

"Maybe you can be different colors of fairies," I said.

Maria looked pleased with that idea, and Jackie threw me a grateful glance.

A few minutes later, my nephew and nieces were excused from the table—before I was ready to let go of their distraction. But not before Jackie pointed out at least three times that Damion was wonderful with kids. I didn't exactly agree; his laughter seemed to scare Eleni a little.

I was more than happy to escape to the kitchen for cleanup following dinner. I took several deep breaths then tied on one of my mother's aprons before opening the dishwasher.

I had about a minute to recover from the gaiety at the dinner table when Damion came in. My heart lurched into my throat.

"Mind if I help you?" he asked.

This man does dishes. My mother is probably having heart palpitations in the next room. I smiled at Damion. "I'll scrub, and you can put them in the dishwasher."

I tried to think of something polite to say while we worked. Without my mother there, conversation was suddenly painful. "What kind of hobbies do you have?"

"Golfing is about all I have time for."

You mean a sport that takes a minimum of four hours to play eighteen holes? But I didn't say it. Karl would think he'd died and found heaven if I told him I wanted to go golfing with him.

I was actually grateful when my mother joined us and insisted that we sit in the living room while she served dessert. Before leaving the kitchen, I wanted to tell Damion that I was not a gifted cook like my mother. But I stayed quiet and decided I could be good and docile Athena for a few more moments. It would ensure that my mother went to bed with a smile on her face that night.

Chapter 5

"ATHENA?"

"Mrs. Crenshaw?"

"Call me Ruby, dear," the woman dripping with chunky jewelry said as she opened her arms wide. I stepped into her embrace, the scent of lemon enveloping me.

"Come in, come in. You're the second one here." She pulled back from me, her bright lipstick smile framing perfectly white teeth. She looked to be in her early 60s. Her hair was cut short, edging her face as if she'd had it salon styled. The rich brown color was definitely a professional job and complimented her hazel eyes. This was a woman who took great care in her appearance.

The nerves in my stomach increased as I followed Ruby through the front entrance. Her home was immaculate, from the white stucco and groomed foliage on the outside to the gleaming cherrywood floors and oriental-style rugs throughout.

"Your home is beautiful," I managed as I ogled everything in sight.

"My late husband was a collector," Ruby said, clasping her manicured hands together. She sashayed ahead, her turquoise tunic billowing behind her.

"Here we are." Ruby turned the corner and ushered me into a high-ceilinged room, complete with a baby grand and a faux fireplace.

A woman rose from the white couch and smiled. She wasn't trim but knew how to dress to her best advantage. Her long blonde hair accentuated her blue eyes, and her tailored cream suit was probably a size twelve but fit so well it looked like a ten, maybe even an eight. I guessed she was in her early forties, but she seemed to be working very hard not to look it—and did a good job of it. She was well put together but didn't come across as fake, which I appreciated.

"Athena, meet Daisy Lawrence," Ruby said.

Daisy stepped forward, tall in her heels, and held out her hand. I grasped her fingers for a second before we both let go.

"I'm always early," Daisy said as if to explain her presence.

"I'm usually early too," I said, wondering if she was a like-minded career woman. I tried to shrug off the feeling of competition. Maybe I was as bad as Karl said.

The doorbell chimed, and Ruby excused herself in a flurry.

I glanced around the room, taking in the museum-quality decorations.

"Do you live here in Newport?" Daisy asked.

"Yes," I said, and before I had a chance to ask her anything, Ruby was back again.

"Olivia," Ruby said, "meet Daisy and Athena."

The new woman smiled and handed over a plate of cookies to Ruby.

"Call me Livvy," she insisted, blowing a stray hair out of her face. Her obviously blonde-dyed hair, cut shoulder length, was a bit frizzy, made worse as she nervously attempted to smooth it. She turned to Ruby. "I know you didn't want us to bring anything, but this was a new recipe I just had to try. White chocolate chip cookies."

Ruby thanked her as the door chimed again. As she swished out of the room saying something about how nice it was to have everyone so punctual, Livvy turned back to us, looking as flustered as I felt inside. She didn't have the cool, calm exterior of Daisy but seemed like a woman who would be easy to get along with.

"It's wonderful to meet both of you. I've been looking forward to this all day," Livvy said, straightening her linen top that looked as if it needed one more pressing.

I immediately liked her after seeing that.

"And this is Paige." Ruby had appeared at the doorway again. "We have one more member, but she must be running late."

We all turned to greet Paige, a young woman who looked like a teenager, though I guessed her to be around twenty-five. She smiled and did a sort of half wave to everyone. Her blue eyes were startling, though she had faint circles beneath them. Maybe she hadn't slept well the night before.

Paige sat down just as the doorbell rang yet again. Ruby hurried out of the room with a smile and returned a few seconds later with a tall woman dressed in khaki slacks and a green collared shirt. She had her brown hair pulled into a tight ponytail and looked to be in her late thirties. I refrained from looking surprised when I noticed the Walgreens logo on the woman's shirt. Was she a cashier there?

Ruby practically beamed. "This is my niece, Shannon. She needs to make room for a book in her life now and again, so I'm thrilled she could come."

The smile Shannon gave Ruby at this introduction seemed a bit indulgent. Her eyes skimmed the tops of our heads as if Shannon was not too enthusiastic about coming to the book club.

"Everyone have a seat, and we'll make the round of introductions," Ruby said, gesturing Shannon to the pristine couches. Shannon sat next to Paige but stayed on the edge of the cushion as if she were preparing to take off at any moment.

Acting as the gracious host, Ruby spread her hands on her knees and said, "Maybe next time we'll get more ladies coming." I smiled at her as she continued. "As you all know, I'm Ruby Crenshaw. I just turned sixty-two last month. I've lived in this gorgeous home by myself since the passing of my husband. It's been nearly two years, but sometimes it seems as if Phil has just left for work." She paused for a moment and took a deep breath. "I have one son who lives in Illinois with his wife." She smiled at Shannon. "My brother and his wife, Shannon's parents, recently moved to Phoenix—I can't imagine why they would want to live in the middle of the desert." She shook her head as if she were truly perplexed. Then she was all smiles again. "Shannon lives in Laguna Hills; it's wonderful to have her so close." She took a breath. "No grandkids of my own just yet."

I shifted in my seat, feeling uncomfortable at the obvious loneliness in Ruby's voice.

She smiled tremulously, twisting the large diamond ring on her finger. "I've always read, especially when my husband traveled." She looked down at her hands. "Since I've been widowed, I haven't socialized like I used to with our friends. They're always there with an open invitation, but I find it harder to enjoy myself around them since I'm always the third or fifth or seventh wheel. So I spend a lot of time cooking for myself and reading, of course." She looked up, her smile bright again. "That's enough about me; let's go around the circle."

One by one, the women took turns. Daisy certainly lived up to her put-together image—two daughters, one a teacher, married and expecting her first child, and the other in her final year of high school. Once she started talking about her job, however, she really lit up. She worked for an insurance company and had been recently promoted. She was divorced but had remarried three years ago. "I belonged to a book club years ago and loved it." She smiled, flashing her excessively white teeth. "And I'm looking forward to getting to know more people now that my kids are older and I have my own life again." She laughed, and Livvy and Paige smiled politely. I worried she wasn't coming across the way she wanted to, but maybe I wouldn't either. I hadn't had my turn yet, and it was hard to introduce yourself to a group of strangers.

Livvy matched my first impression of her. She had four children, and her life centered on them. She spoke in a rush, as if she couldn't make time slow down. "My daughter is babysitting for me tonight, which means the kids will likely be having frozen pizza for dinner, but at least they've got homemade cookies." She smiled, but it seemed a little forced, and even though her tone was upbeat, she looked a little worried. "I haven't read a novel in a long time, so I'm hoping to get a kick-start with the group."

Ruby leaned over and patted Livvy's hand.

Everyone was dead quiet as Paige explained she'd just moved to California after a heartbreaking divorce.

"I'm sort of starting over right now," she said. "See, I'm newly single. I have two little boys—almost seven and three. I still can't believe I'm actually divorced—it wasn't supposed to happen to *me*, you know? I mean, we were married in the temple and everything."

I wasn't sure what she meant by *temple*. Her next words explained it.

"See, I'm Mormon, and marriage is supposed to be forever when the ceremony is in one of our temples . . . The boys miss their dad like crazy, but he left us for another woman, and . . ." She hesitated as if she'd said too much. I felt sorry for her, not just that her husband had cheated on her but that he'd left her with two little kids. "I came tonight because reading is one of my few escapes—or, well, it used to be—and I miss it. I also came in hopes of making some new friends."

She flushed slightly, as though she was embarrassed about being so honest.

I was grateful Ruby interfered with condolences, since I certainly didn't know how to react to Paige's confession. Or her religion. I wracked my mind, thinking of what I'd heard about Mormons. They were a conservative Christian sect, and I'd read some bizarre things in the news lately. My mother had gone to the open house for the Mormon temple in Newport a few years before. She'd tried to talk me into going with her, but I'd had to work, as usual. My mom said once the open house was over, no one who wasn't a member of the Mormon Church could go inside again. Weird.

"I'm a pharmacist," Shannon said once Paige finished.

Wow. I guessed first impressions weren't always right. I felt a little embarrassed for having jumped to the wrong conclusion.

"I live in Laguna Hills, like Aunt Ruby said, and have one son. He's twelve. I've been married for fourteen years, and honestly, I can't remember the last book I read." Her eyes flitted about the room like she was nervous. I could relate. "I think Aunt Ruby's hoping I'll develop some hobbies."

"She works too much," Ruby cut in. "I'm really glad you're here, Shannon."

Shannon shrugged and gave an uncomfortable smile. Then she looked at *me*.

"Tell us about you," Ruby said.

I guess I could just say what I was *not* compared to these women. I wasn't married, had no children, and had never been engaged or even serious with a man, for that matter. I didn't cook, I hadn't read a novel for years, and I hadn't been to a sporting event since college. What did I have in common with these women? *Nothing really*, I decided.

The back of my neck heated as I started to speak, and I realized why I wasn't so great at having girlfriends. I was just too different. Even Paige, at twenty-something, had been married and had two children. *Two.*

I looked down at the plate of cookies on the mosaic coffee table. "I'm thirty-two and single." I glanced up, and everyone smiled at me with sympathy. Great. Just what I needed. Maybe they'd all turn into flagrant matchmakers on my behalf. My voice stuck as I thought about all of them handing me names and cell numbers of their single neighbors.

"Oh, come on," Ruby said in a sincere voice. "There's got to be more to you than that." She smiled, and the images of eager matchmakers faded.

With my heart nearly pounding out of my chest, I said, "I own the online magazine called *Newport Travel*. It keeps me pretty busy . . . so much so that my boyfriend broke up with me a few days ago." I was horrified to have said that out loud, to have admitted that was my reason for joining the book club. How pathetic.

"Oh, I'm sorry," Ruby said, her voice gentle. "I'm sure you won't be single for long."

My stomach dropped. That was just it. I *wanted* to be single. The other women offered a collective murmur of commiseration, and I held up my hand. "It's not exactly what you think. I wasn't ready to move into anything deeper and . . . Karl was . . . so he ended it." I wondered why I was saying all of this—not even my mother or sister knew about what had happened with Karl. Maybe it was Paige's heartfelt words.

I caught Paige's eyes and sensed the understanding.

She knew about breakups.

"He thinks I'm a workaholic." I took a deep breath, looking at Livvy, who nodded with encouragement. "I am. I know it. But I want to do better. So here I am."

Ruby clapped her hands together. "We'll straighten you out." Everyone laughed, though my stomach still clenched from all that I'd confessed to a group of strangers. "Well, now that we know one another, let's eat," Ruby said with a grand smile. "Then we'll talk books."

* * *

Daisy and Livvy stayed after to chat with Ruby. I hurried out the door, Paige right behind me. I thought of her two little kids at home with a babysitter— no wonder she was in a hurry. As for me, I was always in a hurry.

The night air was refreshingly cool, and I felt proud of myself for coming to book club. I was also pleased that the other women seemed enthusiastic about my book selection. Out of all the books we'd discussed, I'd heard of most of them but had never bothered to take the time to read them. In the end, everyone settled on my selection of *The Poisonwood Bible* for this month. I hadn't had the time to start reading it after all, but at least I could thank Grey for that suggestion.

We'd rotate who chose the book each month, and I was relieved to have my turn out of the way.

Paige came down the stairs after me, and I realized I should probably chat with her a little—be friendly—even though it was clear we had very little in common. Thankfully, she spoke first.

"Do you live in this area?" she asked.

I slowed and turned to face her. Her youth struck me again, and it was hard to imagine she'd been married, had two kids, and was now a single mother. I couldn't even keep a boyfriend. "Yes, I've lived in Newport since college. My parents are in Costa Mesa."

She pulled on her purse strap, confusion in her eyes. She must not be familiar with the area.

"It's just north of here," I clarified. "The Costa Mesa freeway runs along it."

Paige nodded, but I could tell I was only confusing her more. She smiled, yet there was something in her eyes that told me it wasn't all that genuine. She was probably still annoyed with the questions some of the ladies had asked her about her religion. I couldn't help but be curious too. Everything I'd heard about Mormons made them seem pretty weird—but Paige looked quite normal, even if she was young and had two kids already.

"Are you all right?" I asked, immediately berating myself. I didn't know the full extent of her problems, and I definitely wouldn't have decent advice for her.

"Yeah," she said in an unconvincing voice. "Just need to get home to the kids—they have a new babysitter."

Our conversation stalled as we continued down the walkway, my heels clicking on the cement rather loudly.

"Do you know how far the Newport Temple is from here?" Paige asked.

I stopped and faced her. "You mean the Mormon Temple? It's not far, maybe a ten- to fifteen-minute drive this time of night." It wasn't hard to miss off the 73 toll road. But if she had driven from Tustin, she wouldn't have seen it. "Do you need directions?"

The sadness in her eyes lifted. "That would be great."

She took a pad of paper out of her purse to write down directions. I was impressed that she seemed quite organized without the huge over-flowing diaper bag I'd seen other young mothers tote around. After she'd verified the directions, I said, "My mother went to the open house. She talked for days about how beautiful it was inside." I shrugged. "I couldn't get there before it closed to the public. But it does look very beautiful from the outside."

A soft smile crossed Paige's face. This was the first time I'd seen her smile—it really changed her face and made her look quite pretty. "I haven't been to the Newport one," she said, "but I've been in a few others in Utah. They're beautiful and peaceful." Her smile faded, and her voice trembled when she said, "It's closed for the night, but I thought if I could just sit outside for a few minutes, maybe I could feel some of that peace again."

I started to feel nervous. Was Paige going to start crying right here on the side of the street? She actually wiped at her eyes. I suddenly wanted to change the subject. "Here's my cell phone number if you have any other questions . . . you know, if you need directions or anything."

We traded phone numbers, and that seemed to brighten her up. At least she appeared to be past the potential-crying stage.

"Thanks," Paige said, slipping the pad of paper back into her purse. "I'm really excited about this book club." Her tone was genuine.

I hesitated then realized I was looking forward to it as well. "So am I."

Paige patted her purse with the pad of paper containing the directions I'd given her. "Thanks again. It will be hard to get away and go to the temple very often, but I think driving by will help a lot."

"So when they say it's closed to the public, does that mean *no* one can go inside except for Mormons?" I asked, surprised that I was actually interested.

Paige looked up at me. "Yes, after it's dedicated."

Now it was my turn to be confused. "Dedicated?"

"The president of our church, or one of his counselors, dedicates each temple with a special prayer. After it's dedicated, only those who have temple recommends can go inside." Paige's entire face changed when she talked about her church. She must be really devoted. One of my friends in college, Kelly, was Baptist. She had invited me to Bible study on weeknights, and I went a couple of times. But I felt uncomfortable since I didn't know enough about the doctrinal points to contribute to the discussions. When I started to make excuses as to why I couldn't go anymore, she dropped our friendship. I had really enjoyed spending time with her, and it hurt that she had based our friendship on my interest in her religion.

"Are you religious?" Paige asked.

The question caught me off guard. I didn't go to church much, but my mother went regularly—at least, before my father was diagnosed with Alzheimer's. "Greek Orthodox."

"That's great," Paige said.

It is? She astonished me. I was ready for her to drill me with questions or tell me what was wrong with my religion, like Kelly had.

"Although I haven't been to church in a while," I said, waiting for her reprimand.

Paige laughed. "If it weren't for my kids, I'd probably be skipping some church as well."

Again she'd surprised me. I gave her a knowing smile; I was really starting to like Paige.

After we said good-bye, I discovered that I was driving home with a smile on my face. It had been awhile since I'd felt so relaxed. I thought about how different each woman was at the book club and how at first I assumed I wouldn't fit in. But if they could accept me, maybe I could accept them.

Chapter 6

MONDAY MORNING I WOKE, MY head pounding, my mind in a haze from being awake until almost 1 a.m. The mocking bird was back and louder than ever, but I smiled as I stretched. I'd spent most of Sunday reading. *Just* reading.

Barbara Kingsolver's writing style was slow and detailed, but she had such a unique way of tying words together that the book was hard to put down. I cringed when I discovered that the character Nathan Price was a Baptist preacher. But I decided to give him the benefit of the doubt. Not all Baptists were like Kelly, I assured myself. At first I didn't like the wife in the story. Orleanna Price had no life of her own. She went where her husband went and gave up everything she knew and loved to live in the Congo with her family.

She was too similar to my own mother, who'd centered her whole life on my dad. She let him tell her what to do, and everything was focused on his care, even before he had Alzheimer's. Since he'd become sick, he'd been every moment of her life.

What about you, *Mom?* I'd asked more than once. But it only upset her, so I stopped asking. I wondered if, like Orleanna Price, my mother had secret places in her heart—a life only she lived and only she knew about.

I re-read part of the book I had highlighted: *My daughters would say: You see, Mother, you had no life of your own. They have no idea. One has* only *a life of one's own.*

Similar to Nathan Price, my father made all the decisions in the family when I was growing up, and my mother went along with him in every case. No, he didn't take us to a primitive village in the Congo, but his word was law.

I could certainly relate to little Ruth May when she talked about her father. *He doesn't like talking back. If that was me, oh, boy. That razor strap burns so bad, after you go to bed your legs still feel stripedy like a zebra horse.*

My father had never harmed us physically, but his disapproving words were sharper than any physical punishment.

It wasn't until my father started to slip into Alzheimer's that my mother truly took charge—even if my father still thought nothing had changed. Over the past two years, I'd never seen my mother more alive and strong, and it was due to my father slipping away.

Spending so much time reading meant I'd be busier today to make up for it. I'd have to get through my usual Sunday errands tonight. I reached for my Blackberry, an impatient tug in my stomach forming as I scrolled through my e-mails again. Nothing new, nothing from Karl either. I'd replied with a "thanks" when he'd sent the pictures over the other day.

Normally, I could justify his silence when he was traveling to a new location, but I knew he was here in Newport. The thought of him out there, so close yet not contacting me, was bothersome. What had he done over the weekend? A good-looking guy like him could go anywhere and get plenty of female attention.

Not going to think about it. I slid out of bed as I automatically went through my call log. I had missed a call last night, but I didn't recognize the number. Had Karl called from a friend's? Or someplace else? It didn't make sense. He knew I didn't answer calls from numbers I didn't recognize.

I skipped my morning run—I had kickboxing tonight. By midmorning, my curiosity burned too much, so I dialed the unidentified number. It went to voice mail. Damion—my brother-in-law's "friend" from last week's family dinner.

I sighed and plopped back on my pillow. He'd been nice. *Nice.*

So really, what was wrong with nice? I should be happy that a man like him was interested in me. Of course, that's exactly who was the problem. Me. I was attracted to Karl, but I didn't want him because he wanted me? I did have a problem. I knew it, but I wasn't going to think about it—too much work today.

Freshly showered and my cup of tea perfectly steeped and steaming in hand, I inserted the pictures from Karl into the article he'd drafted on the Amazon. *Newport Travel* had morphed from local attractions to covering destinations all over the globe.

One of the pictures popped up with Karl himself in it; he was standing next to a translucent pool of water, surrounded by thick jungle. His eyes looked dark green with the emerald escarpment, his hair was longish, and he had definite beginnings of a beard on his face.

I stared at the picture much longer than I needed to. When I finally broke my gaze, I looked through the last text messages he'd sent. Little had I known that he'd ignore me so thoroughly . . . I stared again at his picture, a lump in my throat. Did I want to reconcile?

I wondered if he'd sent the picture of himself accidentally—or on purpose. I decided to use it in place of his formal bio picture. Well, there wasn't really anything formal about Karl, except where he had wanted to take our relationship. Formal. Official.

Despite the butterflies in my stomach when I thought of him kissing me at my doorstep, of his long arms holding me tight, my heart was rejecting him.

What's wrong with me?

I blinked against the stinging in my eyes and quickly placed the pictures in the article layout. Minutes later, I had finished, satisfied with the presentation. With a deep breath, I sent an e-mail to Karl: *Just placed the pictures. They look great. Thanks.* I released my breath. *BTW, I'm reading a book.*

I clicked send before I could change my mind. It was his turn now. Would he take the bait? It would probably be a few weeks before he submitted pictures again—after the elections for the campaign he was covering.

The thought opened a well of loneliness inside me. I gulped the rest of the tea down; it was still too hot, but the scalding helped pull me from further wallowing.

My cell rang. *Damion.* My eyes still smarting, I answered.

Then I did the second spontaneous thing in a single week. I accepted a date.

* * *

I was nearly halfway through *The Poisonwood Bible* by Tuesday night. I'd stayed up way too late the night before, and on Tuesday, I felt lethargic as I read through a half dozen article submissions. I decided to take three of them—not bad progress.

Karl hadn't responded; I guessed I'd have to be more direct if I wanted him to reply. But remembering the hurt in his eyes stopped me from e-mailing him again. Unless I was sure, I didn't want to give him false hope.

By 5:30, I was either ready for a siesta or a five-hour energy drink. The energy drink won out—I still had to proof two articles for the upcoming month's edition, which I wanted ready for publication by Saturday.

First, I decided to grab an indulgent hamburger at Carl's Jr, which had nothing to do with the fact that it was in the same complex as Grey's bookstore. As I pulled through the drive-thru, I glanced over at the bookstore. The lights were on, the open sign displayed. Before souring my breath with onions and the works, I decided I'd just step in and update Grey on the book club like I'd promised. I couldn't break a promise. Besides, now that I was reading novels again, I found myself enjoying it. Perhaps I'd grab a couple more.

A gum-cracking teen sat behind the register, however, bobbing to the earbuds dangling from her ears. In one hand, she held a book with a blue-haired girl on the cover; with the other she twisted a strand of what looked like rosary beads.

The disappointment of not seeing Grey pinched sharp in my stomach.

The teen's eyes fluttered in my direction, but she only nodded at my entrance. I spent a couple of minutes looking through books—apparently, I was in the crime section—every title had "cut" or "bone" in it.

The combination of my stomach growling and the annoyance of being an ignored customer made me approach the register.

The teen looked up, taking one bud from her ear and popping her gum. "Yeah?" She looked at my empty hands, obviously wondering if I was there to shop.

"Will Grey be in later?"

"Mr. Ronning?"

"Yeah, um, Mr. Ronning."

She blew a bubble and shrugged. "I can help you find a book." She put her novel down and turned to the computer.

"Isn't there a schedule that says when he's coming in?"

Her hands halted midpose above the keyboard. She rolled her eyes and slid a pad of Post-it notes in my direction. "Look, just leave your name and number. I'm sure he'll call you like all the others, ma'am."

"Others?"

Her mouth twitched—which might have been a smile, but it was hard to tell.

My face burning, I scrawled my name and number. I wasn't sure what the girl meant about others, but I wanted her to know this was strictly business—or at least strictly about books. "He asked me to . . . I have some information he requested."

She waved her hand, pulled off the Post-it from the pad, and stuck it on the computer monitor. "Don't worry, he'll call." She shook her head slightly, put in the earbud, and picked up her novel.

When . . . *if* Grey called . . .

I hurried out of the bookstore to my cooling burger in the car.

Chapter 7

Grey called two hours later. When I saw the strange number, I hoped but didn't exactly expect it to be Grey. I snatched up the phone and answered.

"May I speak with Athena, please?"

For a second, I didn't answer. I wasn't prepared for my reaction to his voice. Let's just say that I felt like I'd reached the top of a roller coaster—the instant between teetering on the top and plunging down at ninety miles an hour.

"Yes, it's me," I said.

"It's Grey Ronning—from the bookstore."

I was smiling by the time he finished and extremely grateful he couldn't see me. At least the teen-aged employee was right about one thing.

"I know—I mean—I didn't recognize the number, so I assumed—" I cut myself off in the name of self-preservation.

"Chelsey told me you came in."

"Chelsey? Oh, her."

He laughed, and it was like I could feel it over the phone—warm and strong. "Yeah, she's not too friendly, but she's my brother's kid and needs something to do after school."

"I, uh, asked when you'd be in, and she didn't seem to know."

"She's one of those kids who reads a book and doesn't pay attention to much else. Sort of a bookaholic."

Aholics. I knew about them. I walked out of my office and sat on the living room couch, pulling my feet up under me. "The book she was reading looked interesting, although I don't know how she reads and listens to music at the same time." Heat pulsed through my face. Could I sound any lamer?

He was silent for a second, and then we both spoke at the same time.

"Go ahead," he said.

Another second of silence. "I came into the bookstore to give you my report." *Report?* "I went to the book club."

"Ah . . ." The ease was back in his voice. "Ruby Crenshaw. How is she?"

I leaned back on the couch, picturing the vibrant woman. "She's actually quite incredible." I found myself talking, or rather, *blabbing,* about everything that happened in the book club—the women, the white chocolate chip cookies, the discussion about our backgrounds. Grey kept asking me questions, and before I realized what I was saying, I blurted the confession I'd made to the ladies.

"You told them you joined because you broke up with your boyfriend?" Grey asked with a laugh.

"I—" *Did I just tell him that?* "Yes." My entire body went tense. At that moment, I admitted to myself that Grey was an attractive man. Not that I was necessarily attracted *to* him and wanted to date him—or, heaven forbid, have a steady relationship or introduce him to my mother—but suddenly, the awkwardness had returned. I'd spoken about my ex-boyfriend to a single, and possibly available, man.

"So you're on the rebound and decided to bury yourself in novels?" he said, his voice lighthearted.

"Not exactly . . ." I said.

"Then what, *exactly?*" His voice was warm, and I imagined him smiling.

"It's complicated," I said.

He laughed. "It's always complicated." His tone turned serious, quiet. "Are you okay?"

"What do you mean?"

"From the breakup—you must be upset."

"Not exactly," I said before I could stop myself from sounding like a parrot. This wasn't a conversation I'd intended to have with Grey. He was a complete stranger, and except for the fact that I had just unveiled practically my entire weekend to him in ten minutes flat, he knew nothing about me.

"Ah. *You* dumped him."

"Wrong again," I said, my voice trembling as an image of Karl's hurt expression flashed through my mind. I inhaled, steadying my breath.

"Athena . . ."

I said nothing, unsure of my voice. I wasn't going to cry about this, no matter how understanding and friendly Grey seemed to be.

"Are you still there?"

I nodded, then croaked out, "Y-Yes."

He was silent for a second, while I was busy thinking up a way to end the call gracefully.

"I think you need to go flying," Grey said.

"What?"

"When my brother went through his divorce, he came flying with me on the weekends. It helped him."

"It wasn't that serious—"

But he plowed on. "I have a small plane—it's pretty cool if I say so myself."

"You're a pilot?"

"Yep. Are you up for some flying, Athena?"

"I—I don't know," I said. This conversation had taken a 360-degree turn. "What if I get airsick? Plus, this weekend is really busy."

"I have to reserve more than a week in advance, so next weekend would be the earliest."

"Oh." I didn't want to hesitate, but I did anyway. "I'm busy next weekend too."

"Not busy with your boyfriend."

"No, not with him."

"Family?"

"No."

"Then what?"

"Work. November's issue goes into circulation this weekend, but next weekend I need to start on the layout for December's."

"Hmm," Grey said. "That explains a few things."

"Like what?"

"Like why you haven't read a book in so long. Hey, why don't you call me if you want to take me up on the offer? I gotta go. A customer just walked in."

"Okay—" Before I realized it, he'd hung up. My face burned. Was he upset? Had I been rude? I stayed on the couch, staring at the call log on my phone. We'd talked for eighteen minutes. I'd never chatted with anyone that long. And then he'd cut me off so quickly at the end. I flopped back against the couch with a groan.

Chapter 8

SATURDAY NIGHT, AS I PULLED on my classic black dress that fell to just above my knees, I thought of Grey. When I put in my silver standby earrings, I thought of Grey. As I sprayed my favorite tonic on my hair, I thought of Grey.

Although tonight I'd be seeing Damion, not Grey.

I couldn't believe I'd accepted this date.

My heart pounded with guilt or anger or something at myself. Why had I turned down Grey's invitation to go flying?

Should I call and take him up on the offer? Or have I completely blown it? Dressed and ready, I had nothing to do but wait. If I started on a work project, I'd be unable to finish it before Damion came, and it would be on my mind all evening.

When the doorbell chimed, I opened it—probably too fast, which meant Damion might misread my anxiety for excitement.

He stood close to the door, as if he'd tried to look through the peephole backward. Damion wore khakis and a dark pullover. Before he could make a move to come inside, I grabbed my purse, wishing I hadn't dressed up quite so much.

"Ready?" I said with a smile, my voice too bright.

Damion smiled then turned his head and coughed.

My smile froze. He had a cold? This night had better be short. My condo was a certified no-germ zone, and I wasn't about to let him break down the barriers. I started pulling the door closed before I was even all the way out.

"Your car or my car?" I asked, my voice sounding a bit peeved, even to my own ears.

"I'll drive," Damion said.

Relieved that he wouldn't be spreading his germs in my car, I walked a good enough distance from him that there was no chance for touching or, worse, hand-holding, yet I stayed close enough to be polite.

He hurried to open the door for me, and I settled onto the leather seat. *A man with money*, I heard my mother's voice say. Damion climbed in from his side and started the car. All kinds of lights went on in the dashboard, and he fiddled with various knobs, adjusting the A/C and turning down some light jazz-sounding music.

A family man, my mother crooned.

And then he did the unthinkable. He pulled out a tissue and dabbed his nose.

Damion had a certified, bona fide cold. I'm not so shallow that I can't handle a sick person. I've been sick plenty, and my father, well, he only got worse by the month. But this was a first date, and I didn't want to see Damion as *real* quite yet. Was it so wrong to want to wear rose-colored glasses for at least one date?

I exhaled in defeat. I was kidding myself. I'd never worn any type of glasses on a date, not even rose-colored ones. I was always the first to get out, to make any excuse, whatever it took.

"Are you feeling okay?" I couldn't help asking. Maybe Damion would confess that he was sick and he hadn't wanted to let me down by canceling. And I'd say that I understood perfectly and we could do something another time.

But all he said was, "Fine."

You're not fine. I let the thought dissipate; I was going to stick this evening out. And I was not going to think about Grey—I'd show Damion that I wasn't completely devoid of having fun, and I'd have something to share with my mother tomorrow.

Even if that fun consisted of eating dinner with a near stranger.

On the way to the restaurant, Damion started chatting about work. A couple of times, he paused and I got a word in, but mostly he talked. He certainly hadn't been this talkative at my mother's. I just remembered him laughing a lot. Of course, my mother tended to overtake people.

". . . with so many children." Damion's voice reached my ears. He paused as if waiting for me to answer.

What is he talking about? Children? "Uh huh," I said, vague enough that it could be an agreement or an "I understand," and Damion was on his way again. This time I tried to pay more careful attention. Thankfully, he didn't seem to be talking about children that he might have or that I might have but was instead talking about his brother's kids.

I relaxed into my seat. There was one good thing about a man who talked a lot: he didn't expect much from me. That I could handle.

Dinner came in the form of an Indian restaurant, where we sat cross-legged on the floor. Well, at least Damion managed to cross his legs. I was forced to sit more ladylike in my aforementioned black dress—sidesaddle, if you will.

Had he mentioned this restaurant over the phone or anything about the seating accommodations? I didn't think so, but I was having trouble concentrating on his current story of an upcoming golf weekend he was taking with his work buddies at Palm Springs.

I nodded and um-hm'ed as I scanned the menu. The listing was exhaustive, seeming to have so many dishes that I wondered if the chef got mixed up. When the server came to take our order, after bowing several times to each of us, I ordered the same dish as Damion.

Damion smiled at that. "Oh, you like chicken korma too?"

"Yes," I said, offering him a smile of my own in return.

Apparently the smile had been too much effort for him, and he covered his mouth as he coughed.

"Are you sure you're feeling all right?" I prompted.

He took a sip of his drink. "Fine, just fine." Then he suddenly stopped talking. And he stared at me. It wasn't a casual, friendly, how-are-you gaze but a gaze like he was trying to read my thoughts in a Mr. Spock Star Trek way.

I grabbed my glass and took a drink.

Still, he stared. I offered a small smile and took another sip. More staring.

"Do you come to this restaurant much?" I asked.

He shook his head, still staring.

I looked away as if it didn't creep me out at all. A detour to the ladies' room was sounding good right about now, but then he said, "Athena, I just had an idea."

Really. "Oh?" I lifted my eyebrows as if I were very, very interested.

"Why don't you come to Palm Springs with me?"

My eyebrows froze in place. I think my brain was trying to come up with a response, but it didn't translate into any coherent words.

"You could hang out at the spa while I golf with the guys. In the evening, we'll all have dinner together."

Before I could scream out *no* like I wanted to, I said, "So the other guys are bringing . . . friends?"

"Not that I know of," Damion said, his mouth forming a puzzled line as if I'd said something strange. "I mean, one of the guys might bring his wife."

"Then . . ." I literally couldn't bring myself to fashion a reply. I was too dumbfounded.

"It will be great for you to have some fun," he said, his words sounding strangely rehearsed. "You should get out more."

I narrowed my eyes. Only one other person talked to me like that. "Did my mother tell you that?"

Damion's face reddened. "Sh-She . . . It wasn't that."

I creased the napkin on my lap. "Thank you for the invitation, Damion. But I'm afraid I can't accept it." My voice felt a bit shaky, and I hoped he wouldn't notice. First of all, I hardly knew him; second, I didn't know if I could put up with hours of talking on the drive; third, I had to immediately shut down anything even remotely suggested by my mother.

He nodded as if he'd expected me to turn him down. I felt a measure of relief at that. And then he started talking again, something about a previous golf tournament and how he'd bogied three holes.

I took another sip of my drink, tried to pretend interest, and wondered if Grey golfed.

Chapter 9

My mother and I faced off in her kitchen at 5:45 p.m. on Sunday. Father was half asleep in the other room, and I'd come over for dinner, taking the opportunity to set my mother straight face-to-face.

"How could you tell Damion to take me on a golf weekend with his buddies?" I asked.

Mother's face tightened. "Oh, dear, you shouldn't feel bad that I came up with the suggestion. I know he's very interested in you. He said he thought you were nice looking and sweet."

I breathed out. I was anything but sweet, and both of us knew it. "I'm not looking for invitations from men. Especially"—I continued before she could reply—"not from Damion."

"What if it were Karl?" my mother asked.

I hesitated but knew the answer. Although I might welcome a little attention from Karl after his very effective ignoring techniques, a weekend away with a man just seemed too much of a commitment.

"You know, my dear, your father and I didn't exactly . . . wait," she said, opening the refrigerator.

"Wait for what?" At my mother's blush, it hit me. "Please don't tell me you just said that."

She opened the crisper, a smile at the corner of her mouth. "Can you wash the tomatoes for the salad?"

My mother was talking to me about her love life with my father? I was astounded, and I didn't really want to think about my parents in that way. "You're not getting out of this conversation." I put a hand on her shoulder, and she turned, a look of guilt on her face. "Damion and I are not going out again. Don't ask me about him anymore. And Karl and I are over."

Why couldn't my mother understand that I didn't need a man in my life to be happy? She and my dad didn't exactly have the ideal relationship. I remembered plenty of slammed doors and tears. My father dominated the household, and many times, I'd wished my mom had stood up for herself. I loved my dad, but he was a selfish man, or had been. I didn't know what to make of him now.

My mother handed me a clear produce bag containing several tomatoes, but I knew she wasn't giving up yet. "All right, Bee. There are plenty of other men out there—*Greek* men."

She was incorrigible.

"I'll wash the tomatoes," I grumbled.

Dinner was a one-sided affair as my mother prattled on about the neighbor's sick dog, the new yogurt dressing recipe I just had to try (since it tasted good with cucumbers and pita), and then about the new medications my father had started that week.

"So far, there have been no significant side effects," my mother said in a too-bright voice.

I nodded. "That's nice." I looked over at my father, who methodically forked bits of salad into his mouth. He had a dab of dressing on his chin, which my mother quickly cleaned off. He didn't even notice. His iron-gray hair was neatly combed back—again, my mother's doing—and a pressed polo shirt hung off his thinning shoulders.

When he reached for his glass, his hand trembled. It made my heart ache to see that tremble—I knew it was from the medication, which was for his own good, but it was another sign of his dependence.

"Did you read anything interesting today?" I asked in my own too-bright voice. I cringed, knowing I sounded exactly like my mother.

Dad lifted his eyes to me, and for a moment, I saw the depth of intelligence there. Then he blinked. And it was gone. His vacant expression returned. "Olympiacos lost again, Fran."

"Yes, they did," I replied, blinking rapidly against the hot tears. My father had been reading when I arrived; he didn't even remember twenty minutes ago. And he'd called me Fran, his sister's name. I didn't know whether the Greek soccer team had lost this week or not—perhaps it was easier for my father to remember a soccer game than his daily activities.

My mother looked at me with sympathy and understanding, but I didn't want to commiserate with her, which made me feel lousier. My mother and I were in this together—mostly her but me as well. I was the one she should be able to rely on the most and confide in. I knew it was tough on her. I'd visited home enough to see the strain on Mother. She never relaxed any more. Her perfect make-up, her overly cheery disposition, except when she was berating me for not being in a serious relationship with a man, and her habit of dusting when there was no dust.

"I must get you the recipe before you go, Bee," my mother's voice cut through my thoughts.

I mumbled an "all right" and took another bite of salad.

"I would have made it tonight, but I ran out of parsley. Of course, I have dried parsley flakes in the spice cupboard, but fresh parsley makes all the difference."

I nodded and took another bite. My father was back to his own food, dutifully eating.

My eyes blurred as my mother continued to talk about the outrageous price of tomatoes at Ralphs that week—"That's why I only bought two tomatoes for my tomato sauce. If Ralphs thinks I'm going to lay down good money just because they raise their prices, they can think again."

Was this what my life had amounted to? Living in a condo alone, visiting my parents a couple of times a week, listening to my mother's rants about the price of groceries, watching my father slip into a deep abyss of silence, and knowing the only man who'd ever asked me for a weekend getaway did so because my mother had asked him to.

"Can you believe that?" my mother asked, staring pointedly at me.

I swallowed against my tight throat. "Uh . . ."

Thankfully, she didn't miss a beat. "I couldn't either. That's why I told Leslie she needed to go to Kona Dry Cleaners. They've worked out every stain I've ever had trouble with."

I stood. "I should get dessert. It's getting late."

"Will you be having some?" she asked. My mother hailed from the generation of multicourse meals, which always ended with dessert after dinner.

"I can't," I said with a wan smile. "I have an exercise class tonight."

My mother shook her head, directing her furrowed brows at my father. "Women these days—exercising until they drop. A man likes something to hold on to. All these skinny women are no good for loving a man."

I paused to bend over and kiss my mother's cheek, placing my hand on her shoulder. "I'll take some home with me."

She winced at my touch.

"What's wrong?" I looked down at her.

"Oh, my shoulder is a little sore—bumped it last night." She smiled. "Just a bruise."

My father broke in. "Olympiacos lost."

"That's too bad, dear," my mother said, turning to him.

With her attention diverted, I disappeared into the kitchen, where I could let out the sigh I'd been holding back all during dinner.

I put several pieces of baklava onto a plate; then, after eating a small corner piece, I put a few pieces into a Ziploc baggie for myself. I went back into the dining room to put the plate on the table. Then, after saying good-bye to my parents, I slipped out the door into the fresh night air, my baggie of baklava in hand.

A breeze had kicked up, and the smell of salt greeted me. The scent of the ocean wasn't strong all of the time, but the low-hanging clouds seemed to lock in the saltiness closer to the earth.

My mother could make me rant and rave, but I had to admit, I did love her despite her fussiness. And her baklava was heavenly.

Chapter 10

THE FOLLOWING WEEK PASSED QUICKLY, and the only time I realized that I hadn't heard from Damion, or Grey for that matter, was right before falling asleep at night. But I had no such luck on Saturday morning when I found myself sitting on the couch drinking my tea and obsessing over the last conversation I'd had with Grey more than a week ago. Even though I needed to start on December's layout, I couldn't get him out of my mind. This was the weekend he'd wanted to go flying, and Grey's silence told me I'd been too off-putting. And my last conversation with Damion hadn't been much better. Both had been disasters. The Damion disaster, I was grateful for. He hadn't called me all week.

But I felt guilty for the Grey disaster. Yet, I wasn't about to call him. And how could I drop by the bookstore? I didn't know what the next book club choice would be so I had no excuse to buy anything.

Dad. I could get him a book. Even if he wouldn't remember a thing he read twenty minutes later, he still spent a good portion of his day reading magazines. Maybe if I bought him a book on something about sports, he'd read it.

Rising from the couch, I decided I had to somehow reconcile my last conversation with Grey, then I wouldn't have to think about it anymore, and I could concentrate on work.

I stopped cold when I saw the clock. It was only 8:30. Grey's store probably didn't open until 9:00 or 10:00 on Saturday mornings. But there was a good chance he'd show up early.

I hesitated in the doorway between my bedroom and the living room. Work? No, I decided. I was going to go to the bookstore before I chickened out again. A few minutes later, I was dressed and spending too much time in front of the mirror. I needed to look casual—like it was Saturday morning and I was just stopping in. But no matter how disgusted I was at myself, I couldn't pull myself away from primping. I settled for mascara and lip gloss and a casual pantsuit my mother would be thrilled I was wearing. It had been sitting in my closet since the last Christmas. At least it was black and decidedly not velour.

By the time I was ready, it was nearly 9:00. If the bookstore was closed, I'd do a few errands and hit it on my way back. I needed some decent groceries anyway.

Pulling into the parking lot of *Grey's Used & Rare Books*, I noticed two things. Grey's car was parked outside, and Grey himself was outside, standing on the sidewalk, chatting with some woman.

I nearly did a U-turn and escaped, but Grey happened to look over. He didn't wave or anything, but what if he recognized my car? Did he even know what kind of car I drove? I couldn't risk being seen driving past and then leaving. He might get the wrong idea—he might think I was stalking him. Which wasn't true at all. I didn't even want to date him.

Biting my lower lip, I pulled into a stall a few slots down from the bookstore. I spent a minute fiddling with my phone then looked up casually. Grey was still talking to the woman. Now that I was closer, I saw she looked like one of the women from the salon. High heels, tiny figure, long nails. I always felt like a giant next to Asian women.

Climbing out of the car, I kept my phone in hand—as if I had a bunch of important messages to go through and was only dropping in on a quick errand.

I neared the store, glancing at Grey then at my phone. He was still talking. When I reached the door, I tugged it to open it. Locked.

"Here, let me get that," Grey said behind me. How did he get there so quickly?

"Sorry, I thought the store was open."

"Almost," Grey said, and I distinctly heard the smile in his voice.

I wanted to douse my face in cold water.

He opened the door and didn't exactly stand all the way to the side, so I had to pass quite close to him to enter.

Relax, I commanded myself. What was wrong with me? I planned to be nonchalant, browse through the store, then be gone.

The door closed behind me—Grey hadn't come in after all. Through the window, I saw him talking to the nail lady again. I averted my eyes before he could catch me watching.

I crossed to the biography section, and I scanned the titles, looking for something my father might find interest in. But they all looked to be four inches thick. I doubted my dad could plow through one now.

I went over a dozen different conversations with Grey in my head, from outright apologizing to being casual and friendly.

A whoosh of air went through the store as the door opened and closed.

"Looking for something?" Grey asked.

Yes, you, I thought then felt my face grow hot. I wasn't *blushing,* was I? I never blushed. Just in case, I didn't dare turn around until my face had gone down to its normal temperature. "My father likes biographies." At least he used to. "Or memoirs about professional sports players."

I felt rather than heard Grey come stand by me. Glancing at him, I noticed a couple of buttons were undone at the top of his shirt, and it wasn't tucked in, as if he'd dressed in a hurry. His chin and cheeks were scruffy as well, reminding me of Karl for an instant. But the brown of Grey's eyes chased that image away. *Stop staring.* I looked down at the book I held in my hands. *Winston Churchill.*

"That's a good one," Grey said, his breath brushing my cheek. I thought I smelled wintergreen. Toothpaste or gum?

"Does your father like political figures?"

"He'd probably read a president's biography but not necessarily a senator's."

Grey smiled at that. "Republican or Democrat?"

"Greek."

He chuckled and reached in front of me to pull out a book. His arm touched mine, and I instinctively moved back, although I didn't want to.

"Has he read this one?"

"I don't think so," I said, scanning the title on Abraham Lincoln. "At least I haven't seen it around the house, which means if he did read it awhile ago, he probably won't remember it."

"Yeah, I forget a lot of the books I've read too," he said, cracking the cover.

I meant much more than forgetting details in a book; my father wouldn't remember if he'd even read a specific book. But Grey hadn't picked up on it, and I didn't care to expound.

"So do you want to try it?" he said.

"Try what?"

He smiled. "The book—for your father?"

My skin felt warm, and I hoped the heat wouldn't creep to my face again. "Sure." I took the book he held out.

"Or . . ." He stepped around me and pulled another book from the shelf. "Maybe he'd like this one—"

"Are you busy tonight?" I blurted out. I clamped my mouth shut, hardly believing I'd spoken those words.

Grey turned to me, his eyes bright with something I hoped was interest. "I thought you were working this weekend."

"I—uh . . ." My hands tightened into a death grip around the book.

He didn't bail me out but continued to watch me. I was sure he was laughing inside yet was too polite to start guffawing in my presence.

"I am—I will—it seems . . . I have a little time."

He folded his arms—tan arms, by the way. Not that I'm an advocate of tanning without the appropriate SPF, but the tan was quite pleasing to the eye. "How much time is this 'little time'?"

"A couple of hours," I practically whispered then tried to clear my throat without making a sound.

"Sure," he said, his voice seeming very low, but maybe I was imagining it. "I'll be here until 4:00, then I can get away." He straightened, turned, and walked toward the register, adjusting a couple of books along the way, putting much-needed space between us.

I started to breathe easier. "So you don't have any plans to fly . . . or anything?"

He didn't turn until he walked behind the counter, yet I still felt his brown eyes' lingering warmth. Again, I was grateful for the space. I hadn't thought this through at all, and I couldn't believe I'd just basically asked him out on a date. I had no plan.

He propped his hands on the counter. "I didn't make a reservation."

It hit me then—he didn't reserve a flight when I said I couldn't make it. That meant he hadn't invited anyone else to go with him.

"Sorry about that." I looked down at the books in my hand. "I guess I'll take this one," I said. He was watching me—which I knew without looking up—since that warmth seemed to reach across tables of stacked books.

I replaced the other books, likely in the wrong places, and made my way to the register. I hadn't even looked at the price and hoped the Lincoln book wasn't a first edition or something.

Grey was typing something into the register when I walked up. "Just booting it up."

I nodded and waited. I took a peek at the price sticker, but it only had a date on it. "Is this one of those first editions?"

"Oh no," Grey said, looking up from the register. "There's no charge."

"You can't keep giving me free books," I said. "You'll be out of business."

His eyes caught mine. "I didn't say it was free."

"What will it cost me?"

He braced both hands on the counter and leaned forward slightly. "Several hours of your precious time."

My throat felt thick. "All right."

He arched an eyebrow. "What are we doing at 4:00?"

My mind spun. Movie. Restaurant. Did he golf? We might be able to get a twilight tee time. "How about Balboa Island?" I hadn't been there for a long time—probably since my college days, even though it wasn't too far away.

"Done. I'll pick you up then."

I rattled off my address then turned to leave.

"Your book."

Fighting against another rising blush, I grabbed it. "Thanks." I felt his eyes follow me out.

I had to hold myself back from running to my car and squealing once I got inside. I was acting like a silly teenager. I frowned into the rearview mirror, admonishing myself to grow up. I'd been on dozens of dates, many of them first dates, and I had nothing to be nervous about.

But my stomach twisted the entire drive home, and even after I ate a microwave Lean Cuisine meal and the rest of the baklava I'd snatched from my mother's house, the fluttering didn't stop.

Thoughts of Grey wouldn't leave me alone. The only solution to make it until 4:00 was to work.

I opened my document files and started creating bills. *I can't believe I asked Grey out on a date. Where did that come from? Is he laughing at me right now?* I added up the marketing sums and figured in the tax. I decided that in January I'd raise advertising prices by 10 percent. I wrote down a reminder to draft a notice letter. *Why did I suggest Balboa Island? It was something fun for a family with little kids, but what would we do? I can't even remember the places to eat there.*

I opened up the next invoice and filled out the information. This advertiser was on a month-to-month account, and I added a note that if they wanted more space, I could give them a better deal.

How could I almost forget the book I bought for my dad? Did Grey sense how flustered I was? The next invoice stopped me cold. It was for a classified ad Karl put in every month. I didn't officially charge him but created an invoice to show his credit in my magazine for tax purposes and such.

I realized I hadn't thought about Karl in a couple of days. I mechanically filled out the statement and e-mailed it quickly before I could let any memories surface. Things had been near perfect with Karl—until he'd wanted to get more serious.

My head sank into my hands. What was wrong with me? I'd broken up with one guy because he wanted more, and a short time later, I was practically chasing another guy down—asking him out, no less. Was I setting things up to be dumped again? Was I being masochistic? How could I expect a guy to ever feel comfortable with me if I couldn't even figure myself out?

Chapter 11

AT 3:00, MY MOTHER CALLED. My hand hesitated over the phone, but then I decided to answer it. She probably knew I was at home—her eyes were like lasers and, I swear, could see across freeways and through buildings. If I didn't pick up, she'd keep calling. Every ten minutes.

"Bee, I must tell you something before you come over tomorrow for Halloween," she said before I could say a proper hello. I didn't know I was planning on going over to her house tomorrow, but I let that slide. It was a fair assessment on her part. I always pleaded work on Saturdays, which theoretically left Sundays open for church, but definitely not in practice, and visiting my parents.

"All right—" I started.

"Apparently, your sister mentioned your disappointment to Andrew about Damion, and last night Andrew and Damion talked—"

I groaned—quite loudly, in fact—but my mother didn't seem to notice one bit.

"—and it was all a misunderstanding. Damion is very interested in you, and yes, he did ask you about the golf weekend at my insistence. But he told Andrew that he probably would have asked you anyway."

What's your point, Mother? Instead I said, "It doesn't matter. We aren't dating anyway."

"That's just the thing, Bee. Tomorrow, Andrew and Damion said they'd stop by for some dessert after a round of golf."

"Mother!"

"And I thought it would be nice, since you're planning on coming over anyway, of course, if you could maybe be here around 2:00?"

"*Mother!*"

"I'm planning some fun Halloween games for the kids, so Jackie will be here too. Later, Andrew will take them out trick-or-treating around the neighborhood. I'm sure Damion and you can chat in private on the back porch to clear all this up or even take a drive up the coast—"

"Mother, that's not going to work." I hated to interrupt, but then again, it was quite necessary at this point. Before I could take stock of my reasoning, I rushed on. "I'm bringing a date."

"So if you'll just . . . What?" Dead silence.

I could practically hear her mind working, after the shock subsided, of course. *My* shock *and* her shock. How was I going to pull this off now? Had I really thought I could bring Grey to meet my parents—my whole family? Maybe he already had Halloween plans. And was I really giving my mother advance notice so she could possibly invite several aunts and uncles to witness the great Athena miracle? This was giving her plenty of time to turn her Halloween games into a full neighborhood party.

I could hear my mother on the phone speaking to every living relative, saying, "Athena, yes, my thirty-two-year-old single daughter, is bringing a *man* over. To meet us!" I was grateful she didn't use e-mail.

Crud. What had I done? My mind had tricked me. How could I ask Grey to come over? What would he think? Of course it had to be Grey; it couldn't be Karl. That would be too complicated, and my mother would never understand that I was using an ex-boyfriend to avoid Damion.

My mother recovered with a remarkable swiftness that impressed even me. "That's absolutely wonderful, dear! I'll let Andrew know, of course, that he might want to put off the after-golf visit with Damion. But I'll be sure to tell him Damion isn't off the list yet. Maybe he'll be fine on the backburner until we see how this new man plays out. With your record, Athena, I hope he'll last more than a few weeks." She paused, because, after all, even my mother had to breathe. "Is he Greek?"

I almost didn't hear the last question. My mind was spinning in a thousand different directions. I looked at the clock. 3:03. Impossible. It felt as if an eternity had passed since I'd interrupted my mother with the declaration that I was bringing a date to her home.

"Uh—he's not Greek, but he loves to read books."

Silence again. The clock changed to 3:04. Good. At least I knew that something was moving forward.

"All right, dear," she said in her too-bright, everything-is-okay voice. "Maybe you can still talk to Damion sometime just to straighten it all out. I'd hate for him to—"

"Mother, I have to go now. I'll call you later to let you know what time we'll be there." I hung up before she could ask me more questions. Like what

Grey's name was. Whether he'd been married before. Or what his annual salary was.

I buried my face in my hands and groaned. How would I get up the courage to invite Grey over to my parents'? This was not going well at all.

Chapter 12

I WON'T ASK HIM TO come to my parents' house. I'll just show up tomorrow and say the guy had to cancel at the last minute. I didn't even tell my mother his name. But then I pictured my mother stealing into the kitchen, where Andrew was on speed-dial, and telling him to hurry over with Damion.

Scrap that plan. I shook my head then scrutinized my reflection in the bathroom mirror. I'd been working on my hair for twenty minutes, and it still didn't look right. *Twenty minutes.* I had a feeling I was coming down with something.

I checked the time on my Blackberry. It was too late to call Grey to cancel. He should arrive any second. As if he could read my thoughts, the doorbell rang.

My heart skipped a beat. My hair still wasn't right, but I didn't want to leave him waiting in the hallway. I resorted to shoving my hair behind my ears.

I hurried to the door and opened it, hoping it would be windy on Balboa Island so my hair wouldn't matter.

I stopped my greeting midsentence when I saw that it was not Grey standing at my door but Damion.

"Uh—Damion? Um . . ." I stared into his green eyes. Definitely not Grey's.

"Athena, how are you?" he asked with a wide grin. He shifted from one foot to the other, shoving his hands into the pockets of his khakis.

He looked nervous, but I wasn't about to feel sorry for him. He'd shown up unannounced at my door just minutes before Grey should be coming over. My body froze as I heard unmistakable footsteps coming up the stairwell.

"What do you need, Damion?" I asked rather brusquely. I was already formulating the phone call that I'd be making to my mother as soon as I had a free moment. But first, I had to deal with Grey walking down the hall toward me, glancing back and forth between Damion and me.

I couldn't believe it. This only happened in movies—bad movies at that. I had sunk to the lowest of the low, and my life had plummeted into a bad movie.

Damion blundered on. "Just stopping by—in the area—and I thought . . ."

What had my mother told the guy? His attention moved to my approaching date.

I smiled at Grey, although it might have technically been a grimace. "Damion, I'd like you to meet Grey," I said in a voice about as loud as a mouse.

Stopping next to Damion, Grey held out his hand. The two men shook hands, quite awkwardly, I must say.

"Are you Athena's brother-in-law?" Grey asked in such an innocent voice that I immediately became suspicious.

I'd never seen someone turn so red before—except for maybe a teenaged girl. If there were blue ribbons given for blushing, Damion was a clear winner. "No, I—we're, ah, dating. Just visiting to see if Athena . . ." Then he stopped talking. Which really did everyone a favor.

I felt Grey's eyes on me, and I didn't dare meet them.

I also felt Damion's eyes on me, and you can only guess what I did. I couldn't believe it myself. But like I explained earlier, my life had been demoted to a bad—a very bad—movie.

I shut the door on both of them. Then I leaned against it, taking deep gulping breaths. Apparently, my lungs were working, and I was still alive, even if my quality of life had just taken a nosedive.

"Idiot!" I said to myself, possibly loud enough for the two men on the other side of my door to hear. How had this happened? *It's not my fault*, I wanted to scream at someone. *I don't know how this happened.* Well, maybe I did, and I'd be speaking to that source very firmly tonight. Then something told me there might not be any date if I didn't open the door and try to salvage something.

Damion's green eyes and self-conscious grin were on the other side when I flung the door open for the second time.

"Where's—" I hurried past Damion with a, "Sorry, I've got to go."

I didn't have time to stop and let the poor man down properly. Hopefully he was taking the hint.

I hit the stairs three at a time, which was quite the athletic feat when one was going *down* the stairs. "Grey!" I called out as I nearly tripped on the curb.

He paused, his hand on the door of his Jeep.

"Sorry!" I said in a loud enough voice that I'm sure all of my neighbors were suddenly drawn to their windows to watch me flounder.

I couldn't read Grey's expression. Was he mad? Annoyed? Disgusted? Would he laugh?

"I—I can't believe he came over," I said, out of breath as I reached the other side of his Jeep. His gaze met mine across the leather upholstery, still not revealing much. I continued. "I'm really sorry about that. I wasn't expecting him."

Grey said nothing, but at least he was gentleman enough to listen and not get into his Jeep and roar away.

I felt like an idiot, sounded like an idiot, but I'd lost all semblance of dignity already. "We went out once—well, twice if you count dinner at my parents'—but I don't count that." My dignity was gone for sure now. "Damion asked me to go on a golf weekend, and I turned him down. End of story."

Grey's eyes assessed me as if he were deciding whether or not to believe me. "I don't think *he* knows the story is over."

"That's because of my mother," I rushed on. "She's really pushing for us to date."

One eyebrow lifted.

"Damion's Greek." As if that explained everything. But really, it did. At least for my mother.

Grey stared right through me. I almost turned around to see what he was looking at. But then he seemed to focus. "Is there going to be a problem if I'm not Greek?"

"Yes, but only with my mother."

His eyes were warm, teasing. Something inside me melted, and until now, I hadn't realized how much I liked Grey and how much I wanted him to like me back.

His mouth turned up just slightly. "Are you okay with that?"

I smiled. But I really wanted to hug him. Fortunately, I was able to control myself, besides the fact that there was a Jeep between us. I didn't need more idiot points. "I'm definitely okay with that."

He nodded toward the Jeep, his gaze fully on me now. "You'd better get in before 'end-of-story' comes down those stairs."

My heart nearly stopped. I looked behind me like a skittish deer, but no one was there. Grey laughed at my reaction.

I opened the Jeep door and climbed in. In my sprint out of my condo, I'd forgotten my purse, which incidentally contained my money. At least I had my keys. I checked my pockets to see if I had a forgotten twenty.

"Don't worry, this is on me," Grey said, putting the Jeep into reverse.

Relief flooded me. There was no way I was going back to my condo, where, apparently, Damion still lurked.

When Grey pulled out on the street, I finally caught my breath. "I'm very sorry about that. I didn't know—"

"Athena," Grey said, cutting me off. "You already explained. Don't worry about it." And then he did the most extraordinary thing. He grabbed my hand and slipped his fingers through mine.

I sat there in disbelief, holding his hand and feeling warm all over as the wind tossed my twenty-minute hairdo about my face.

My bad movie had just earned a four-star rating.

Chapter 13

BALBOA ISLAND WAS A BIT of a tourist trap, but really, it was quite fun for the locals as well. Not that I'd been there recently to enjoy anything. In fact, I hadn't done much lately that would fall into the category of "something to do for fun." I might go so far as to say I was fun-challenged.

Grey parked the Jeep at the ferry loading dock. He bought our tickets, and I felt a tad guilty for making him pay, but that was nothing compared to my embarrassment over Damion. At least Grey had seemed to forgive that part of our date so far.

As we boarded the ferry, I wondered why I was so worried about Grey forgiving me. It wasn't like we were serious or really even in a relationship. But my hand still pulsed from him holding it on the drive over. And I couldn't stop smiling—or wanting to smile. I forced myself to hold back a little. After all, Grey hadn't met my parents yet.

Dread pitted in my stomach at even thinking of saying the words to Grey: *Would you like to have dinner with me at my parents' home tomorrow?*

What would his expression be then? Would he say yes out of politeness? Would he have a ready excuse?

Grey touched the small of my back, guiding me in front of him as we navigated through the crowd to the railing. I shivered at his touch, which made me realize my real fear. Grey might *want* to meet my parents.

And then I'd be faced with what I hadn't allowed myself to do for a long time: entertain the possibility that I wanted Grey to be a part of my life—and that he wanted me to be a part of his.

My heart pounded as we reached the railing. I didn't want to think of how much I wanted Grey to hold my hand again. I leaned on my elbows and looked at the churning gold-and-green water. The clouds had burned off from the morning, and now the sun touched everything.

Grey's hands grasped the railing as he took his place next to me. We were a couple of inches apart, not too close but close enough that I could imagine his shoulder brushing against mine. I glanced at his hands; they were strong, tanned, and had light golden hairs, as if bleached by the sun.

I bit my lip and looked back at the water. Could I just think normal thoughts? Maybe about work? I hadn't even checked my BlackBerry since the Damion/Grey incident.

I had no desire to. But maybe it would help me snap out of whatever daze I was in. I pulled it out of my pocket—thankfully I hadn't stowed it in my purse—but there were no new e-mails. So much for that distraction. I'd have to start thinking about Grey and the two-inch distance again. The ferry's engine revved, then we started slowly across the harbor.

My hair blew into my face, and I pushed it behind my ears.

"What a perfect day," Grey said.

I looked at him, my eyes narrowed.

"Well, almost perfect," he amended.

"I am really sorry about—"

"Athena, just enjoy the rest of the day." The corner of his mouth lifted into a smile. His eyes searched mine as if he was wondering if I could enjoy the day. Great. Our first date, and he already had me figured out.

I exhaled and looked out across the water. The people behind us and the screech of the seagulls faded into the background. Could I enjoy the day? It felt good to feel the sun and wind on my skin. I closed my eyes and lifted my face toward the sun, trying to soak in the moment, forget work, forget my sick father, forget the disastrous run-in with Damion, forget the inevitable confrontation with my mother.

"So . . ." Grey's voice cut into my revelry. "How old are you?"

My eyes snapped open, and I blinked to adjust to the brightness of the sun. "What did you say?"

"How—"

"Um . . . thirty-two." I peered at him, wondering why he was asking my age and also wondering how old he was.

He nodded, a half smile on his face.

"What? You aren't going to tell me your age?"

"Thirty-one."

I'd thought, or maybe hoped, that he was a couple of years older than me. But . . . younger? "So I'm out with a younger man?" I pretended to scrutinize him. "I don't know if my mother would approve."

He laughed. "Forget your mother; what do *you* think?"

I watched a seagull land a couple of feet from us, scrambling for a crumb on the ferry deck. "I think I can handle it." I lowered my voice. "What do you think about older women?"

He lifted his hand and brushed a blowing lock of hair from my face, tucking it behind my ear. His hand lingered. "I guess it depends on how much gray hair she has." He leaned forward, examining the color of my hair.

I couldn't help but breathe in his warm, sunbaked scent.

"You won't find any gray," I said.

"Is this a color job?"

"Only the highlights." I wished he'd move away so I could breathe normally, but, then again, I didn't want him to move at all.

"Hmm." He kept looking at my hair.

"I thought you'd like the color gray."

He slowly smiled. "Any color would look good on you."

I shook my head, a smile escaping. "That's completely cheesy."

"Yeah, but it made you smile. Though I'll apologize if you really want me to." He dropped his hand, but he didn't move back. He stood extremely close.

I kept my hand on the rail to keep steady. "Okay, I'll accept your apology, then," I said, trying to look serious.

He stared at me for a few seconds as I tried to come up with something else to talk about. Thankfully, he spoke first, "Do you want to rent a boat and take it out?"

"Sure. But you have to let me pay you back."

"Nope. You're not paying me back." His hand touched mine, and before I knew it, he'd threaded his fingers through mine.

"Then at least half," I said, momentarily distracted. "I can't let you pay that much."

"Athena," he said, his fingers tightening around mine. "Don't worry so much. Let someone take care of you for a change."

"What are you talking about?" How could he say that? He hardly knew me.

"I have very fussy sisters," he said. "Sometimes women just need to let go a little."

"So you're an expert on women?"

He laughed, squeezing my hand. "Hardly. But I do have plenty of advice."

"For me? Or for other men?"

He tugged my hand and pulled me close, leaning down to speak in my ear. "For you."

I played along. "So what's your advice, Mr. Grey?"

"A girl needs to have some fun once in a while," he said.

I stiffened. He was sounding like Karl and Damion. Was I really so transparent, so uptight, so awful to be with?

I peeked past Grey to the other passengers on the ferry. Some kids were wearing Halloween costumes already, and parents seemed to be happily chatting away. How did they live their lives? Did they maintain the balance between work and family and having fun? Was there really that much wrong with me?

I pulled my hand away from Grey and saw the surprise in his eyes. This date might be shorter than I thought.

I turned toward the railing, staring at the choppy water.

"What's wrong?" he said.

Don't ask me what's wrong. That meant I had to answer. "Nothing," I said in a firm voice.

"That's woman's talk for *you were just a jerk and don't even know it.*"

How could he do this to me? Make me angry and happy in the space of a few seconds? I refused to smile. He moved next to me, his shoulder nudging mine. "If I promise not to give you any more advice, will you promise not to push me into the water?"

"I promise." I smiled despite myself. "But only because you're a younger man and seem to have a lot more to learn about women."

"Does that mean you'll be my teacher?"

I cast a narrow glance at him. "You're really pushing it."

He kept his gaze straight ahead, but his lips quirked into a smile. "I have a feeling that might be what it takes to get a second date with you."

My mouth fell open. He was already thinking of a second date? My neck grew hot, and I turned to look at the water again, willing myself not to blush. I felt him watching me, and I didn't know whether I loved it or hated it. Well, maybe I did know, but I wasn't ready to admit it. The second date Grey had referred to might be much sooner than he anticipated. And it might be at my parents' house.

Once off the ferry, we passed a sign that announced a Halloween parade the next afternoon. "We don't want to miss that," Grey said.

"Definitely not," I joked.

He glanced over at me. "Are you dressing up tomorrow?"

"I don't even get trick-or-treaters," I said. "There'd be no one to see me."

He chuckled. "I could knock on your door."

I smiled. I didn't tell him that we might be knocking on my parents' door and playing Halloween games with my nephew and nieces.

We rented a small ski boat, and I completely gave up on my hair. In fact, hat hair would have been preferable to the rat's nest it was becoming.

Grey expertly steered the boat out of the harbor slip and guided it into open waters. "Do you want to drive?" he asked over the wind.

"No thanks," I said.

"Have you ever driven a boat before?"

"Not that I remember."

He gave me a funny look then rose from the captain's chair. He reached a hand toward me. "Come on."

"No, really, I'm perfectly happy."

He kept his hand extended.

"Are you giving me advice?" I asked.

"No, I'm inviting you."

I sighed and grabbed his hand. He pulled me up, and I sat in the captain's seat. Leaning close to me, he explained the gears and throttle.

When I had the hang of it, he sat in the seat behind me, propped his feet up on the side and linked his hands behind his head, eyes closed.

"Enjoying yourself?" I called back.

"Yep," he said with a laugh. "Just don't run into anything."

The entire ocean was before us. Several other boats were out but none close enough to make me worried.

Besides, Grey was right there.

See, Karl? I can be spontaneous with just a little coercion.

I pushed Karl out of my mind. There were some things I missed about him—but I wouldn't have met Grey if Karl hadn't challenged me to read. It was easy to believe I didn't have work or other things to go home to when there was a vast expanse of blue ocean surrounding us.

After awhile, Grey took over the driving, and I relaxed as we headed into the harbor.

Grey helped me off the boat, my legs a little unsteady. The sun was much warmer on land. I tried to finger-comb my hair, but I don't think it made too much of a difference.

When we returned the boat, Grey said, "I'm starving. Where do you want to eat?"

"You choose since it's on you," I said. Truthfully, I wasn't sure what kind of restaurants there were.

"What are you in the mood for?" Grey asked.

"I'm not picky," I said, still hedging.

He tilted his head. "I find that hard to believe."

I raised my eyebrows. "What do you mean by that?"

"We'll find out soon enough." He held up a guide he'd grabbed from the marine shop.

"Japanese? Mexican? Pizza?"

I took the guide and leafed through it. "How about the Island Grill?"

"Don't you want a sit-down restaurant?"

"Like I said, I'm not picky." *Because I'm always in a hurry.*

"All right. Sounds great to me." We walked through town, passing quaint shops and candy stores until we reached the Island Grill. There was a short line at the walk-up window. He ordered a steak sandwich with onions. I ordered a steak sandwich without onions.

"Don't like onions?" Grey asked.

"Not cooked ones."

"I thought you were Greek."

"Yeah, it's quite a tragedy," I said.

"Well, you *are* named after the goddess of war," he said with a wink.

"She was also the goddess of wisdom."

"Touché." He led me to a small rickety table. We sat on cold metal chairs, but the shade felt good after being in the sun all day.

After eating, we decided to explore a few of the shops before heading back across the harbor. I had never been much of a window shopper; I left that sort of stuff up to my mother and sister. But since I was already here . . . and I didn't quite want the day to end after all—no matter how much work I might be missing.

We walked through a small art gallery, a scented candle store that made Grey's eyes water, and a novelty shop with trinkets piled from floor to ceiling. I smiled at a lady in the novelty shop who clutched her toddler's hand in a death grip. One wrong move and a glass configuration would certainly shatter.

Grey stopped outside a candy store called *Too Sweet*.

"Are you a chocolate girl?"

"Sometimes."

"Caramel?"

I smiled.

"Let's go in."

We stepped into the shop, and before the door had shut behind us, I'd melted into a heaven of smells. I stood there in a daze for a few minutes, staring at the array of chocolate treats, caramel apples, candy, and nut popcorn.

"Athena?" Grey's voice sounded far away.

Someone touched my arm. "Are you okay?" Grey's voice was closer.

I blinked and saw Grey's concerned expression as he watched me. How could he know how I deprived myself of sweets and instead ate unsalted granola, plain yogurt, dressing-free salads, and lean meats? Only when I was at my mother's did I eat anything dessert related.

"I'm okay," I said, walking forward to the glassed-in displays of mouth-savoring beauty.

Grey stayed by me as I looked at each divine creation. He occasionally glanced at me with concern.

"I'm okay," I insisted. "You don't need to hover. It just smells really good in here."

He looked relieved. "What do you want?"

I let out a sigh. "Can you come back in an hour?"

He folded his arms across his chest. "Wow. I just found your weakness."

I couldn't answer him. My senses were on overload. How could someone work in a place like this and exist on the outside? I would have a cot in the back room or just set it in the middle of the store at night and sleep surrounded by the smell of vanilla caramel.

"Athena?"

Grey was trying to interrupt my thoughts again.

I think I said, "What?"

"Come on." He was pulling me with him. "You're scaring the employees."

"What employees?"

Outside, the salty air snapped me out of my dazed state. I turned away from Grey, trying to go back inside.

"No you don't," he said. In his hand, he held a white sack I hadn't seen before. From it, he pulled a gigantic caramel apple drizzled with white chocolate and rolled in miniature butterscotch chips. "This is for you."

I hadn't even noticed him buying the caramel apple. I took a huge bite, savoring the sweet and tangy. My teeth stuck together for a second as I tried to chew through the thick caramel, and apple juice ran down my chin. Grey laughed and handed over a napkin.

"Thanks," I mumbled.

He grabbed my hand, and I reluctantly let him lead me away from the candy store.

I took another huge bite. There was no going back now.

"Athena?" Someone had called my name.

I looked up and stared at Karl.

Not as much as Karl was staring back at me though. I couldn't really blame him. I had caramel oozing out of my teeth, white chocolate smeared on my chin, and my hand in Grey's.

"Hi," I said, feeling mortified and sure that spittle was flying out of my mouth.

Then I noticed he was with another girl—woman. Tall, thin, blonde. She had a bit of a sharp, narrow face, but her body made her look like she'd stepped out of an Adidas commercial. Perfect timing.

Karl's normally blue eyes seemed to glitter black. He had said something. Was it, *how are you?* or *nice to see you?* or *why are you on a date with this guy when I thought you were a workaholic?*

All I knew was that everyone was staring at me. I didn't know what had been said to know how to reply, so I said, "Karl, this is Grey. He owns a bookstore."

He owns a bookstore?

They just nodded at each other.

I think Karl introduced the woman next to him—who he *wasn't* holding hands with, by the way.

I might have said, "Nice to see you," or maybe it was, "Nice to meet you" to the blonde girl, but I was too focused on not opening my caramel-stuffed mouth too wide.

Somehow, they moved on, passing us, and somehow, I finished chewing and swallowing. I'd never look at a caramel apple the same way. And sometime during the exchange with Karl, I had let go of Grey's hand.

I glanced over at him, hoping to see his easygoing expression, but it wasn't there. He'd definitely noticed the hand dropping, and he'd definitely noticed that Karl was not a Damion-who-only-went-out-with-me-once.

One part of me wanted to sit on the sidewalk curb in the middle of all the people, cover my face with my hands, and wish for everyone to disappear. Maybe if I couldn't see them, they couldn't see me.

The other part of me wanted to chase after Karl and ask him why he had to come to Balboa Island today of all days. And besides, he was with a date too. Did he expect me to stay home and pine for him? He hadn't even spoken, texted, or e-mailed me with anything more than submitting pictures for the next magazine issue.

I tried to catch Grey's eye, but he wouldn't even look at me. He walked a little in front so I was out of his peripheral vision.

I was back to the bad movie.

Chapter 14

THE FERRY RIDE BACK SHOULD have been beautiful and possibly even romantic. The sun had set, and the lights on Balboa Island twinkled against the violet sky. Let's just say it was night and day compared to the ride over, no pun intended. Grey went right to the railing and leaned against it. I stood by him but allowed a careful distance. I didn't want a bunch of complete strangers thinking we were in a fight.

I tried to think of what I could say, how I could say it, to explain, but standing in the wind, with seagulls screeching and Grey's stone face, I was terrified.

This was new to me. I wasn't in control. Even when Karl had broken up with me, I knew it was really my choice. I hadn't wanted to commit. If I had, we'd probably still be together.

Once off the ferry, I followed Grey to the Jeep. He opened the door for me, surprising me a little but also making me feel worse. Why did he have to be a gentleman? Especially now?

I climbed in and said, "Thanks."

He nodded but didn't even look at me.

The drive home was pretty much silent, except for the radio, which I was grateful for. Out of the corner of my eye, I watched every movement Grey made, trying to gauge if he was mad or really mad. Or maybe annoyed. Or maybe irritated. And then I wondered what exactly the difference was. He wasn't talking to me—not that I had really tried to talk to him or explain anything. Well, I had tried in my mind, but that didn't count.

When Grey pulled the Jeep up to my condo, he shut off the engine. I don't know what I was hoping, maybe for him to drop me off but not for him to turn off the engine.

That meant I'd have to explain, I'd have to talk, I'd have to peel off a layer of my history—expose myself. And I didn't know if Grey would like what was underneath.

"I'm really sorry," I said, fighting back tears. I didn't need one more embarrassment.

"Stop apologizing," he said quietly but not accusingly.

But what else could I do besides apologize?

"I wish I could explain," I said after an uncomfortable silence, looking straight through the window at the shrubs between the sidewalk and the side of the building. I'd never noticed how evenly they had been trimmed.

"Then why don't you?"

I took a deep breath. Every instinct in my body wanted to get out of the Jeep, run up the stairs, and slam my door. Shut out this whole day.

"I guess that's my answer." He started the engine.

"No. Wait. I mean, I do want to explain."

He looked over at me. "I'm not going to force you to do anything you don't want to, Athena."

"I know," I said, looking down at my lap. "Karl is my ex-boyfriend."

"Another Damion?"

"No," I said in a faint voice. "Damion was just a blind date. Karl and I dated for about a year. He's the one I told the book club ladies about."

Grey blew out a breath. "You still love him?"

My heart jolted. *Love?* What was Grey talking about? "No," I said. "I— He—It's complicated."

He laughed. It wasn't a mean laugh, but there was an edge in it. "It's always complicated, isn't it? Not that I want to give you any more advice."

I relaxed just a sliver. I'd heard the amusement in his voice, although I didn't dare look at him quite yet.

"He dumped me because I didn't want to get serious. He told me I only cared about my work, that I couldn't even take the time to read a novel. And that's when . . ." I couldn't finish.

"When you came into my bookstore with the look of a woman on a serious mission," he finished for me.

I bowed my head in defeat. "Yes."

"And now?"

My head snapped up. "Now?"

"Now that you've joined a book club, started reading a novel, took half a day off of work on a Saturday to go to Balboa Island . . . Now have you proven Karl wrong?"

I looked at Grey. There was no humor in his eyes. He was dead serious. And he was dead right.

"Yes, I proved him wrong," I finally whispered.

"Are you going to check me off your prove-Karl-wrong list too?"

"It's not like that," I said, feeling mortified.

"Look, Athena," he said. "I like you, but you have to fight your own demons, or whatever they are. Don't worry about today. Don't worry about me. I think there are things you need to take care of before you"—he waved his hand—"do any more dating."

I nodded. Did I agree? The alternative was something I wasn't sure I was ready for—actually admitting that I liked Grey more than Karl. More than I thought was possible. That scared me.

"Okay," my voice sounded meek to my own ears. "Don't worry about walking me up. I think all lurkers are long gone." It was a bad joke with bad timing. I popped the door handle and slid out of the seat. I was suddenly freezing, and my legs felt shaky when I stood up.

"Thanks, Grey." I hoped he knew how sincere I was, although I couldn't think of anything else to say that didn't sound like another weak apology. He nodded but didn't say anything more. I stepped onto the sidewalk and just stood there, looking at the pavement.

Grey reversed the Jeep and pulled out of the parking space.

"Wait!" I stepped toward the Jeep, and he braked. I ran around the front and stopped next to his door. If I didn't tell him now, I'd probably never see him again. Even a guy as cool as Grey had a tolerance limit.

"I just—" I took a deep breath. "See, I do like you. A lot. And I don't know what to do about it." Grey opened his mouth to respond, but I rushed on. I had already gone this far, a little further wouldn't matter. "Even if Karl came over tonight and wanted to get back together, it wouldn't matter. I didn't want to get serious with him then, and I don't want to now. He *was* right that I'm a workaholic and that I have serious 'fun' issues. And I *did* have to prove to him I could do something different, but it was mostly proving it to *myself*." I took a much-needed breath. "I know you're sick of me apologizing, but I'm so sorry about Damion and Karl. But seeing them both in the same night, while I happened to be with you, made me realize something . . . Something I wasn't 100 percent sure of until tonight. Karl and I are over. Completely over."

I couldn't stand the way Grey was looking at me. Even in the moonlight, I felt the warmth of his eyes. "Athena—" he started to say, but I didn't let him finish.

I leaned forward, moving my hands to his shoulders, and kissed him . . . He didn't pull back, but he didn't respond either for a few seconds. And then he took over. Which I found out was a very, very good turn of events.

The only thing that stopped me from possibly passing out on the spot as he kissed me was the Jeep door between us. It kept me from igniting because if I had felt anything more than his lips on mine and his hands on my face and neck, I would certainly have ceased to exist.

Grey kissed me until we were both out of breath. It was nearly impossible for me to let go, but somehow I did. And somehow I let him drive away into the night. And somehow I made it into my condo without collapsing.

After shutting the door, I leaned against it.

I was in big trouble.

* * *

I woke up in a tangle of sheets, sweating and feverish.

It took me a minute to remember what day it was—Sunday—and what had happened the night before—kissing Grey.

Despite the achiness and general misery running through my body, I smiled. My heart fluttered as I remembered what I had said to him and how I had kissed him first and how it had taken me at least an hour to fall asleep after that.

I climbed out of bed to get a drink of water, and a wave of dizziness rushed through me. I sat back down and groaned. I was sick. My stomach roiled with flu-like nausea. A glance at the clock made me groan again. It was almost noon. I couldn't afford to miss work tomorrow. I'd put off plenty of things yesterday that I'd planned to do today.

Sunday was the only day I truly took off work and caught up on minor irritations like grocery shopping.

I wanted to crawl back into bed, but I knew I needed to get a drink and take ibuprofen. Where was my mother when I needed her? I grimaced at myself. If she had any inkling that I was sick, she'd be over with a gallon of herbal tea.

Just as I staggered into the kitchen, the phone rang, but it was back in my room and out of reach. By the time I made it to bed again, the phone was on its second call. I picked up and sighed as my mother's voice blared through.

Damion had apparently shared our encounter with my brother-in-law.

I groaned for the third time in less than a few minutes.

"What's the name of the man you're bringing tonight, Athena?" she asked.

I gathered my thoughts, hoping my voice didn't sound too shaky with the chills running through my body. I didn't want my mother to know how sick I was, or I'd be fending off the soup parade as well as the tea.

Sleep sounded so good.

"His name is Grey, but I don't think I can make it. I've got a fever."

My mother didn't take a breath for at least the next three minutes as she first asked me the origin of the name *Grey* and then drilled down a list of health-related questions—did she find them in some health magazine? Impressive. Also impressive was the way I was able to talk my mother out of coming over right away but stopping by after dinner when Jackie could stay with my father.

That would give me a few hours of sleep and hopefully a whole lot of recovery.

After hanging up with my mom, I drifted into a feverish sleep, the ibuprofen slowly easing the pain.

The sound of someone knocking at my door jarred me awake. It took me a moment to orient myself, and then I made my way to the door. My mother was early, although I couldn't say I was too surprised. It was around 5:00 p.m.

But it wasn't my mother on the other side of the door.

It was Grey.

Even though I thought I might fold over with weakness, I smiled, and then I frowned. I was a mess.

"I guess you didn't get my message?" he asked.

I shook my head, which hurt quite a bit, frankly. The ibuprofen had worn off. I decided to stick with using words instead of head gestures. "I'm not feeling well." I felt my legs go extremely shaky, and I hoped I wouldn't collapse with Grey standing there.

"I can see that," he said.

"You shouldn't be here. I'm probably contagious."

"I'm coming in."

My pounding heart went up a notch as he led me to my bedroom and helped me into bed. I didn't have the energy to think about what he thought about the décor—or the lack of décor, to be exact. Tan walls that were bare, white blinds, lavender bedspread. I tried to protest, but he just shushed me.

He disappeared for a few minutes then came back in. Somehow he'd put together a cup of herbal tea and made some toast. I didn't even remember having bread.

"Have you eaten today?" he asked.

I shook my head. Painful mistake. "Not yet," I croaked.

He placed a hand on my forehead like he was checking a little kid's temperature. "That must have been some kiss last night. You're burning up."

I wanted to hug him but was sure it would do me in, in more ways than one. I wanted to think of a good comeback, but nothing came. I could barely smile.

His hand moved along my face, brushing back my hair. I knew I looked awful. Why didn't he just make his escape now?

"The tea will take a few minutes to steep," he said.

"Okay," I whispered. "Thanks for coming."

He leaned over and kissed my forehead, which, despite my miserable condition, actually made me feel better. "I'm not going anywhere," he said. "You're too beautiful to leave in distress."

"Oh." My stomach fluttered. How could he think I was beautiful at a time like this? I didn't have the energy to contradict him.

He moved around my room, adjusting the blinds and straightening the bedspread. I wanted to tell him he didn't need to do anything, but I didn't think he would listen to me anyway. When the tea was ready, he propped pillows behind me and handed me the cup.

I took a few sips. The warm tangy liquid soothed my throat.

"I hope it wasn't the caramel apple," he said with a sly smile.

"I don't think so." I wasn't even sure what I did with it. Probably threw it away on the ferry.

The tea made me feel a little more stable. "My mom is coming over— she'll probably bring enough tea for the whole building."

"Should I get out of here before she comes face-to-face with your non-Greek friend?"

"She knows you're not Greek."

His eyebrows shot up. "She knows about me?"

"Just a little." I paused. "Or I should say, she knows just enough to keep the blind dates at bay."

Chapter 15

GREY STAYED UNTIL NEARLY 7:00 p.m. I don't really know if he was hanging around to meet my mother or if he was that concerned for me or just extremely bored.

The combination of the tea, a few bites of toast, and having Grey nearby—who knew he was such a great nurse?—made me feel quite a bit better. In fact, I even cleaned myself up, and we sat on the couch together with the television on mute.

"What do you think about *The Poisonwood Bible*?" Grey asked, having noticed it on the end table.

I picked up the book and opened to the place I was reading. "I'm halfway through. Just started reading the part about the ants." I shuddered. "I think I'll wait until I feel better to read any more."

"I agree," he said. "Some parts of the book are kind of hard to stomach."

I noticed Grey had moved quite a bit closer to me. He took the book from me and set it on his other side. "When you finish, you'll have to let me know what you think of the ending."

"Is it a happy ending?" I asked.

His expression grew thoughtful. "For some."

"No hints?"

He shook his head and reached for my hand. I started feeling dizzy all over again, but this time it wasn't from any illness. He leaned in, a bit hesitant, maybe wondering how sick I really was.

"You're going to catch my germs," I whispered when our lips were only about an inch apart.

"Then you'll have to make me tea," he whispered back.

He kissed me gently, as if I were fragile and he didn't want to break me. I could tell he was holding back, which was a good thing, since I was pretty much at his mercy.

When he slowly pulled away, he kept his hand on my neck, his thumb stroking my jaw. "I think I'm getting a fever now."

"Really?" I studied him, looking for any sign of paleness.

He chuckled. "You're definitely contagious."

I took a swipe at him, but he caught my hand and pulled me closer. "And you're definitely hot," he said and kissed me again before I could respond. My body shivered.

"Are you okay?" he asked.

"Getting better," I mumbled, feeling a little dazed.

"You should get some sleep; you've been up for a while."

I nodded but didn't want to move out of his arms. *Maybe I could fall asleep in them . . .*

Then I brought myself back to reality, thinking of my mother coming through the door and seeing me in this position. Actually, she'd probably be happy.

"Athena?" Grey said.

"Hmmm?"

"Do you want me to help you to your room?"

"No. I'll just stay here."

"Okay, I'll grab a blanket."

He released me, and his warmth was gone. I immediately missed it. I curled up on the couch and closed my eyes. A few seconds later, Grey put a blanket over me and tucked it around my feet.

He kissed my forehead. "Call me when you wake up."

"Okay," I said, already half asleep and feeling completely spoiled.

"Even if it's late; I want to know if you're feeling better."

I opened my eyes just a little and nodded, wondering if I really deserved this guy. He touched my shoulder for a second then left the condo, the door shutting quietly behind him.

I must have fallen asleep because I woke in the dark to a ringing phone. At first I was confused that my mother hadn't come over. Surely I'd remember that. A quick glance at the clock told me it was 8:30 p.m.

Recognizing my sister's cell phone number, I answered.

"Athena? Tell Mom I have to get the kids home to bed."

I sat up on the couch, feeling disoriented. Then I remembered Grey putting a blanket over me and leaving. "What do you mean? Mom's not here."

"Okay, how long ago did she leave?" Jackie asked.

"She never came over." I still felt weak, but I wasn't feverish, and I would have certainly remembered. "Maybe she stopped at the grocer's first to get fresh tea leaves or something. You know how she goes all out."

My sister didn't laugh. There was a long pause instead.

"Mom left here at 7:00," she said. We both knew that while Mom was thorough in her mothering ministrations, she wouldn't have spent ninety minutes at a grocery store on a Sunday night with me sick and my sister watching over Dad.

Cold flashed through my body, settling into my stomach with a tight grip. "Did she take her cell phone?"

We also both knew she'd never learned how to use the cell phone Jackie had bought her for her birthday. "No," she said in a quiet voice.

"If I wasn't sick, I'd come over and watch Dad so you could leave." I pushed up from the couch. No dizziness, just weakness. "I'm feeling a little better."

"Maybe she ran into a neighbor at the grocery store," Jackie said, but there wasn't much confidence in her tone. Still, we both knew how much my mother could talk, and if it wasn't someone she'd seen in a while . . .

"If she shows up there," Jackie continued, "call me immediately."

"Okay." My voice shook a little. "And you do the same if she gets there first."

There was no good-bye, just a few seconds of silence and then a click.

I turned on a lamp and shuffled into the kitchen for a drink of water. The tea that Grey had left was cold. I leaned against the sink, wondering where my mother had gone. Then I wandered over to the couch and curled up in the blanket Grey had brought out. I checked my phone to see if my mother had called and I hadn't heard the ring for some reason.

She hadn't called. Only a message from this morning from Grey. I'd missed it when I'd first come into the kitchen. I played it, smiling at the sound of his voice. *Hi, Athena. Just checking to see if you've recovered from yesterday yet. Call me if you have. I have the day off.*

I held the phone to my chest, swathed in the blanket, and I must have drifted to sleep again because the phone jarred me awake a second time.

Jackie again. I glanced at the clock before answering. 9:15 p.m.

She didn't wait for me to answer. "It's Mom." And then she started to cry.

I bolted up from the couch. "Jackie? What's wrong?" She kept crying, her sobs turning hysterical.

Tears filled my eyes, and my chest constricted, making it hard to breathe. "Tell me . . . w-what's wrong?" I choked out.

Her husband's voice came on. "Athena, your mother was in an accident. We just got a call from College Hospital. They don't think she'll make it through the night."

The phone slipped from my hand, and I sank to the floor. I could hear Jackie's cries coming from my phone, sounding like a Halloween CD playing in the background. I covered my face with my hands as my mind closed off.

Chapter 16

I DIDN'T KNOW HOW LONG I'd been sitting in my car. I wasn't even wearing shoes, but I had somehow started the engine, although I had not moved from the condo parking lot.

Jackie's sobs rang in my head, and I couldn't shut them out. Then I realized they were my own. I forced myself to take several deep breaths then reached for the gearshift with a trembling hand and automatically checked the rear window. I couldn't see anything. My vision was too blurry.

I collapsed on the steering wheel, more sobs rising. Maybe my mother would be okay. Maybe the doctors were wrong. Maybe I'd get to the hospital and she'd be upset that I'd left my condo wearing my pajamas and no shoes.

I lifted my head, but my body shook all over, and I knew that if I drove, there was a good chance I'd get in an accident too. I picked up my phone and, with trembling hands, managed to call Grey.

"How are you feeling?" Grey answered.

I stumbled over my words. "I—Grey—It's my mother."

I heard the instant alarm in his voice. "What's wrong?"

"She's in the hospital," I said then started crying again.

"Where are you?" he asked.

I couldn't catch my breath to answer. The tears just kept coming.

"Are you home?" he asked. "Tell me where you are, Athena."

"Home," I whispered.

"I'm on my way," he said.

I let the phone fall into my lap and leaned back in my seat. This wasn't happening.

I didn't know how much time had passed when my car door opened. Grey was standing there. He pulled me out of my seat and drew me into his arms. I clung to him as he rubbed my back.

"She was in a car accident," I gasped. "They don't know if she'll make it."

"Which hospital?"

"College."

He guided me around the car and sat me in the passenger seat. We drove to the hospital in silence. I'd stopped crying, but I was numb all over. At one point, Grey put his hand on my forehead. I was hot again, still sick, but it didn't matter. My mother was fighting for her life.

We pulled up to the emergency entrance, and Grey stopped the car.

"I don't think we can park here," I said.

He climbed out and put his arm around me, guiding me into the emergency entrance. The bright lights blurred my vision, and I blinked against them, trying to focus. Grey spoke to the woman at the front desk, and soon we were on our way to the intensive care unit.

We stopped at another desk, and again, Grey spoke to the nurse. "Only family members are allowed in," the woman said.

Jackie was coming out of a room down the hall. Her eyes were swollen and red. My heart lurched.

Grey released me, and I walked toward my sister.

Jackie collapsed into my arms, and somehow, I held her up. "They say . . . They say there's nothing they can do."

I clenched my teeth together as the air left my body. This was not happening; this was a dream. But Jackie's trembling body said otherwise. I squeezed my eyes shut, blocking out the fluorescent lights overhead and their reflection in the gleaming floor below.

We stood there for a long time, but finally, I was breathing again, and there was space between my sister and me. Arm in arm we walked together to my mother's room. I didn't want to step through the doorway because once I did, I knew I'd have to face whatever was on the other side.

Jackie tugged me through, but then I stopped, staring from across the room at my mother, where she lay helpless on a sterile bed. My mother who never sat down. My mother who was always busy, always taking care of someone, always full of advice.

Her eyes were closed, her body covered in a white blanket. Her head was bandaged, hiding her carefully coiffed hair, making me think she wouldn't be happy about her appearance when she woke up.

Jackie led me to the bed, holding my hand. I stood there for a moment, watching my mother's chest move up and down, breathing, living. But it was artificial. She wore a hospital gown, but there was blood on the sleeve and the neckline. I reached out and straightened the blanket over her, pulling it a bit higher. Then I took her hand. It was warm and soft.

Every part of me burned with denial. Maybe she'd wake up. Her hand was warm, her chest moving with breath. "What happened?" I whispered.

"Someone turned right in front of her," Jackie said in a trembling voice. "Witnesses said she didn't have time to stop. Andrew is trying to find out more."

I blinked back tears as I thought of what it would mean to have my mother gone. "Does Dad know?" I asked.

"Leslie is staying with him right now. I don't think we should tell him . . . not until after . . ." She leaned her head on my shoulder, her voice catching.

I stroked my mother's hand. Her eye shadow and mascara were smeared; her red lipstick had faded. She'd always taken such pride in her appearance, even when taking a sick daughter some soup. I felt dizzy and weak. I sank into the only chair next to her bed, keeping a hold of her hand.

"Do you think she can hear us?" I asked.

"I don't know," Jackie said, a sob in her voice. "They say the machines are keeping her alive. There is no function in her brain, and her organs are shutting down."

Jackie moved to the other side of our mother's bed and grasped her other hand.

Tears fell onto my cheeks. Where was she now? Was her spirit still in her body? Was it hovering in the room? My mother was breathing, yet she didn't look like herself.

Jackie murmured something about Pastor Peter coming. Andrew had called him to administer the last sacrament, the Euchelaion.

I didn't want to hear about that now—to even think about it. I leaned over the bed and lay my cheek against my mother's hand. Closing my eyes, I concentrated on the warmth and softness of her hand again, wishing it could forever be like this.

Then Andrew entered the room with the pastor. Andrew's eyes were bloodshot and his face solemn. My eyes watered at the sight of him— thinking of all he was handling while Jackie and I spent time with Mother. Seeing the pastor in his robe and full beard made me realize this was really the end.

He greeted us quietly then crossed to Mother. As he administered the Euchelaion, we stayed silent. My heart twisted as I wished my father could be here to say good-bye to his wife.

When the pastor finished, we sat in silence for several moments, then Andrew went to speak with the doctor.

I gripped my sister's hand as the doctor and a nurse filed in. Andrew stood on the other side of my sister, holding her other hand. Then the doctor turned off the machines that were keeping her alive.

It took only seconds for my mother's breathing to grow sporadic. We all stared at her chest, watching it rise and fall, listening as her breathing grew more labored and shallow.

I couldn't move or speak.

Pastor Peter whispered more prayers, blessing her soul and her journey to paradise.

Jackie sobbed, and tears coursed down my cheeks.

My mother took a staggered breath, and then her chest was still. It was quiet, except for Jackie's cries and the pastor's murmurs. I pressed my cheek against my mother's hand as it grew cold.

The nurse came back in and pronounced the time of death. 12:44 a.m. November 1.

Jackie clung to Andrew, but I couldn't move. I stared at my mother's still face, waiting for her to take a breath, open her eyes, say something. Say anything.

* * *

Just after 6:00 a.m., Grey sat next to me on the couch in my condo. I leaned my head on his shoulder, and he stroked my hair.

"I need to get in the shower then call Jackie to see how I can help her," I said.

"You need sleep," Grey said.

I turned my face against his neck, and his other arm came around me. "You'll be able to think more clearly, and you need to get better."

"I know," I whispered. "But Jackie and I need to tell my father."

"He doesn't know?" The surprise in Grey's voice was plain. "Wasn't he at the hospital last night?"

"No," I whispered.

"I don't get it," Grey said, his hands stroking my arms.

Tears burned against my eyelids again, and I blinked against them.

"My father has Alzheimer's," I said, the word sounding foreign, as if this couldn't really be happening. I waited for the world to shift, for Grey to drop his hands as if he had just touched fire, but he only moved closer.

"I didn't know . . ." His voice was soft, tender, which made my eyes burn even more.

"And my mother—she took care of him at home." My voice wavered. After a deep, steadying breath, I continued. "She did everything for him . . . *everything*." I didn't want to sound selfish, but there was no other way to say it. "I'm not my mother. I don't know if I can pick up where she left off."

Grey pulled away from me. "What about your sister?"

"She has three little kids. I can't place the burden on her—my relatives already think I'm a failure in the daughter department. It's my responsibility to step in and care for my father. It's how it has to be."

His hands slid down my arms and grasped my hands. "You're not a failure."

A sob bubbled up in my throat. I knew he was just being nice, but no one had ever said that to me. I had always felt I was falling short of my parents' expectations. And now my mother had died before seeing her greatest wish fulfilled. If only I'd married a nice, successful Greek man like my sister had, produced a couple of grandchildren . . .

"Athena, where are you?"

I looked into Grey's eyes. "I'm someplace far away, being a horrible person."

He pulled me into a hug.

I tightened my arms around him, wishing I could reverse time. Why did my mother, of all people, have to die? Why not me or even, heaven forbid, my father—who was already going downhill? My vibrant, beautiful, caring mother was gone.

"Athena, you're not alone in this. You have me."

I started crying again.

Chapter 17

LONG AFTER GREY LEFT ME curled up on the couch with a blanket pulled around me, his words played over and over in my mind. *You're not alone in this. You have me.* But I couldn't let them into my soul. It wasn't fair to him. We'd just started dating. Yes, we'd kissed a couple of times—and I'd probably never forget them. But this relationship was different from any I'd experienced—at least on my end. Grey was different. And I didn't know if he knew that or even suspected it. He'd certainly witnessed enough to know I was a bit of a mess and didn't warm up easily.

I, the responsible, working president of my own company, could barely contain my emotions around this man. He made me want to curl up next to him, block out the world, and talk about nothing. *Who does that?* Definitely not Athena Di Jasper.

And now he'd unconsciously offered me a hand up to the next level in our relationship. Because telling him the truth about my father was definitely the next level. Karl hadn't even known about my father.

Focus, Athena, I chastised myself. *One thing at a time.* I needed to get cleaned up and get over to my parents' house. Telling Dad about Mom's death was the hardest thing I could imagine doing.

I rose from the couch, feeling weak and numb, but I had to push forward. I took a shower then dressed. I smoothed my hair back into a clip and left the condo.

My hands shook on the drive to my parents', and twice I pulled the car over to let the tears subside. When I arrived at the house, Jackie's car was in the driveway. For an instant, I wondered where my mother's car was; then I remembered.

I bit my lip to keep the crying at bay and climbed out of my car.

Andrew opened the front door. He looked like he hadn't slept either. He murmured something about taking the kids to his mom's. Jackie was in the kitchen, her head bowed over a cup of coffee. When I entered, she didn't even lift her head, but she held out her hand. I grasped it and squeezed.

"Where's Dad?" I asked.

"Still asleep."

"How do you think he'll take it?"

"I don't know," Jackie whispered. "He may not even understand."

My breath caught just thinking about it. My mind worked overtime as I wondered about how we'd pull all of the details together: the funeral, the arrangements, notifying our relatives.

We heard the toilet flush.

"He's awake," Jackie and I said at the same time.

She stood and linked her arm through mine as we waited for my father to shuffle into the kitchen.

A minute later, he came in. His iron-gray hair stuck up on the side, and his eyelids were puffy. He was wearing only pajama bottoms. I hadn't seen my father so undressed in a long time. My mother always insisted he at least wear a T-shirt.

My father stopped and looked at Jackie. He didn't say anything as he stood still for a moment then continued to shuffle to the table.

Jackie turned away, sniffling.

"Come sit down, Dad," I said. I pulled out a chair. "Do you want some oatmeal?"

He didn't answer, but at least he placed his hands on the table like he was waiting for something to eat.

I mouthed to Jackie, *Let's feed him first.*

There was nothing "instant" in my mother's house, so I had to boil water, add in oatmeal, then include a couple pinches of brown sugar, hoping that's how my father still liked his oatmeal.

Jackie busied herself slicing a banana.

We watched our father eat. He didn't ask for anything, just took several bites in a row. He only ate about half the oatmeal, and he didn't touch the banana. "Are you still hungry, Dad?" I asked.

He shook his head.

Jackie sat across from him, and I sat at the end of the table so I could see them both.

"Dad," Jackie began. "Mom was in a car accident last night."

He raised his head, his eyebrows drawn together. "She didn't wake me up."

"I know, Dad," Jackie said. She glanced at me, and I reached for Dad's hand.

He pulled his hand away as soon as I touched him.

"Mom was seriously injured, and she . . . she died this morning," I said.

Dad looked at the place on his hand that I had touched, then he looked up at me. "Carmen died?"

I nodded, tears burning in my eyes.

Jackie covered her mouth, stifling a sob. I looked back to Dad. His eyes were watery. Then he buried his face in his hands and started to cry.

I never thought I'd feel my heart break, but as I watched my dad cry at the kitchen table, the pain in my chest radiated through my whole body, making me want to double over.

I put my arm around him, but he didn't move, just cried into his hands.

Jackie was crying just as much. We stayed at the table for more than an hour with my dad. He asked a few questions, but mostly he grieved.

When I was able to lead my father to the front room, he sat down and stared at the blank television. I asked if he wanted to watch anything, but he didn't answer.

The room was so quiet, I heard Jackie puttering around in the kitchen, occasionally sniffling as she worked out her grief. I finally turned on the television so the house wouldn't feel so empty. I sat on the couch near my dad's recliner. After a few minutes, he reached over and patted my hand.

I looked over at him, and he said, "Tell Mother I want an egg and tomato sandwich for lunch."

My heart froze. *Mother is gone*, I wanted to say, but the calm look on his face stopped me. Did he really not remember spending the last hour crying over his wife's death?

"Just a minute," I said and left him sitting in front of the television.

In the kitchen, Jackie was scrubbing the spotless sink. She turned when I entered.

"He told me to ask Mom to get him a sandwich for lunch."

Jackie's face paled. "He's already forgotten?"

I sank into a kitchen chair, exhaustion catching up with me. "Do you think he'll remember later?"

Jackie closed her eyes briefly. "I don't know. Mom always knew what he'd remember or what we could talk to him about."

I ran my fingers through my hair and felt the still-damp roots. "Who can we ask?" I didn't have any friends in the medical profession.

Jackie let out a sigh. "We could call his doctor, but it might take awhile to get through. Google?"

"Okay," I said. "I'll look some things up to see if there are ways to help Dad through this when he's already forgotten what we told him."

The sound of the front door opening reached us. Andrew poked his head around the corner. "You gals in here?"

Jackie held her arms out, and he crossed the kitchen and stepped into them.

A lump formed in my throat. Even after all that had happened, they had each other.

"The kids are settled at my parents," Andrew said. "Jackie, why don't you take a nap? I'll hang out with your dad."

Jackie drew back, her face flushed with relief. She looked over at me, and I glanced away quickly, embarrassed she'd caught me in a moment of longing.

"Why don't you go home and sleep too, Athena," she said. "I know you're still sick."

I looked from her to Andrew. "Are you sure?"

They both nodded, their arms around each other's waists.

"I'll fix him a sandwich," Jackie said. "I guess the oatmeal breakfast didn't do it for him."

I went into the front room to say good-bye to my father first. He was watching the television with some interest. I kissed the top of his head, and he looked up at me. "Tell Carmen I want an egg and tomato sandwich."

"I will," I said in a thick voice.

I left the house, my heart heavy. I needed sleep. I needed to get better. And I needed to help my father.

Chapter 18

WHEN I WOKE UP, I was surprised to see that I'd slept through most of the day. Putting off checking any messages, I called Jackie right away.

"Andrew talked to Dad about Mom after you left," she said. "He started crying again."

My throat tightened as I imagined my father's emotion. "Did he say anything?"

"Not for a while. But later, when Andrew was watching a game with him, he wanted to look at one of the photo albums."

I exhaled. Maybe my father was remembering some things. Mother had kept photo albums of us as kids, and now the newer ones were mostly of Jackie's kids.

"How are the kids doing?" I asked.

"They keep asking questions," she said, her voice sad. "How are you feeling?"

I didn't quite know. I hadn't given myself enough time to wake up and assess my situation. "Better." I climbed out of bed, the phone still in hand. No dizziness. No nausea. "Much better."

"That's good," Jackie said. "Andrew is staying overnight with Dad." She fell silent for a moment. "But we'll need to figure out what to do . . ."

I was nodding. "I know."

Jackie and my mother were closer friends than I was with my mother, but neither of us knew the full extent of what my mother had done every day to care for Dad. We had a lot of work ahead of us.

My sister was speaking again, and I tuned back in. "I don't want to pressure you, but we need to discuss it soon," she said. "Andrew and I can trade off staying with Dad for now, until we can get things worked out. We too need to make some important decisions."

I nodded, although she couldn't see me. She continued talking. I was listening but not letting it soak in.

"It would be really crazy to bring Dad to my house," Jackie said. "I'd have to put all three kids in the same bedroom. Plus, he needs to be around familiar things. And we really can't move in with him. The kids are already established in school and with their friends . . ."

I massaged my temples as Jackie spoke. I was still in disbelief that my mother was truly gone, and Jackie already had the next year planned out.

"Athena, are you listening?"

"Uh, yes," I said not too convincingly. "What do you want me to do this week to help?" I couldn't discuss what she wanted to, not yet. I had to get through today, tomorrow, the funeral, and then I'd face the discussion. But not now, not yet.

"Andrew already called the mortuary," Jackie said. "We were thinking of holding the funeral next week on Wednesday."

I looked at my calendar. "That's over a week away."

"We need to give Mom's brothers a chance to get here. They'll probably want to fly over from Greece. And the funeral home is booked until the weekend anyway."

I let out a sigh, looking at my calendar. "So November 10?"

"Yes, I'll call Pastor Peter right now to see if the date works for him."

The image of the fully-bearded pastor we'd seen the night before came to mind. My heart swelled with gratitude at all that my sister was doing. I'd slept the day away while my sister had arranged our mother's funeral. "Thank you, Jackie," I said.

Her voice lowered. "Did you get some sleep?"

"Yes, I feel mostly normal, at least considering . . ." I paused. "How's Dad now?"

She sighed into the phone. "I haven't told him about Mom again. We've been able to distract him for the most part. But I worry about the day of the funeral."

"I do too."

After hanging up with Jackie, I opened a can of soup. While it was heating in the microwave, I checked my messages. There was one from Damion, expressing his condolences. He must have spoken to Andrew.

I straightened when I heard the next message. It was from Karl. The message was brief and completely open-ended. "Hi, Athena. It was good to see you . . . the other night. Hope you're doing well."

Nothing more. But he'd obviously taken the first step, and now the opening was for me to take. He likely hadn't heard about my mother either.

I clicked through to the next message as the microwave chimed. My hand paused on the microwave handle as Grey's voice came through my phone. It washed over me with warmth, and my eyes pricked with tears. There was real compassion in his voice . . . and maybe something more. My heart pounding, I tried to ignore the knots of fear beginning to form in my stomach.

I saved the message and carried the steaming bowl of soup to the table. After grabbing a spoon and a glass of water, I sat down. Hearing Grey's voice made me miss him.

That's where the worry was coming from—worry that I liked him too much, too fast. I'd just seen him the night before, and I was an emotional wreck, but I still knew I missed him.

I rubbed my forehead as the soup cooled. I had little to no willpower at the moment, and what was going to stop me from clinging to Grey, especially in the next few days? And then what would happen when I started to feel better and realized I had fallen into a relationship? My breathing quickened. It would be so easy, and I wouldn't even blame myself. *Don't even consider it.* Tomorrow I'd be able to think clearer. I took a sip of the hot soup and was glad it scalded a bit as it went down. I needed the wake-up call.

As I ate, I listened to Grey's message again. Then a third time. Tears slipped down my cheeks. I needed him. The image of my sister embracing her husband and my father forgetting my mother's death came to mind. They each had their coping mechanisms. What was mine?

Next week I'll worry about if I was letting him get too close, I decided. Next week I'd sort out my feelings for Grey. After the funeral. But right now, I needed his support.

When I finished the soup, I called Grey.

"How are you feeling?" he asked right away.

I was about to say, "Much better," but it came out as a raspy "Terrible."

"I'll be right there." He hung up.

Closing my eyes, I pressed the phone against my chest as if I could feel him next to me.

I suddenly felt weary again, despite the soup, so I walked over to the couch. I pulled up my feet and tucked them under me as I gazed out the window. My mother had always complimented my view—majestic trees with glimpses of the ocean. I'd been lucky to get into this condo right after it was renovated a few years ago. It was only about fifteen minutes from my parents' home yet separate enough to give me my own life.

What kind of life had it become? I had buried myself in my own work and only graced my parents once or twice a week, and I rarely bothered to see my sister, who was married and busy herself. I wondered at my mother and how she'd managed to keep it all together. She hadn't left my father's side in months, and I had barely noticed the increasing burden of her caring for my father.

The fact that Jackie felt either Andrew or she had to be with my father night and day proved how neglectful I had been. I grabbed my laptop from my office and sat back down on the couch to Google the stages of Alzheimer's. When my father was first diagnosed, my mom had given Jackie and me some pamphlets. I had skimmed through them and decided the disease was so slow moving that I didn't need to research it too much at the time.

But now, reading through the stages of Alzheimer's on the Internet, I realized my father was more advanced than I'd thought. He hadn't called me by name for a very long time, yet I assumed he recognized me. The websites said an advanced stage was when the person stopped caring about their appearance and cleanliness. My father was always dressed and clean—but he probably had my mother to thank for that. Also, I couldn't remember the last time my mother had taken him any place other than the doctor's office.

My stomach twisted. I had so much to learn. Could I even do half of what my mother had done? Maybe Jackie and Andrew would take him into their home after all. It was selfish of me to wish that, but I couldn't push the thought away.

I was in some sort of a self-hatred daze when a soft knock sounded on the door. I logged off of the Internet and rose from the couch to open the door. Grey stood there, wearing a worn T-shirt, faded jeans, and sandals. In his hands, he held a bouquet of white roses.

I steeled myself against the sudden rush of emotion. "Didn't have to work today?"

"I left a little early." He held out the flowers. "These are for you."

I took them and inhaled the heady fragrance then opened the door wider. "In that case, you can come in."

Grey's smile was tender. Instead of passing me and entering the living room, he stepped close to me and wrapped a hand around my waist. His other hand brushed my cheek and rested on my neck. He bent down and kissed my cheek.

I breathed in his nearness.

"You look better," he said.

I leaned into him, and he wrapped his arms about me. I practically melted against him right there in the doorway. No matter how much I chastised myself for relying on him so much, I couldn't make myself pull away.

Grey stroked my back and, after a moment, since I wasn't about to budge, led me into the living room. I sat on the couch and watched him with a blank stare as he set the flowers on the kitchen table then came over to me.

"What do you need?"

For my mother to come back and my father to be cured, I thought. But I didn't say anything.

He noticed the open laptop. "What are you working on?"

"Researching Alzheimer's. I need to know as much as I can about it."

His eyebrows lifted. "Have you decided to take care of your dad?"

My lips trembled. "I don't see another solution." I looked down at my hands, wishing I wasn't such a weak person. "Jackie and Andrew will help, of course, but someone needs to be with him full time."

Grey reached for my hand. "That's a major commitment."

Looking at our clasped hands, I realized that he was only talking about half of it. "But he's my father." I felt Grey's gaze on me.

"Athena, my great-aunt had Alzheimer's. I was pretty young, and I know that there are medications that slow the progression now, but taking care of someone full time is a really big decision."

"I know," I whispered, my chest constricting. I couldn't even take care of a relationship. My sister had always been the strong one in that department, caring for a husband and three kids and managing to keep it all together. "It's the least I can do for my mother."

Grey was quiet.

I looked over at him. "What was it like with your great-aunt?"

"I was only about ten or eleven, although I remember thinking it was strange that she didn't know my name," he said.

"I can't remember when my dad last spoke my name, but he still remembers my mother's name."

Grey nodded. "Everyone's progression is probably a little different. You should meet with his doctor and find out where he is exactly."

"I wouldn't be surprised if my sister already has that arranged," I said, not able to hide the bitterness in my voice. Here I was, barely able to fix myself soup, and my sister was making phone calls.

Grey caught the tone. He slipped an arm behind me and kissed my forehead. "I think you're pretty great."

"Ha," I said. "You don't even know me."

He lowered his head so that we were eye to eye. "I know enough."

I looked down, feeling tears threatening. "Why are you so nice to me?"

"I thought we already established that," he said in a teasing voice.

"I mean, I'm a mess right now." I closed my eyes. "I'm sure you have better things to do than babysit me."

"Not really," he said. "Babysitting is a top priority."

"You know what I mean."

"Athena," his said, his tone serious. He touched my chin and lifted my face. "I like you, okay? Mess or no mess, I still like you."

"I don't want to drag you through this—maybe in a couple of weeks when I'm feeling better, we could go out again or something."

Grey stared at me for a moment; I couldn't tell what he was thinking. As much as I wanted him to stay and baby me, I needed to give him an out. I needed to know if he really liked me or was just feeling sorry for me.

"A couple of weeks, huh?"

I nodded, swallowing hard. It took everything I had not to sink into his arms and keep him by my side over the next week while I tried to wade through my grief.

"Athena, you're so frustrating."

My heart pounded, and I wanted to cry. He was angry and had every right to be. But it was better this way. I liked him too much to make him miserable along with me.

"I'm sorry," I said. "I didn't plan for any of this."

His brows pulled together. "Neither did I."

I waited for him to stand up and walk out the door. Instead, he placed his hands on each side of my face and kissed me hard. Before I realized what exactly was happening, I kissed him back. Tears ran down my face as we kissed, and I decided I had finally, truly, lost it.

When Grey pulled away, we were both quiet for a moment. Then he wiped the tears on my cheeks and said, "Let's get out of here."

"But I—"

"I'll carry you out if I have to," he said in a hoarse voice. He stood up and pulled me along with him. "You have two minutes to get ready."

He released me, and I went into my room, every part of my body trembling from his kiss. I changed from my sweats into jeans and pulled on a fresh shirt. I washed my face but didn't bother with make-up—my eyes were too swollen. My phone rang from the living room, and I walked out to see who was calling. Grey held it out to me.

Karl's name flashed on the screen. Grey had obviously seen it. I pushed the End button, sending the call to voice mail.

"He probably heard about my mom," I said.

Grey nodded, reached for my hand, and gripped it possessively. I didn't tell him about the previous message—when Karl was just calling to say hello.

We walked to Grey's Jeep, and I burrowed down in the warm seat. The sun was just beginning to set, throwing oranges and pinks across the sky.

"Where are we going?" I asked.

He looked over at me. "I don't know."

"That sounds perfect," I said, and despite myself, I smiled.

Grey started the Jeep then grasped my hand.

Chapter 19

"SORRY I WON'T BE ABLE to make it to the funeral," Karl said in a low voice.

I stared out the window at the innocence of the clear blue sky. The trees on the edge of the parking lot rustled in the breeze, and a car pulled into a parking space—as if life could go on when I was getting dressed for my mother's funeral. It had been a week since my mother's death, a week of struggling through work deadlines and spending the rest of the time in tears. Karl had called to tell me his flight into LA was delayed. He'd planned on coming, but I felt nothing one way or another. Karl could come, or he could sit in an airport.

I wondered if Grey wasn't around—seemingly every minute—if I would have turned to Karl. But our relationship had never had much depth—at least on my part. Would we have grown closer together during this time if we hadn't broken up beforehand?

I never asked Karl about the woman he was with on Balboa Island, and he didn't ask about whom I was with. For now, the elephant would stay in the room.

"I'll call you when I get in," Karl said.

"All right," I said.

After hanging up, I slipped on my heels, realizing I'd forgotten panty hose. The effort seemed too much all of a sudden. If the church was cold, maybe it would have a numbing effect.

The phone rang, and seeing it was Ruby from book club, I answered it. I'd already called earlier in the week to tell her I had to miss Saturday's book club because of my mother's death. When Ruby's voice flooded through the other end, I let her motherly tone envelop me.

"I just wanted you to know that I'm thinking of you today," she said. "And I'll see you at the funeral."

I hardly knew her, yet she was so sweet. And for a moment, I allowed myself a measure of comfort.

"Thank you, Ruby. That means a lot to me."

When we hung up, I silenced my phone. I didn't want any more calls.

Grey said he'd pick me up, but I talked him into meeting me at the church. The first part was for the immediate family anyway, and despite my reliance on and gratitude for Grey, I didn't want my sister reading into our relationship any more than I was able to handle explaining right now.

I left my condo and stepped into the sunny day. The sun always made me feel better, no matter how gloomy my thoughts or how stressful work was. But today it seemed to mock me. It was unusually warm for a November day, even in Newport. I jumped on the 5 freeway and headed toward Irvine, where St. Paul's was. It was the same church where my sister and I were baptized as infants, where my sister was married, and where my mother attended before my father started declining.

As I pulled into the parking lot of the grand church, my throat tightened. A hearse was parked at the side entrance; a floral company van sat next to it.

This is really happening.

I chose a shady place to park and walked slowly into the dim interior. Maybe if I moved slowly enough, something would change, time would reverse, and I wouldn't really find myself here.

I entered the church, and an usher directed me toward a side room. My footsteps echoed off the massive white ceilings as I walked. It had been awhile since I'd been inside this church, and it was impressive. When I stepped inside the side room, I saw Jackie first. She rushed to embrace me, and I don't know who held the other more tightly. When we pulled apart, I noticed that her kids were dressed nicely and that Andrew wore a full suit. Behind Andrew stood Damion. I almost did a double take. Why was he at the family gathering? Before we could enter into any sort of awkward greeting, the room filled with all my Greek relatives.

My mother's two brothers had flown in from Greece, and my father's sister, Fran, who lived in Northern California, had come with her children and a few grandchildren. Perfumes, colognes, and aftershaves all blended until I thought I might be a good asthma candidate.

The number one question asked of me was not how I was holding up but whether or not I was dating someone special. More than a few significant looks were thrown in Damion's direction when he was introduced as Andrew's friend *and* my friend.

My father arrived, walking in with Uncle Jon, Aunt Fran's husband. A hush fell over the room as they walked to the casket together. His eyes looked sunken and hollow, his expression utterly bereft. Uncle Jon must have told my father recently about my mother . . . again.

The confusion and pain in his eyes tugged at my heart, and I had trouble catching a full breath. People moved out of the way so he was the only one standing next to the casket. My eyes connected for a moment with Jackie's, and with her affirming nod, I agreed that we'd done the right thing by having our father at the funeral, even if as early as a few hours from now he might forget everything completely. It was important for him to honor his wife's memory.

My father stood in front of the casket, looking stunned for a few seconds, then he started crying. Uncle Jon's arms went around him, and Jackie and I hurried to help. No one in the room spoke as my father cried; everyone's eyes were wet with tears.

Thankfully, my father calmed down when the time came to enter the chapel behind the wheeled casket. Everyone was standing as we entered, and I looked for Grey, hoping to see something in him that might keep me held together. But it was hard to distinguish him among all of the assembled black-dressed mourners.

We stood by the casket, and a few more family members came forward to greet us. Kisses on both cheeks and hugs went all around.

As I took my seat between my mother's brothers, I chanced another glance behind me. I still couldn't see Grey.

Pastor Peter stood up in front of the congregation, his long robes commanding attention, and the services officially started. Around me, my relatives repeated some of the words the pastor said, whispering them over and over. I found myself joining in, "May you have an abundant life, and may her memory be eternal."

Mother's life had been abundant—I could see that now. I had felt that she sometimes catered to others too much, gave of herself more than she should have, but her memory would definitely be eternal. I wondered if her spirit was present—if it would linger during the funeral and internment. I had no doubt her spirit would be escorted to paradise. If anyone was an angel, my mother was.

Father grasped my hand with his trembling one as the service concluded and the family rose to their feet. He seemed to have lost his strength in his grief. At this point, he was still remembering where he was and why. I wondered at his memories of my mother, of when she was much younger—I'd love to hear some. Jackie came to my aid and stood on Father's other side, and we walked with him down the aisle, following the casket out of the chapel.

I swung my gaze around again, searching for Grey, but instead, it landed on some very familiar-looking women. It took me several seconds to realize who they were—since we'd only met once.

Ruby stood with Daisy, Paige, and Livvy. They all offered small smiles, and I smiled back, feeling touched that they had all come. Tears pricked my eyes, and I nodded to each one, mouthing a thank you. I didn't know these ladies well, but the fact they had come to show their support meant more to me than I could have thought.

"Where are we going?" my father asked, pulling my thoughts away from the book club ladies.

My heart skipped a beat, and I glanced over at Jackie. She shook her head but kept her composure. I vowed to do the same. Then I saw Grey. He was near the back of the chapel, standing next to the aisle. As I passed, he touched my arm. My throat was too thick to speak; I hoped he'd come to the graveside service.

Outside, Andrew guided us into a limo, and we pulled out behind the hearse. We moved through the traffic slowly, and on the way, Andrew explained in quiet tones to my father what was happening. I don't know what Jackie or I would have done without Andrew at that moment. I could barely stand to look at my father's stricken expression.

By the time we arrived at the cemetery, my father was subdued and somber. We walked with him toward the gravesite, although it was Andrew he hung on to now. The floral arrangements were magnificent. My breath caught as I realized my mother would have been impressed.

Jackie and Andrew surrounded my father, so I took my place off to the side of the casket. Closing my eyes, I inhaled the scents coming from the flowers and let the breeze stir around me. The warmth of the sun enveloped me as I wished my mother were still here—walking and talking, even ordering me around.

Tears tumbled down my cheeks; it wasn't a desperate sorrow any longer but a healing sorrow. It was good to have my uncles here and other relatives. It was good to honor a great woman.

A shadow crossed in front of me, and I opened my eyes to see Grey. He gave me a gentle hug. I was sure all of my relatives now had plenty to speculate on, but for once, I didn't care.

"Thanks for coming," I said.

He just nodded as if he knew there weren't many words to be said. I took his hand, noticing his pleased expression, and led him toward the chairs where most of the family was seated. We sat together, and I knew there was no one else I'd rather be sitting with on a day like this.

Chapter 20

"Ruby," I said into the phone, my feet propped up on the packing boxes in my office. I was nearly done packing to move in with my father. "Thanks so much for coming to the funeral."

The voice on the other end of the line gushed with sympathy. I assured her that I was okay, sounding far more confident than I felt, until she changed the subject and got down to business. "Everyone loved *The Poisonwood Bible* choice. We're so sorry you couldn't make it to book club the other night, but of course we know how awful that week must have been for you."

I thought of the book club ladies at the funeral, all offering smiles and a show of support. It would be nice to see them again.

"I wasn't quite finished with it when my mother died," I said, surprised that my voice didn't break. Regardless, I took a deep breath before continuing. "My heart connected with Orleanna Price."

"I imagine it did," Ruby said in a hushed voice. "I thought of my husband when I read about Orleanna's grief."

Tears filled my eyes. I crossed to the box I'd just placed the novel in. Picking it up reminded me of another time and place, when I'd first met Grey and my mother was still alive. Another lifetime.

I thumbed through the pages as Ruby shared some things about her husband's funeral. Normally, the intimacy of this type of conversation would make me uncomfortable but not now. Talking to Ruby was comforting. She understood my pain. My hand stalled on a passage I'd marked.

When Ruby paused, I said, "I don't know how the author did it—she captured the emotions so perfectly." I let out a breath. "I underlined a few sentences . . ."

"Which ones?" Ruby asked in quiet voice.

"'As long as I kept moving, my grief streamed out behind me like a swimmer's long hair in water. I knew the weight was there, but it didn't touch me . . . So I just didn't stop.'"

"She stayed busy," Ruby said, her tone reverent. "She kept going, moving forward. It's all any of us can do."

"I know," I said, turning a few more pages. I'd treasure the book, and it would never end up in a used bookstore again. "What are we reading next?"

"*My Name Is Asher Lev* by Chaim Potok," Ruby said, her tone brightening. "It was Livvy who recommended it, which surprised me, frankly. I thought she'd recommend something by Dr. Phil. But no matter."

Ruby continued to chatter about the book, and I couldn't get a word in, so I leaned back in my office chair to listen. Truth was, she reminded me a little of my mother, and I was going to soak in every busybody word.

I'd read the book in high school, but it had been so long ago that I'd forgotten everything about it.

"And you won't believe this, but we have a new member named Ilana, who is Jewish!"

I wasn't sure if she was exclaiming on the religion or the coincidence of the group having just chosen a book about a Jewish boy. I said the most noncommittal thing possible. "Interesting."

"She's a lovely young thing—works in the trade show industry though. I don't know how she stands being around all those vast warehouses, setting up booths. It must be the most dreary job, ordering cases of water bottles and such . . ."

Minutes later, I hung up with Ruby, feeling lighter and happier than I had in days. I still felt the weight of responsibility on me, but it was nice to hear about other peoples' lives and troubles for a change.

The phone rang again, and I hesitated a few seconds after seeing the caller ID—Karl. I had to talk to him sometime, so I answered.

"Hi."

"How are you? I've been trying to call."

"It's been pretty crazy," I said.

Karl rattled on for a few minutes, offering condolences, giving excuses, and just as I dreaded, he said, "I wondered if we could go to dinner sometime this week."

Here it was. I had to do it, and I knew it had to be now. "I can't; I'm dating someone."

The silence made my stomach wrench.

"That guy at Balboa?"

"Yes," I said, forcing out the words. "It's not serious, and I don't know where it's going, but I can't—"

"You don't have to explain," Karl said, sounding hurt.

I would have rather taken anger, not hurt. "It's just—"

"Really, don't worry about it. I obviously don't want to force you into anything. I hope you'll be happy."

"I'm really sorry."

"Take care, Athena."

I opened my mouth to reply before realizing he'd hung up. I took a deep breath and stared at the phone. What had I told Karl? That it wasn't serious with Grey—and it wasn't. I had felt close to him over the past couple of weeks—that was true—and I didn't know how I'd be handling all of this without him, but maybe he was a distraction. Maybe I was trying to avoid grief—what were those stages of grief?

Just get through moving, and then I'll make the decision about Grey.

An urge came over me to call Ruby back. Maybe we could talk about the Jewish trade show coordinator woman again and speculate about all the nametags she'd printed out. Or I could get updates on Daisy or Paige or ask what kind of dessert Livvy had brought.

I groaned and slumped over my desk. I had done the right thing in being direct with Karl, but now I felt lousy. The hurt in his voice had been real. And before the hurt? There had been hope.

And now I was thinking about doing the same thing to Grey.

I had to work harder on becoming the new Athena. The one who didn't lead men on, the one who took her responsibilities seriously. I lifted my head and looked around my almost bare office. I was taking most of my office stuff to my dad's. Jackie and Andrew would spell me off every other weekend, so I was leaving some stuff here.

Packing had brought me some sanity in the days after my mother's funeral—that and spending time with Grey. But back to that, was I just leading him on?

A knock sounded on the door. I leapt from my chair, hoping it was him, and hurried out of my office. I forced myself to slow down and walk normally. I didn't want to appear too eager to see him. He might start thinking I really liked him.

Grey smiled when I opened the door. "Took you long enough."

I smiled back and was immediately enveloped into a hug. When it turned to kissing, the guilt over rejecting Karl faded rather quickly, as well as any thoughts of dumping Grey as soon as I was settled at my dad's. After a few minutes, I had to push Grey away. "I thought you came to help move boxes."

"Oh yeah," he said with a grin.

My heart thumped, and I had to restrain myself from kissing him again.

Within an hour, we had his Jeep and my car stacked with boxes. Grey followed me into Costa Mesa and helped me unload at Dad's. It was a strange feeling to be moving back home after so long. Dad sat with a neighbor, Mr. Durfey, watching television the whole time we went in and out of the house.

Once I got things semi-organized, I went back into the living room. "Mr. Durfey, thanks for staying until I could get here."

He was a short man, coming up to only my chin. "You're welcome. Your sister left a list in the kitchen—mostly his schedule—and she wants you to call her."

I nodded as if this was all new information to me. I had spoken to Jackie several times a day, and this morning she'd had to leave extra early, so she asked Mr. Durfey to come over until I could arrive.

"Thank you. We really appreciate your help," I said.

Mr. Durfey glanced over at my dad. "He's on one today."

I didn't dare admit that I wasn't sure what he meant, so I just nodded.

When Mr. Durfey left, I crossed over to my father. "Dad, there's someone here I'd like you to meet."

He looked up, his eyes a bit bloodshot, as if he'd been staring at the TV for too long. "The Olympiacos lost."

I nodded and leaned over. "Dad, this is Grey."

Grey didn't extend his hand or anything, which was probably wise since my dad barely looked at him. Here was the first man I'd actually wanted to introduce to my father, and my father didn't even acknowledge him.

I stood there, feeling horribly embarrassed, even though I knew better—it was the illness.

"Come on, Athena," Grey said in a quiet voice. "We can try later."

Grey followed me into the kitchen. My eyes were swimming by the time I looked at the note with Jackie's neat handwriting. I took a deep breath and tried not to think of the enormity of what I was undertaking. Focusing on the list, I realized everything on it looked pretty basic, not too daunting. "It looks like Dad wants a cheese and cucumber pita pocket." I could definitely fix that. Because I didn't know how to tell Grey to leave so I could have a good cry, I said, "Are you staying for lunch?"

"If you want me to."

I kept my gaze on the list. "I'll be all right here alone, unless you really want me to make you a cheese and cucumber sandwich."

"I should probably get to work," he said in a quiet voice, but he didn't sound too much like he was in a hurry.

"Thanks again," I said, "for your time and helping carry the boxes and everything."

Grey took the list from my hand and pulled me close to him. "I can come by later."

I leaned against him, relaxing into his warm chest. Maybe I could let him do this—be here for me—let us do this together. He didn't seem to mind my father's behavior. But I was scared that things were moving too fast and that I wasn't in the right mind to process it.

I pulled away from him. "Call me first." I waved at the list on the counter. "My sister might be coming over later to go over some things."

"Okay." He held his hands up. "I won't interfere with the sister. Call me if you need anything, all right?"

When he left, I stayed busy fixing my father's lunch. Then I walked into the living room to fetch him. My mother had always insisted that all meals be eaten at the table.

But my father wasn't in his chair. The television droned, set to the same station it had been on when I'd arrived. I switched it off and walked down the hall, assuming my father was in the bathroom.

I made a quick search in all the rooms on the main level, but he was nowhere to be found. "Dad?" I called out over and over. I called into the backyard, but there was no sign of him.

Just then, the house phone rang. I didn't have time to answer it; then I paused, wondering if it might be about my dad. I answered.

"Jackie?" a female voice said on the other end.

"This is Athena."

"Oh. I thought Jackie was staying over," the woman said. "Your father just passed my house in his bathrobe."

"Who is this?" I asked, panic pounding through me.

"Mrs. Markland."

Three houses to the north. "Thank you very much." I hung up and ran out of the house, heading north.

Thankfully, he was walking slowly, but I still had to sprint to catch up. By the time I reached him, I was too mad and too out of breath to say much. I just steered him toward the house, and once we got inside, I said, "Where are your shoes, Dad?"

"I can't find Carmen," he said, his eyes pleading.

My breath caught. "Mother is . . ." How could I tell him again and put him through more torture? "She's running errands," I managed. Was it the best thing to say? Probably not. I definitely had to call Jackie to get her advice.

I led my father to the kitchen and hovered over him as he ate. He yawned several times, and I looked again at the list. *Dad might need a nap after lunch.*

After he finished most of the pita, I led him to his bedroom and settled him beneath a light blanket. He closed his eyes immediately, and I looked around the room. I hadn't been in here since . . . well, since Jackie and I had selected Mom's funeral clothing, but before that, it had been months. I could still smell the gardenia perfume my mother wore faithfully every day, even when she wasn't going anywhere in particular.

My chest felt tight, as if grief were trying to press its way in. So I tiptoed out of the room, leaving my father sleeping. As I pulled the bedroom door shut, I noticed something I hadn't paid attention to before. There was a latch on the outside of the door, and the thought came to my mind that my mother had used it to lock my father in.

Understanding what her reasoning might be—the risk of a wandering man in a bathrobe—I latched the door closed.

Chapter 21

My name really had no particular meaning to me growing up. It was common enough among Greeks, and once in a while, a teacher would say, "That's a pretty name." My mother's shortening to "Bee" had bothered me once I hit puberty, but now . . . Living in a household where my name was never spoken was unsettling, and I would have taken Bee.

My father called me either Carmen or Jacqueline, which was also the name of his mother, so I wasn't sure if he was referring to my sister or my grandmother. Sometimes he called me Fran, his sister. But never Athena. It was as if I was just there to find his shoes, check the locks on the doors several times a day, and prepare a wide variety of sandwiches—some my mother must have invented.

It's interesting what the human mind remembers—names of sandwiches—and what it forgets—name of own daughter.

Our routine was down to a science after only a couple of weeks. Dressing, medication, breakfast, television, reading while watching television, lunch, nap, walk around the block, television, hoping that someone would come to visit—my sister or brother-in-law or Grey . . . really anyone. I set up my laptop in the kitchen, where I could keep an eye on Dad while at the same time getting work done.

But I wasn't able to get everything done in those short working spurts during the day. When he was asleep I'd move into the office for variety. So, I also worked from 9:00 p.m. until at least midnight each night, plowing through my work to-do list and reveling in the hours of quiet after my father went to bed.

With funds from my new investor, I hired a new editor. I still double-checked her work, but it did allow me to save time and focus on advertising contracts and billing.

Three times a week, we had a home nurse come in and lead my father in exercises and shower him. During those times, I peppered the young man, Scott, with questions. He was the one who told me to keep all of the doors locked at all times.

It was Saturday night, and I'd almost forgotten there was an outside world when Grey showed up at the house. We'd talked every couple of days, and he'd stopped in once in a while. But there had been no real dating, even when Jackie offered to come over. Truth was, I'd been too tired to do anything but fall into bed after working.

"I came to see if you were still here," Grey said, coming into the house while I held the door open. He glanced toward the living room, where my father sat in front of the television. "How is he?"

"He hasn't told me," I said, not meaning to sound so sarcastic.

Grey smiled with sympathy. "You look tired."

"You're never supposed to say that to a woman." This time I *was* making a joke, but he didn't smile.

He just stood in the foyer, a bit awkwardly, like he didn't know if he was allowed to hug or kiss me anymore. It had been a strange couple of weeks. I hadn't even had the energy to think about our relationship.

"I'm worried about you," he said.

"I'm fine," I said, feeling the warmth of his concern spread through me. "Just tired—like you already pointed out."

He must have noticed the dejection in my voice that I had tried to suppress. "Can someone come over for a while so I can take you out?"

I shook my head. "Not on short notice." I looked toward the living room, where my dad sat in his oblivion. "I'm too tired to do much anyway."

"All right," Grey said. "Let's go in the kitchen. I think you need something to eat." A corner of his mouth lifted. "You can go that far, right?"

"The kitchen is within limits."

I sat down, and while Grey moved around in the kitchen, "fixing something" for me, I told him about my dad. I didn't tell him any of the nitty gritty of what caregiving entailed—I didn't want to be a boring complainer.

"So you're able to get work done, then?" Grey asked after offering sympathetic comments.

"Yes, although it takes more hours in the day to fit everything in." Not that I was exactly missing a massive social life. But I did miss my kickboxing class and the freedom to go out and jog. I'd been trying to make do with the antiquated treadmill in the guest bedroom.

Grey set a plate of what looked like a gourmet salad in front of me.

I examined the fancy arrangement. "You know how to make salad?"

He sat across from me and shrugged. "Just needed the right ingredients." There was a new distance between us. I didn't know if I liked it; even though I had been planning on giving him the get-out-of-jail-free card, I hadn't mustered up my courage yet. Actually, I had just been too exhausted and consumed with making it from one hour to the next.

I took a bite of the salad—bits of chicken, sliced almonds that he must have found in the recesses of my mother's cupboards, feta cheese, and onions, topped by a vinaigrette that I knew wasn't in the fridge. "Mmmm. Did you make the dressing?" I'd been rambling so much about my dad that I hadn't paid much attention to what he was fixing.

"It's only vinegar spiced up."

"*Only?* My mother would love this," I said then caught myself. I had almost asked him to write down the recipe to give to her. Here I was in her kitchen, with a man she would have loved to meet—but never would. I had been too late to make her happy. Life was horribly ironic.

I took a shaky breath, but I couldn't meet Grey's eyes without succumbing to tears.

After a long moment of silence, Grey said, "I spent a lot of time at a friend's house while growing up. His mom was a gourmet cook—we used to sit at the counter and eat everything she set in front of us. Pretty soon, I'd ask her how to make stuff so I could make food at home."

"I'll bet your mom loved that."

"I don't remember if she did," he said in a quiet voice. "After . . . my father left, she didn't notice much of anything."

I looked at Grey. "I had no idea. I'm sorry."

That shrug again. "I don't tell many people," he said, his eyes on mine. "It's not something I bring up on a first date."

"And we've only been on one date, technically."

He nodded, his gaze still on me, intense and vulnerable at the same time. It tore at my heart, and for a moment, my problems faded. "How old were you when your dad left?"

"Nine. I'm the youngest, so I probably took it the hardest out of the kids."

Even with my resistance against my father's rules, as well as my mother's, over the years, it was better than having one of them gone.

"So you learned to cook?" I asked, keeping my tone light.

His face relaxed a little. "It helped me through a pretty tough stage. When I was younger, I kept everything buried inside. But when I hit the teen years, it all came out." He turned his arms over, and in the bright kitchen light, I noticed the fine scars along his wrists.

My eyes pricked with tears, and I reached out and touched the faint ridges. "That must have been horrible."

"My sisters saved me, literally."

I was speechless. This was not the Grey I had imagined—the happy and relaxed man that I knew. "How did you get through it?"

He grimaced. "Avoiding things and some therapy. A couple of anger management classes."

"They must have worked."

"For the most part." He pulled his arms back and folded them on the table. "I'm still pretty edgy around my mom."

I tried to imagine Grey angry. The only times I knew he'd been upset at me, he'd gone silent. "How's your mother now?"

He looked away. "She's never held down a job. She isn't what I'd call highly functional. But she seems to manage as long as we kids pitch in to pay her house payment." His eyes met mine again; the brown had darkened. "She's more interested in feeling sorry for herself—takes whatever medication she can to dull her conscience."

"She suffers from depression?" I asked in a quiet voice.

"Who knows what it is. She decided to check out a long time ago, seems to think life is better when she has no part in it."

I swallowed. His mother might be mentally ill, but clearly, Grey didn't see it that way. His insensitivity surprised me a little since his aunt had had Alzheimer's and he'd seemed so understanding of my father. Regardless, the challenges with his mother couldn't be easy on him or his siblings. "Where does she live?"

"In Lake Forest."

I knew the area—about a twenty-minute drive from Newport. Grey's entire demeanor had changed, and I was starting to feel uncomfortable, like I was opening a wound I shouldn't be.

"So you cook? That's really great," I said, steering the conversation.

Grey's mouth moved into a tentative smile. "I cook."

I took a few more bites of salad, letting the silence grow.

Grey leaned toward me from across the table. "I also have an innate ability to detect when someone is avoiding me—since I'm an expert in that art."

I lowered my fork, my heart racing. I hadn't expected him to be so direct, yet I hadn't thought such a warm person could be so cold toward his own mother. "Yeah, I guess you could say that I haven't exactly been available."

"And I completely understand," he said. The old Grey seemed to be back, the one who had a heart of gold. "You already know that I like you, Athena. And I know you're having a really tough time right now, but I just wish you'd let me in a little more."

My throat tightened, and I set my fork down. The expression on his face was serious and endearing at the same time—definitely hard to resist. "It's hard," I said. "Even though I *want* to let someone in," I looked up at him, "like *you* . . ." I couldn't finish. He was looking at me in a way that made it hard to breathe.

"What are you afraid of?" he asked in a quiet voice.

I exhaled. My eyes stung, and I had to look away. "Everything." Tears escaped, and I brushed them away, feeling stupid. "You've probably never been around a woman who cries more than me."

"I think you have a pretty good excuse."

"Maybe." I rose to clear my plate. Grey met me at the sink, and we just stood there for several seconds. My heart was pounding, and I was sure he could hear it, but my throat had frozen, and I couldn't speak.

"Athena," he finally said. "I'm afraid of everything too."

I nodded numbly, holding back any future tears. Where was my speech about how I needed space and wanted to be friends and didn't want to bring him into my messy life? Why had the kitchen shrunk around us so that it felt like there was nothing but Grey in the room?

I touched his arm and turned his wrist over, then I brought it to my lips and kissed the scars. His other hand went behind my neck, threading through my hair. We were standing so close that although our bodies didn't touch, it was as if I could feel every inch of him.

"I wish I could help that nine-year-old boy," I said.

He leaned down, touching his forehead to mine. "You already have."

I closed my eyes as he kissed me—so gently that I wondered if it was really happening. When he pulled away, I felt like I was in a trance. His hands moved around my waist, and I leaned against him, letting his arms envelop me.

"Now what?" I whispered.

"We just take it slow."

"Okay," I said, not believing I was saying it.

Chapter 22

AFTER GREY LEFT, I COULDN'T sleep. My father was snoring lightly in his locked room, and I piled under some blankets in the guest bedroom. It had long been converted from Jackie's childhood room, and many years before, my old bedroom had been converted into my father's office.

Even though it wasn't cold, I found comfort in Grey's absence under the weight of the blankets. I felt scared and nervous about where things were going with him, although it was strangely reassuring that he did too. I couldn't get the image of a young boy learning that his father had left him out of my mind. Or the image of an angry teen cutting his skin because the physical pain dulled the pain in his heart.

I told myself that I hadn't changed my mind about Grey because of any sympathy. It just endeared me to him more. It also conjured up a different image of the Grey I had perceived. He was still a self-assured man, but he hadn't arrived there easily.

It did explain, perhaps, why he'd never married. We were quite the pair; that was for sure. I couldn't commit because I didn't want the demands and subservience of marriage; he couldn't commit because he was afraid of reliving his childhood.

I burrowed deeper into the blankets and started reading *My Name Is Asher Lev*. The story came back to me as I read, and it was eerie how domineering the father was. I wondered how many books out there cast the fathers as dark characters. Between Grey and me, it reflected reality quite accurately, but there must be other fathers out there, ones who didn't abandon children or dominate women.

I understood Asher's father and his horror that his son didn't treat his artistic skills as a mere hobby. They were Orthodox and steeped in tradition. Mr. Lev was an important and devout man in the community with all eyes on him and his family.

My heart stilled as I read about Asher's mother's nervous breakdown. I found myself weeping at 1:00 a.m. as I read about Asher's fear and how his father brought in a housekeeper to instill routine and order. Grey didn't have that. He'd told me his sisters had literally saved his life, and he had coped by spending a lot of time at a neighbor's. In so many respects, the young Asher and the young Grey seemed one and the same.

* * *

Morning came too soon, with my father shouting and pounding on his bedroom door. I had overslept, and I rushed to let him out, still bleary-eyed.

He shoved past me as soon as the door popped open, and I fell against the wall, my shoulder throbbing where he'd pushed me. My eyes smarted, and suddenly, I remembered something: my mother's injured shoulder.

He went into the bathroom, and I straightened and hurried to the kitchen. Instinct told me that my father would be more calm after he'd eaten his breakfast. He'd had a temper when I was growing up, but he'd never physically hurt anyone that I knew of.

My heart pounded as I prepared his oatmeal with shaking fingers. I could still hear him ranting about something in the bathroom.

I'd replaced the rolled oats with instant since moving in, so by the time Dad blundered into the kitchen, it was steaming in his bowl.

"Where's Carmen?" my dad shouted, his face red.

"She's—out running errands."

"She didn't make the bed," he said, still in an angry tone but not shouting.

"I can make it for you, Dad."

He grunted, not acknowledging that I'd called him Dad, and he sat down and ate. He seemed to calm down after a few minutes, and I let out a breath of relief.

Through my research and meeting with the doctor the week before, I knew violence was one of the stages of Alzheimer's. Yet I wasn't sure that shoving me against the wall because he was desperate to get to the bathroom was a sign that he'd entered a new stage.

When he settled in front of the television, I slipped into his room to make the bed. A sour stench met me, and I had to cover my mouth as I looked around. What had happened in here? Nothing looked out of place. I pulled back the covers, thinking he'd brought food into bed. Then I checked underneath the bed but couldn't see anything. As I stood up, I caught a glimpse of a shiny spot in the corner of the room.

My stomach knotted as I crossed the room to inspect. He'd urinated there. It must have been in the middle of the night because his urgent pounding on the door this morning was for another visit to the bathroom.

I felt sick, not only that he was probably in a panic during the middle of the night but also that this was something I had to take care of myself.

I hurried out the room, ready to arm myself with plastic gloves, 409 cleaner, and maybe even a face mask. I knew I'd be putting face masks on my next shopping list if I couldn't find any for this job. Of course, I'd read about the possible need for Depends, but I hoped I didn't have to face that now.

Thankfully, today was one of the days the home aide came. My father could get cleaned up properly. By the time Scott arrived, I was exhausted. I called Jackie while Scott and Father were busy with exercises.

Hearing Jackie's voice helped me feel calmer and stronger. I took a shaky breath. "He had an accident—well, he urinated in the corner of the bedroom."

"Because the door was locked?" Jackie asked.

"I'm assuming. Although he didn't try to get out of his room—I didn't hear anything."

Jackie was quiet for a moment. "Maybe we should install key locks on the outside doors so you don't have to lock him in his room at night."

"All right," I said, relieved that the solution might be so simple. Another thing to put on my to-do list, but I was ready to try anything.

"Are we still on for cleaning out Mom's stuff this weekend?"

"Yes," I said, pushing back the dread. It was easier for me to skirt around her belongings and not think about actually touching them or going through anything.

"Is Grey coming to Thanksgiving?"

"I haven't asked." My stomach fluttered at the mention of Grey. I doubted he'd say no, unless he had plans with his family.

"Great. What food assignments do you want?" Each year Jackie and I brought a couple of dishes to dinner. My mom did the traditional turkey—yes, we're Greek and we celebrate the holidays of our current country—and the pies.

"Ummm. Let me talk to Grey first. He cooks, you know."

"He does?"

A bit of pride swelled in me. "He's pretty good too."

"Wow, that's great," she said. "Let me know if he wants to bring anything."

I smiled to myself, not realizing my sister was waiting for me to respond. "I'm really happy for you, Athena," she said. "He seems like great guy."

"Yeah," I agreed in a quiet voice. "He is." I didn't add, *And I think we're in an official relationship.*

Chapter 23

After hanging up with Jackie, I couldn't stop thinking about my relationship with Grey. It wasn't that I was looking for any sort of excitement, but having him around had certainly helped with the monotony of my days, although I didn't want our relationship to be like that—where I was essentially using him.

I wanted to understand what my feelings were for him.

While working on cleaning the kitchen, I ran over the things he'd said the night before. Thinking of him made me feel strange . . . I couldn't wait to see him again. I realized that I missed him—a phenomenon I wasn't sure I'd experienced with another man.

So what was the difference with Grey? Was I acting the part of a mother bear and wanting to protect and heal him from his past? This made me realize that if I had any intention of breaking things off with him, I'd only make it worse.

I checked my phone, half expecting to see that he'd called, although I hadn't been far enough away from my phone to miss a call or text. With Jackie's question about Thanksgiving in mind, I called Grey. Or maybe I just wanted to hear his voice, to know that last night had been real.

"You made a mistake," I said when Grey answered.

"What's that?"

"You let me know you can cook, and now Jackie said you're welcome to bring something to Thanksgiving tomorrow, but I told her it might be too last minute for you to cook. Plus, we pretty much have all the food."

He was uncharacteristically quiet.

"You have plans already?" I ventured.

"Nothing I can't change," he finally said.

I swallowed, feeling like an idiot. He did have plans, and here I was inviting him at the last minute. Backtracking, I said, "I'd love to have you over if you can come. If not, I'm sure Jackie will survive. I will too."

The sound of his chuckle loosened the nerves in my stomach.

"You do realize that inviting me for Thanksgiving is considered moving our relationship up a notch," he said.

I closed my eyes; just listening to his voice sent darts of warmth through me. "I'll take the risk." I pictured him in my mind, leaning against the counter at the bookstore, phone to his ear.

"What time's dinner?"

I pulled out of my reverie. He was coming. "About 4:00?"

He breathed into the phone, and I almost felt it on my end. "Tell Jackie I'll bring the pies."

"Homemade?" I couldn't help asking. Baking pies was an art form to my mother. I had been planning to make a cake, but pies would be better.

"You'll have to wait until tomorrow to find out."

I laughed. I wanted to see him, to ask him to come over tonight or even right now. But it would be better to wait.

After loading up the dirty towels I'd used to clean Dad's bedroom, I carried them to the laundry room off the kitchen. I was still thinking of the conversation with Grey when I started the washing machine. Standing there for a moment, I replayed what he'd said and the way his voice had sounded. It was then I noticed a thick black book on the laundry shelf. I picked it up, surprised to see it was a Bible. Why had my mother kept it in the laundry room?

I carried it to the kitchen and opened it. Another surprise—it was well marked. I sat down and thumbed through the pages slowly. Notes were written in the margin in my mother's flowery writing. I paused when I reached the Gospel of John and read the verses that were underlined twice: "And shall come forth; they that have done good, unto the resurrection of life; and they that have done evil, unto the resurrection of damnation."

A lump formed in my throat. How long ago had my mother marked the passage? Had she any inkling on that last day that her time had come? I still struggled with whether it had been "her time" or if it had all been a big mistake.

I had heard my mother say such things when a neighbor, Mr. Labraro, had passed away. "It was his time," she'd said. "It was God's will." But how could God orchestrate a car wreck to take a wonderful woman who had many healthy years left ahead of her, a woman who was the center of her family?

My mother had always done so much for others, often with very little thanks, as I was discovering firsthand. Just managing the household and my father was a full-time job. Even when Jackie and I were growing up, she'd always been busy hosting family events and managing to keep extended family closely bonded together.

The lump in my throat grew as I fought back tears. Other passages were marked, and in one margin, she'd written "Finding peace." She'd underlined a verse in 2 Peter: "Wherefore, beloved, seeing that ye look for such things, be diligent that ye may be found of him in peace, without spot, and blameless."

The conversation I'd had with Paige after book club replayed in my mind. She was young to be going through such hardships as divorce and single motherhood. She'd spoken about finding peace as well—what had she said? Something about the Mormon temple and if she could just sit outside for a moment . . .

Without exactly knowing why, I picked up my phone and scrolled through the contacts until I found Paige's phone number. Was she working? I wasn't sure what she'd said about a job. Then I remembered—she worked in a dental office, but maybe she was off for the holiday. Before I could second-guess myself, I dialed Paige's number.

My heart pounded as it rang, and I chided myself for being ridiculously nervous. I was glad when it went to voice mail. As I listened to the cheery message, it was interrupted with a slightly breathless, "Hello?"

"Paige? It's Athena . . . from the book club." The introduction was more than awkward, but I took a deep breath, determined to ask her my questions.

"Oh, hi . . . I'm really sorry about your mother," Paige said in a sincere voice. The sympathy came through, genuine and heartfelt. "I know we didn't have a chance to talk at the funeral service, so I'm glad you called now."

"I—I am too," I said, realizing at that moment that it was nice to talk to her. She was someone I hardly knew, but somehow, I felt I could ask her religious questions and she wouldn't laugh at me. "I found a Bible of my mother's," I said. "She went to church pretty regularly, except for the past couple of years, so I guess I shouldn't be surprised."

"Did she attend that church in Irvine?" Paige asked.

"Yes, my sister and I were baptized there as well—forever ago."

"It's a gorgeous building, and the flowers were amazing," she said.

I babbled on about how my sister had arranged it all and how I was now living with my father, caring for him. I told her about his Alzheimer's. Paige seemed surprised but didn't ask any awkward questions. Finally, I gathered the courage to tell her about the passages my mother had marked in the Bible. "I guess I was curious about what you believe in—as far as the afterlife—if Mormons believe in that sort of thing."

"We do," Paige said. "We believe that when someone dies, their spirit goes to heaven—that is, if they were righteous."

"So you believe in Hades too? You know, hell?"

"Not like most Christians think of it," she said. "We believe God's merciful. Good people who die aren't suffering on the other side."

It sounded straightforward, similar enough to what my mother had believed in.

"Your mother was a good person, Athena," Paige said in a gentle voice. "I heard the tributes at the funeral, and she is a woman to be proud of."

Tears pricked my eyes at the mention of the tributes. "It's just hard," I said, "to think she might be happier in heaven than she ever was here."

"In heaven, there aren't all the earthly trials to weigh us down."

I agreed with that. "But she could have been happier. She let my father run her life. He made all the decisions. Even for us kids. It was like she never did anything for herself." Tears fell, and my voice trembled. "I wish I could go back and demand that she find something she loved to do, just for herself. I wish I could explain to her that there was so much more."

"More what?" Paige prodded.

"More to life than being a housewife and cooking and cleaning for a man who could very well do it himself, but she never complained. She just served everyone. In fact, since my father's illness, she seemed happier than ever—as if the fact that my father wasn't himself made her happier. She could boss him around for once."

Paige let out a breath. I'd probably said too much. "I think you need to give her more credit, Athena. Your mother sounds like an intelligent and educated woman. Maybe it was her choice."

I grunted while shaking my head. "She was a peacekeeper, that's all. She wanted to stay married and not be labeled as a divorcee." I exhaled. "I don't know if she even loved my father." It hurt my heart to say it, to even think it, but despair had completely taken over.

Paige was quiet, though I felt that she had listened and was truly considering what to say. "Athena, I think you need to forgive your mother."

My breath halted. "Forgive her for *what*?" My mother had been too good, too giving, too subservient. There was nothing to forgive.

"Forgive her for leaving you with so many unanswered questions."

My head drooped, and I closed my eyes. "Maybe you're right," I whispered.

We were silent for a moment, then Paige continued. "Someday when you're both on the other side, you can talk to her and find out why she acted the way she did. But you can't move on if you're stuck in the past. And with your mother gone, there's no way to find the answers. Maybe she did have dreams she reached. Maybe she knew exactly what she was doing. But for *your* sake, you need to forgive her for the fact that you'll never have the answers, at least in this life."

Was Paige right? I didn't know how to respond exactly. Finally, I thanked her and hung up, hoping I wasn't too abrupt. Did I have to forgive my mother for being so weak? For not standing up for herself? For not following her dreams? I didn't even know if she'd had dreams.

After talking to Paige, anger at myself replaced my despair. I hadn't even asked my mother what she dreamed about. Had my father? Had anyone?

* * *

I stared into my parents' room, not wanting to walk through the door. With Thanksgiving the next day, I still had plenty to do to get the house ready. I wasn't a horrible housekeeper, but I'd let things slide while trying to fit a full workday in around caring for my dad.

Before Jackie and I tackled my mother's things, I wanted a few moments to myself. Paige's words had really struck me. Mother had been a wonderful person, despite the weaknesses I'd seen in her. Just as she'd seen weaknesses in me.

Maybe if I went through some of her things now, it would prevent me from having any meltdowns around Jackie and whomever else she recruited to carry boxes around—like Andrew.

My father was watching television. Today, he'd been quiet, and that was just fine with me. I took a few steps into the bedroom, my heart twisting as I turned toward the closet. There were two—*His* and *Hers*. Opening my mother's closet, I was struck with the scent of gardenia. She never believed in wearing dry-cleanable clothing only once, so she wore her best clothing several times in a row, which kept the perfume in the fibers.

On the floor, her shoes were lined up neatly, and a small suitcase was stashed in the back. The imprints of my mother's feet were in the shoes, and I knelt down, picking up one of her favorite pumps. I ran my hand along the worn sole, imagining my mother walking around the house, to the car, to a neighbor's, in these shoes.

Finally, I straightened and noticed that above the hanging clothes was a long shelf holding stacks of shoe boxes. I'd never seen the boxes before and assumed my mother was just saving them. They'd be easier to throw away than the actual clothing.

I took one down and was surprised to feel the weight of it. Maybe my mother rotated shoes? I opened the top and found a stack of note cards. All different colors and sizes. There were no envelopes with them, just cards. I carried the box over to the bed and sat down, expecting to find thank you cards from all the people she'd done things for over the years.

Maybe I could make a scrapbook with them to honor her memory—it wouldn't be a gorgeous creation like Jackie would do but a modest contribution from me.

The first card stopped me though. It wasn't a thank you card from a neighbor or friend. It was in my dad's handwriting.

I read the slanted words slowly.

> My Carmen,
> I hope you're feeling better. I'll come to the therapist with you, even though you said you don't want me to. We're in this together.
> I love you.
> Dimitri

Why had my mother been seeing a therapist? There was no date on the card. Not knowing if any of the cards were in order, I read the next one, my stomach tightening in confusion.

> My Carmen,
> I know you're having a hard time right now. But don't worry about the girls. We'll keep the household going, and you take all the time for yourself you need. The doctor said the new medication might take weeks to help. I'll be here when you need me.
> I love you.
> Dimitri

I set the card aside and exhaled. What had been wrong with my mom? How old had I been? The words of my father were so kind and gentle—a side I didn't remember seeing. I picked up the next card; I couldn't stop reading, even though I felt I was trespassing on some secrets I wasn't sure I should know.

Card after card detailed my father's concern and encouragement for my mother as she went through some trial that was never clearly defined. Therapy? Medication? I could only guess at what she'd endured. And she'd hidden it well. My eyes blurred with tears as I felt my father's anguish and love through his writing.

My mind raced as I tried to put the pieces together. But it was impossible. When I finished reading the cards, I searched through the remaining shoe boxes in the closet. They were filled with other things, like spools of thread, shampoo samples, and buttons.

I read through each card again, trying to tie together anything else, but I was dumbfounded. The image I had of my impatient and demanding father collided with the gentle and loving words on the cards. I read through a few of them again, trying to process this new perception. From my father's words, it seemed that he wasn't dominating my mother but holding her together. Protecting her secret and running a household all at the same time.

How was this possible? My mother had always had it together. My father seemed to be more of a burden to her than a help. At least when I saw them together, it seemed my dad was the one being served and waited upon. He was the one my mother catered to.

Then something clicked in my mind. I remembered coming home from school one day—it must have been fifth or sixth grade—and my father was unloading a desk from a moving truck. He said he'd be working from home sometimes and needed to have a desk in his bedroom. After I left for college, my room had been quickly converted into his office.

I exhaled, thinking of what my father might have really been doing. Cleaning, cooking, and caring for my mother?

I read through each card again until my vision was too blurry to read anymore. Finally, I replaced the cards and returned the box back to the closet.

Chapter 24

THE LOCKSMITH COULDN'T COME UNTIL Monday, so I decided to move the recliner to block the front door each night and place a ladder at the back door. If my father tried to leave in the middle of the night, at least I'd hear him.

Caring for him changed for me. I had been determined before, but now I was dedicated. I watched my father closely, wondering if I could catch a glimpse of the man who'd written such heartfelt letters to my mother, the man who kept her secret faithfully for so many years and protected her from everyone. Even from her daughters.

When I awoke to my father shouting early on Thanksgiving morning, the softness growing in my heart took on a sharp edge. It was coming from the bathroom and was not, thankfully, directed at me. I crept toward the bathroom door but couldn't make sense of what he was upset about. Glass crashed, and I visualized the soap dish fractured on the tile floor.

I hurried to the kitchen, my pulse racing as I prepared his breakfast and hoped he would calm down quickly. He came into the kitchen, grumpy and disheveled. He held his toothbrush in one hand. I sighed. At least today there would be a reprieve with everyone coming over for dinner.

He hardly touched his oatmeal and only took a few bites of a banana.

"Dad, do you want me to put your toothbrush back?"

He gripped it and pulled it to his chest, his eyes narrow. "No," he said in a loud voice. "I need to go to the office, Fran. Did you move my desk?"

I resisted the urge to tell him I wasn't his sister, Fran. "The desk is in your home office." I led him to the converted office that now had my stuff in it. He sat in the chair for a few minutes, looking around with a confused expression.

"Do you want to watch some television before Jackie gets here?" I asked. "She's coming with her family for Thanksgiving."

He nodded, but I wasn't sure if he understood that the house would soon be filled with people. I slipped into the bathroom, and sure enough, the soap dish was broken on the floor. I swept up the pieces and made a mental note to put a plastic one down on my shopping list.

By the time Jackie arrived, I was more than ready to turn everything over to her. It was heavenly having people around doing things—and not me doing it all myself. I'd prepared a couple of dishes and stored them in the refrigerator. Andrew carried in the turkey and placed it in the warm oven. The kids ran to the backyard to play after saying hi to their silent grandfather.

It was only 3:00, so I had time to get ready before Grey arrived. I decided to tell Jackie about the cards in Mom's room later, maybe when we were cleaning it out over the weekend. I hesitated to tell Grey about my mother's problems. I wasn't exactly sure what had been wrong, but my best guess was depression. And if that's what Grey's mother suffered and he didn't understand it, what would he think of my mother's secret? For now, it would stay that way.

I stopped in to check on my father before my shower. He sat in the recliner, staring at the television. I leaned over and kissed his cheek. He didn't seem to notice. I wondered what was going on in his mind, what he was thinking about, what he felt.

After a shower, I felt like a new person. And Grey arrived, with four pies—definitely homemade. As Jackie and Andrew oohed over the pies, I watched Grey out of the corner of my eye. He was dressed up more than usual: dark slacks, polo shirt, and loafers. Now that I knew what to look for, the scars on his inner arms were quite plain. My heart tugged again, reminding me that life wasn't quite what it seemed. Not Grey's, and not my parents'.

Grey caught me looking at him, and he smiled. My breath stalled. How could he do that to me with only a smile? As Jackie and Andrew debated on whether the gravy was thick enough, he crossed to me.

"I think you have flour in your hair," I said and reached up to brush the imaginary dust away.

He grabbed my hand and pulled me into a hug. I was about to protest the public display, but he kissed me before I could. Just then, Jackie's kids came scampering into the kitchen.

"Eww!" eight-year-old Andy said.

Jackie spun around as I pushed Grey away. "What?"

"They were kissing!" Maria pointed right at me.

I turned so no one could see my red face. I stayed as busy as possible setting the table, but Grey was every place I moved, standing in my way.

"I think you need something to do," I said, looking up at Grey.

"Anything."

I handed him a stack of plates. "Put these on the table."

He took them, his hands touching mine. "I missed you," he mouthed.

My heart thudded, and I looked around. Jackie was telling Andy to find all the matching glasses, and Andrew was sitting with Dad in the living room.

"I missed you too," I whispered back. He leaned forward, and I leaned back. "But no more kissing right now."

"Later?"

I smiled and turned away, scooping up the utensils to set around the table. The doorbell rang. I looked over at Jackie, who shrugged. Everyone was here.

I could hear Andrew welcoming someone at the door, and a few seconds later, Damion walked in. If I'd been holding a dish of food, I probably would have dropped it.

Andrew looked from my shocked face to Jackie's equally shocked face. "I was texting Damion, and he said he didn't have any Thanksgiving plans."

I tried to neutralize my expression. Obviously Andrew had no clue how inviting Damion over might make me feel awkward. I didn't even dare look over at Grey. "Hi, Damion," I said in a weak voice.

"Come on in," Jackie said in a tone much more welcoming. "There's plenty of room."

As soon as Damion saw Grey, his expression turned guarded. The greeting between them was awkward at best. I shot Jackie dagger looks, but she refused to meet my eyes. It was plain she didn't have anything to do with the invitation, but hadn't she trained her husband better?

My face felt too hot. *Relax*, I told myself. I didn't want Damion to know how bothered I was. After all, we'd only been out on one date, and I'd made it pretty clear that I wasn't interested in him. Twice. So there was nothing wrong with *Andrew's* friend joining us for dinner.

Except . . . no matter how I tried to calm myself down and pretend like it wasn't a big deal, I realized that it was a big deal. It was a big step to invite Grey over in the first place, and I'd hoped that I could see how he interacted with my sister. And now Damion would be in the middle of it all.

I finished setting the table as Damion wandered into the living room to join Andrew.

I looked over at Grey, who was rubbing a glass with a cloth napkin, making it spotless. He caught my gaze over the glass, and his eyebrows lifted slightly.

I motioned for him to follow me. We stepped into the laundry room, and I shut the door. "Sorry," I whispered. "I had no idea."

Grey folded his arms. "You really owe me now—inviting me to dinner with your ex-boyfriend."

"He's not—"

"I know." Grey chuckled, sliding his hands to my waist. I tingled down to my toes. "But you still owe me. For that and because I spent the whole morning baking pies."

I smirked. "How can I repay you?"

"I have a few ideas," he said, leaning down, his lips moving dangerously close to mine.

A voice called from the other side of the door. "Dinner is ready," Jackie said.

"Come flying with me this weekend," Grey said into my ear. "The weather is supposed to be nice."

My heart stuttered at Grey's nearness, and I tried to keep my breathing even. "Jackie and I are cleaning out my mother's things."

"Good," he said. "Then maybe she can stay and watch your father when we go."

"Grey—"

Commotion rose outside the door; the kids were inside the house.

"Dinner's ready," I said.

But Grey didn't let me go. "At least think about it."

"All right," I said, staring into his warm eyes. "Those pies better taste good."

He released me with a laugh, but before I could move away, he cradled my face and kissed me. When he finally let go, I was ready to skip dinner altogether. But we were expected on the other side of the door.

Grey opened the door, and we walked through the kitchen into the formal dining room that we hadn't used since my mother's death.

My father sat at the head of the table, and for a moment, it was like other Thanksgivings in our home. All except for the vacant look in his eyes and my mother's absence.

Damion sat across from me, and Grey sat next to me, which gave him plenty of opportunity to talk only to me. He casually draped his left arm around the back of my chair and ate with his right hand, making our "relationship" obvious enough that Damion hardly spoke to either of us.

The food was delicious, the pies even better. The menu change from oatmeal and sandwiches was very welcome. Grey intently watched me eat a slice of pumpkin pie.

"Is it good?" he asked in a quiet voice.

Damion and Andrew were talking about golf, and my father had long since left the table.

I glanced up at Grey. "Are you going to watch me eat the whole thing?"

"Yes."

I suppressed a laugh. "It's good. Satisfied?"

"No," he said in a serious tone. Underneath the table, his hand touched my leg.

"Did you ask your sister about going flying with me yet?"

I glanced pointedly at Damion and Andrew. "I will later."

He squeezed my leg, and I wished that everyone would leave the room—the house—instantly. But I satisfied myself with eating every last morsel of the slice of pie. My mother would have loved it.

Later, when Jackie left, she promised to return in the morning. Thankfully, Damion left at the same time as the others.

I went back into the kitchen to find Grey loading the dishwasher. "You really don't have to do that."

He turned, and I noticed he was wearing my mother's red apron tied around his waist.

I pretended to grimace. "You've permanently ruined my image of you."

He looked down at the apron. "This bothers you?"

"I don't think it's your color."

"Should I have gone with the pink floral?"

"Definitely not," I said. He was walking toward me, holding a wet sponge from the sink. I ducked away before he could reach me and fled to the far side of the kitchen table.

He kept coming around the table. I made a move toward the hall, but he caught me before I could get too far. He pulled me back into the kitchen, squeezing the sponge over my head.

I screeched and covered my face with my hands as the water dribbled down. "You're getting me wet!"

He dropped the sponge into the sink then slid his hands up my arms and behind my neck. I tried to wriggle away, but he pushed me against the counter, locking me in.

"Okay, I surrender," I said, water dripping from my hair.

"Then we'll go flying tomorrow?"

"Yes," I said, still trying to catch my breath. I wiped the dripping water from my chin. I'd have to tell Jackie that we'd do the cleaning Saturday and Sunday.

I wrapped one arm around Grey's neck and kissed him. He lifted me to sit on the counter and pulled me closer, kissing me back. Every complaint I had about the day—the unexpected company of Damion and my father's nonparticipation—seemed to be in another life now.

Kissing Grey was another existence.

But I couldn't let him get away with getting me wet. Sitting level with the sink, I reached for the water sprayer with my free hand, while keeping Grey distracted by kissing him.

Seconds later, I had him running for cover.

Chapter 25

IN THE MIDDLE OF THE night, I awoke to a crash. In my sleepy stupor, it took a second to orient myself. I climbed out of my covers and hurried to my father's room. He wasn't there.

I ran to the back door and saw the ladder on the ground, pulled away from the door. My father had just opened it and was about to leave.

"No, Dad!" I grabbed his arm. "We'll go for a walk later."

My father swung at me, knocking me across the temple with his forearm. I stumbled, dizzy and gasping. Tripping backward over the ladder, I landed on the floor.

My father shouted something, but my head was too fuzzy to understand. I got to my hands and knees and pulled myself up, bracing against the wall. When my head cleared, I went outside, turning on the deck light. Thankfully, my dad hadn't opened the yard gate but was kneeling in the garden, digging in the dirt with his bare hands.

Every part of my body trembled as I walked toward him. I was poised to flee into the house if he tried to lash out again. Stopping a safe distance away, I said, "What are you doing, Dad?"

He didn't answer, just continued digging in the garden. I stood there, hugging my arms around me, shivering in the breeze that rattled the fruit trees. My eyes still smarted from the blow, and my hands were shaking. He was so much stronger than I'd expected, and it hadn't even occurred to me that he'd strike out so forcibly.

I took a deep breath, trying to decide what I should do. It was the middle of the night, and I didn't want to wake up Jackie. Besides, I knew what Jackie would say—that it was time to put him in a nursing home. Now that I knew all that my dad had done for my mother, I understood why she had been so determined to take care of him. I needed to carry on what she would have done and what my father would have done. I hadn't been the best daughter while Mother was alive, and this was the least I could do—even if the sacrifice was more than I'd anticipated. In truth, my dad had probably already forgotten about striking me.

I stared at my father's back, battling the emotions inside of me. Watching over my father was something I had to do for my mother, to hopefully repair all of the disappointments she'd had in me. Putting up with my father was minor compared to what she had endured over the years with her depression and a daughter who went against all good things Greek.

After several minutes, I went inside and pulled on a jacket then sat on the back step, waiting for my father to finish his digging. I didn't dare try to convince him to come inside until he was ready of his own accord. Even though he was more than sixty years old, his strength exceeded mine.

He dug until he was out of breath, and then he let me lead him into the house. He went straight to his room, dirt covering his hands and pajama pants. I'd have laundry to do in the morning. I locked the door and set the ladder up again.

Taking a couple of ibuprophen for the pain in my face, I went to bed, hoping that tomorrow I'd wake up and it would all have been a terrible dream.

* * *

I gasped when I looked in the mirror and saw my face in the morning. My eye was swollen and bruised. I touched the swelling, and hot pain shot through my head. There was no way I could keep this from Jackie now. I had more ibuprophen with breakfast, and by the time my dad shuffled into the kitchen, I was ready to confront him.

But he didn't even look at me, just sat down and ate every bite of oatmeal in his bowl. He didn't remember. He didn't know what he'd done. With tears in my eyes, I led him to the living room, where he seemed content to watch television.

It was before 9:00 a.m. when I called Grey to cancel. I told him I was sick. He sounded disappointed but offered to come over. I was able to talk him out of it, telling him Jackie was already coming over. I didn't want him to see me—to know the truth.

Jackie was upset when she arrived.

"You should lie down," she said.

"No, the ibuprophen is helping fine." I just wanted to get cleaning out my mother's things over with.

"Tell me what happened again," Jackie said.

I explained how he'd tried to escape. "I don't blame him for smacking me," I said. "I shouldn't have grabbed him—it startled him."

"Has he . . . is this the first time?"

I nodded, not exactly being truthful. It had happened with my mother. But after reading about the way my father had cared for my mother, I knew my mother would be protective of my father if she were alive. In fact, she had probably been protective of him for a while.

"Athena," Jackie said. "This isn't fair to you—even if he doesn't know his own strength and doesn't know what he's doing. He could really hurt you." Her eyes watered. "We need to look into nursing homes right away."

I turned away. I couldn't look at my sister. "I'm not ready to put him in a home. Mother would have kept him here." I thought of Mother's sore shoulder and knew it was true.

"Athena—"

"Another month or two keeping him here will save us money." December and January were coming, the worst months to try to sell a house. And we'd have to sell it in order to pay for my father's medical care. Andrew had already looked into all of the possible financial avenues.

"Andrew and I can cover the house payments until it sells," Jackie said.

The walls seemed to be closing in around me—to sell my childhood home and to put my father into an uncaring environment—I wasn't ready. "I'll let you know if it gets too bad, Jackie."

"You'd better, sis," she said, giving me a hug. She pulled back, her eyes moist. "Now let's tackle Mom's things."

Before we started, I showed Jackie the notes written by my dad, and we both had a good cry over them. It took us hours to go through my mother's things, broken up only by fixing lunch from the Thanksgiving leftovers.

Grey called twice. The first time, I let it go to voice mail. When Jackie overheard our conversation on the second call, she put her hands on her hips after I hung up with Grey.

"You're not telling him?"

"He wouldn't understand," I said. "His aunt was in a nursing center almost from the beginning." I let out a sigh. "He's been very supportive of me during all this, but I can tell he doesn't exactly approve." My hand subconsciously went to my bruised face. "I don't think he'd take this lightly."

"*I* don't take it lightly," Jackie said.

"I know," I agreed. "I just need more time. Please."

Chapter 26

By THE NEXT BOOK CLUB on December 8, the bruising on my face had faded enough that make-up easily concealed it. I had managed to avoid Grey for almost a week, making one excuse after another. I felt horrible about it, but I knew he'd freak out if he saw my face.

So it was with relief that I drove to book club, knowing my face looked quite normal and that the next day I'd probably be safe enough to see Grey. I also wanted to ask him more about his mother. Even though it was too late to change his past, maybe I could help him understand that his mother's neglect of her kids may not have been on purpose. If she really did suffer from mental illness, it would do Grey some good to understand that.

And me. If he couldn't be compassionate toward his mother, could I tell him about mine?

When I arrived at Ruby's, I was impressed with the Christmas decorations. The outside lights were obviously done by a professional, and they looked great. Lighted candy canes lined the front walkway, and an extravagant wreath hung on the front door. It reminded me that I hadn't done one thing for Christmas yet.

As soon as Ruby opened the door, she enveloped me into a tight cinnamon-scented hug, like we were long-lost friends. Did she coordinate her perfume with the holiday seasons? She pulled back, all smiles. She wore a soft red sweater with a cowl neck and what looked like matching ruby earrings and a delicate necklace.

"Come in, come in. So glad you're here." She looked me up and down. "You're looking skinny, my dear. You'll have to eat two helpings of our refreshments tonight."

I smiled. It had been a long time since I'd worried about my weight. It felt nice to think about something I *could* control.

Ruby quickly introduced me to Ilana, the woman who'd first come to book club when I was gone. She was petite, with to-die-for curly black hair—all natural.

Livvy and Daisy said hello as I stepped farther into the living room. Daisy looked a little uncomfortable—more so than the first time I'd met her. She wore one of those trendy baby-doll shirts that hid a lot on a woman who was more filled out. Daisy's figure didn't need any hiding.

Paige came up and touched my arm. "How are you?" she asked.

"Doing better," I said. The room hushed, and I realized everyone had heard me. "Thanks again for coming to my mom's funeral." I swallowed against my thick throat. "It really meant a lot to see you all there."

Ilana hadn't been there, of course, and she quickly added her condolences.

The doorbell rang, and everyone became distracted again. Ruby swept out to answer it and returned with a woman I hadn't met before. She had gorgeous mocha-colored skin and gigantic brown eyes.

"Ladies, I'd like you to meet Victoria Winters," Ruby announced. We each took a few seconds to introduce ourselves. "Victoria has assured me she's a great reader and ready to dive into whatever we're in the middle of."

Victoria had a low, mellow voice and a ready laugh. "I was really excited when Ruby invited me to the club. I hope I can contribute a little and not bore you all to death."

We laughed, and Ruby swatted Victoria's arm. "She's far from boring," Ruby said. "She works in the film industry and has some amazing—and horrific—stories."

"That's true," Victoria said with a smile as she took her seat. "But before telling you any of them, I'll need you all to sign a nondisclosure form."

We chuckled at that. My mind raced, wondering what types of situations she dealt with each day. If it was anything like the screaming headlines on the tabloids, it must be quite horrific. But Victoria did seem to be well put together, calm, and collected. She was probably great at her job.

"Well," Ruby said with a clap. "Let's get started." She looked around the room, where we had all settled on various couches and chairs. "Anyone have anything new to share?"

Paige rushed through her update, saying work and family were the same as usual, but I felt like she was holding back.

"Not much going on with me," Livvy said.

When it was Victoria's turn, she said, "Since it's my first time here, everything about me is new. Trust me; you don't want all the details at once."

I smiled. Victoria seemed to be easygoing, someone who would be easy to be friends with. When everyone looked at me, I straightened my back and said, "Last time I was here, I made an announcement about my pitiful dating life." I stole a glance at Ruby, wondering how she'd react to the news. "The fact is, things have turned around. I'm dating a man named Grey Ronning."

"From the used bookstore?" Ruby asked, clapping her hands together.

"Yes." I couldn't help smiling.

"That's simply wonderful," Ruby continued.

Everyone started to congratulate me.

"It looks like you're on Santa's good list this season," Victoria said with a wink. "A man for Christmas."

I snorted, which made everyone laugh. Ruby hooted in delight. "How perfect. And you know you're not allowed to return any of Santa's gifts."

For a moment, I let myself revel in everyone's enthusiasm and even said, "I think this is one gift I wouldn't want to return."

"Any pictures of your man?" Victoria asked, her eyes bright.

"Not yet," I said, and the other ladies smiled. I couldn't really imagine telling Grey that the ladies at the book club all wanted to see a picture of him. He'd definitely find a way to tease me endlessly about that. But I still said, "I'll try to work something out though."

"Just e-mail them so I don't have to wait until the next meeting," Victoria continued.

It probably wouldn't happen, but I said I'd try anyway. When their exclamations died down, Ruby said, "Keep us updated, Athena. This is no small news." She turned to Livvy. "Now, let's start with Livvy, who chose the book. What are your thoughts on *My Name Is Asher Lev?*"

Livvy offered a brief, nervous smile. "This book seems to revolve around the suffering caused from conflicting traditions. The story really deals with the decisions these three people made in their lives that ended up affecting not only their traditions but the people they loved the most. And yet . . . none of them could have chosen differently, or they would have been betraying themselves." She took a breath then looked over at me.

I nodded and opened the copy I'd brought with me. "After a few pages, I actually started underlining some of the sentences." I bit my lip for a couple of seconds. "The relationship between Asher and his father really affected me." I looked up at the women. "You see, my mother was always pushing me to get married—to a Greek man. Time after time, I dated men who didn't have marriage potential for me. Maybe it was a rebellious act to show my mom I could make my own decisions."

"Is the bookstore guy Greek?" Daisy asked.

"No," I said.

Daisy nodded knowingly.

I flipped toward the back of the book, looking for something I'd underlined. "When Asher goes against his parents' wishes to not only become a painter but to paint the Crucifixion, I guess I was reminded of myself." I took a breath. "Listen to what he says, 'I turned my back to the paintings and closed my eyes, for I could no longer endure seeing the works of my own hands and knowing the pain those works would soon inflict upon people I loved.'"

The room was silent.

"I guess it really hit me hard," I said. "I was doing the same thing. Living a life or, more accurately, rejecting a life those who loved me wanted me to have." I blinked back hot tears. "I don't want to turn my back anymore. Although I don't know if marriage or children are in my future, I'm willing to open my heart at least and consider the option."

Next to me, Livvy patted my hand.

"I found some letters that my dad wrote to my mom." The tears escaped now. "Their marriage wasn't what I thought it was. They had their challenges but loved each other dearly." I wiped at my cheeks. "What I saw as a child was only a glimpse. I misunderstood greatly."

"Isn't that true of many things in life?" Paige asked quietly. "We go around assuming we know or understand another person. When we find out the truth, our whole perception changes, for better—or for worse."

I wasn't sure what had exactly happened with Paige and her marriage, but what little she'd shared about her cheating husband made her words feel weighted.

"This book is filled with layers of family dynamics," Livvy added, her tone serious. "Each character has intense flaws, yet you can't help but relate and understand their motivations for doing what they do, even when it tears down another family member."

Livvy's comment was completely accurate. It also surprised me a little. I'd viewed Livvy as somewhat scatterbrained, but she was quickly proving me wrong.

"Families are sticky," Victoria said, and we all nodded in agreement.

We talked for several more minutes about the book, and Ilana shared some thoughts on growing up in a Jewish home. I realized that no matter what religion or background each of us had, our parents still had expectations for us to follow in their paths—be it Jewish, Mormon, Greek Orthodox, or anything else. Our parents wanted what they thought was best for us.

Victoria jumped in again and said, "You know when Asher got in trouble with his Mashpia, which I took to mean as his school principal—I didn't take the time to look it up . . ." She paused, glancing at Ilana. "So this Mashpia is talking to Asher when he's in trouble for drawing a rabbi on his scriptures . . . Can I borrow your book for a second," Victoria said, reaching for Paige's copy of the book. She opened it and turned a few pages. "Here it is. So this Mashpia says, 'Many people feel they are in possession of a great gift. But one does not always give in to a gift. One does with a life not only what is precious to one's self but to one's own people. That is the way our people live.' Don't you think that's sad?"

She handed Paige her book back. "To have a gift and not use it because you might feel selfish doing something that makes you happy? I'm around artists all day: writers, directors, actors, set designers, costume designers. They use their gifts because it makes them happy. The side benefit is that their art makes other people happy too. I guess I just don't understand Mashpia's attitude."

Ruby grinned and let out a contented sigh. "You read the book!"

Victoria lifted a shoulder. "Told you I'd jump in wherever you were all at. I have a lot of downtime on the set, so I'm up for reading whatever's next."

We talked for a while longer, and then Ruby smiled and singled out Paige. "Paige has the next book selection; would you like to tell us a little about it?"

"Sure," Paige said with a nod. "I chose a classic that some of you might have read in high school or college. *Silas Marner* by George Eliot."

"Oh, I love that one," Ruby said. "It's definitely worth reading more than once."

While Ruby and Paige discussed a few things about the book and the female author with her chosen pen name, I noticed Daisy looking more uncomfortable. She kept tugging at her shirt as if she were self-conscious of how she looked.

Livvy obviously noticed the same thing. "I think those kinds of shirts are so cute, Daisy. But I can't wear them; anytime I try, I totally look pregnant."

Strangely, Daisy glanced over at Paige. What was the look that passed between them?

"I wonder if you are," Ruby said to Daisy. "How exciting!"

Daisy smiled, but she didn't look very happy. I wouldn't be excited either if it were me—especially if I had two grown children. "I'm *not* pregnant; trust me," Daisy said in a firm voice. "I got that taken care of permanently fifteen years ago, remember? I can't get pregnant."

Ruby didn't seem to be paying attention. "I had a friend back in '87 who had a tubal ligation, and then ten years later, poof! There she was, expecting a surprise little caboose! He's a teenager now."

I cringed for Daisy—but she had to know that was just how Ruby was—overly interested in the details of everyone's lives. In fact, I was a bit worried about Ruby going into the bookstore to have a chat with Grey.

"That's pretty rare," Daisy said with a faint chuckle. "I'll just make a point of not wearing this shirt again."

"Well, let's serve up the dessert," Ruby said, standing. "Or, rather, the refreshments, since potato latkes aren't sweet. Ilana brought them for Livvy. Wasn't that nice of her?"

While we ate the latkes, which were quite delicious, Paige turned to me and asked about my father. I must have hesitated too long because, once again, the room hushed and everyone waited for my answer.

"It's getting harder," I said quietly. I thought of the concealed bruise on my face and knew they'd all be horrified if they really knew the truth. "He doesn't sleep well and usually thinks I'm my aunt Fran, his younger sister. I don't know how my mother did it by herself for so long. Since I've stepped in, it feels like it's all been downhill. I can't work as much as I need to, so I'm always behind, and I can't seem to get a routine figured out to save my life."

Getting the bulk of my work done late at night was probably not the best thing when I was barely awake. I looked around the room and tried to smile over my pounding pulse. "My sister thinks we should put him in a care center now. But it's so expensive, and this is a bad time of the year to put my parents' house on the market."

"Had your mother ever talked about a care center?" Livvy said.

"Not that she told us." Now that I knew what I did about their relationship, I could picture my mother caring for my father to the end. I stalled and pushed the last bits of latke around on my plate.

"Have you checked into any of them?" Daisy asked.

"It might be worth looking into," Paige added.

I took a stuttered breath. If nothing else, I was grateful for their obvious concern. "I looked up a couple of locations, but I feel so . . ." I glanced at the ceiling, trying to find the right word. "Guilty." That was it. "I'm his daughter;

he raised me and took care of me my whole life. I'm the only one who can really take care of him—my sister has three kids. It's not his fault my mother is gone; I have to take her place as best as I can. I just can't bring myself to put him away."

"You're not putting him away," Paige said quickly.

"Nursing homes are awful," Ruby said, her lips a little tight.

"Not all nursing homes are the same," Paige rushed in. I didn't dare glance at Ruby to see what she thought of Paige contradicting her. "Back in Utah we had a care center that my church provided worship services for. It was beautiful, and the residents were happy there." She looked at me, determination in her eyes. "The thing is, your mom was his caretaker, and she did what she thought was best. You're his caretaker now, and it's not wrong to make a choice in both of your best interests."

I nodded. She was right. But I wasn't ready.

We finished our dessert, and no matter how much Ruby cajoled, I only had one serving. Leaving book club, my heart felt lighter. They had been so supportive and had given me a lot of things to think about. I'd heard some of them from Jackie and Grey, of course, but these were women who weren't emotionally connected to my family, so it was good to hear their opinions.

When I turned the corner onto my street, I saw Grey's Jeep in the driveway next to Jackie's car. My heart hammered as I pulled to a stop and checked the vanity mirror. I decided that the bruising wasn't noticeable, even though some of my make-up had likely faded by now. I'd just stay out of the kitchen and its bright lights.

I hoped Jackie hadn't said anything, but who knew how long they'd been visiting together. Thinking back to book club, I realized it had felt good to talk to those women as friends.

But Grey was different. He was more than a friend to me. He was part of my life, and his opinion mattered more and more.

I parked on the street and unlocked the front door. Jackie came into the foyer just as I stepped in. "How's Dad?" I asked, though I really wanted to ask about Grey.

"Sleeping." She hugged me. "Did you have a good time?"

"Yes." I released her, tempted to tell her about my new friends, but Grey's Jeep in the driveway had driven all girl talk from my mind. "How long has Grey been here?"

"A few minutes," a male voice said. Grey stepped into the foyer, his arms folded. He didn't look very happy. His eyes scanned my face, and I knew Jackie had told him.

I shot a glare at her, but she ducked behind me, squeezing my arm. "I've got to hurry home. Call me later, Athena."

I didn't answer her. When the front door shut, I met Grey's stare.

"What were you thinking?" he asked after a few seconds of silence.

The hurt in his voice pierced through me. I looked down at the ground and sighed. "I don't know." I closed my eyes and leaned against the wall. Why had Jackie told him? Why hadn't *I* told him? Was it really better to avoid him and lie to him—than this . . . How could I consider this a relationship if I couldn't talk to him?

I heard him move but didn't open my eyes until he was standing in front of me. He ran his hand along my face. "I'm really sorry this happened."

"Me too," I whispered. "He doesn't even remember."

"I know," Grey said. His other hand brushed back my hair, and he leaned his forehead against mine. "I know you love him, and you want to take care of him, but—"

"Don't say it," I said, pulling away from Grey. "I need more time."

"Athena—"

"You don't understand. I need to take care of my father as long as possible. He deserves to be taken care of by someone who . . . cares." My voice broke.

Grey stepped back, studying me with an incredulous look. "You've read about the deterioration—he'll only get more violent. There will be more instances, and you're living here with him by yourself."

"I can handle it," I shot out, my heart and head pounding now.

"Can you?" His words hung in the air, twisting my stomach.

My eyes burned, but I refused to cry about this in front of Grey.

"You've locked yourself into this fortress—no one can get in or out without a key. You've given up too much, Athena." His gaze bore into mine. There was nothing warm or gentle in his look. "You've even gone so far as to avoid me this whole week."

I couldn't look at him anymore. He was right. Was taking care of a father who didn't even know who I was most of the time really worth all of the sacrifices? I couldn't give Grey any good reason except that I wanted to do something that would make my mother proud.

Grey reached out and touched my shoulder then ran his hand down my arm. He grasped my hand. When I didn't, couldn't, respond, he let go.

"I wish that you could've trusted me enough to tell me when your father struck you." His voice held an exasperated edge now. "Why can't you let me help you?"

I slumped against the wall. I couldn't move, even though every part of me wanted to hold on to him. Let him in completely.

Tears budded and fell onto my cheeks.

Grey pulled me against him, and I buried my face against his chest, feeling his warmth and his strength. Why had I pushed him away before?

It was a habit. I wanted to be in a relationship with him, yet the more real it became, the more afraid I was.

"I don't think anyone can help me," I murmured, the tears coming faster.

Grey tightened his hold. "This is a good start."

Chapter 27

AFTER GREY LEFT, I STOOD in my father's bedroom doorway for some time, listening to his soft snoring.

What did my father dream about? Did he know my name when he slept? Was it just the daytime that brought the confusion?

What I hadn't told Grey, or Jackie, was that the ladies at book club had given me the courage to call the nursing centers. At least, I'd felt courageous during book club. Now . . . in the peace of night . . . I wasn't so sure.

I swallowed back the painful lump in my throat. Grey had said he'd be here at 7:00 a.m. He wasn't going to let me do this alone, he'd said. My throat hurt for a different reason.

Being away from Grey for a week, then feeling his arms around me tonight and hearing the concern in his voice, had made me realize I did need him.

A lot.

I pulled the bedroom door shut, muffling the sounds of my father's snores. My heart ached. This was all that was left of my father's life—a nursing home and family who wanted to help but whom he couldn't remember. What did he have to look forward to?

I headed to the office and turned on my laptop, bent on researching nursing homes. There were a couple of them in Costa Mesa. As I read about their "missions" and looked through the staff bios, my head started to pound.

Was I really going to do this? Could I really drop my father off at one of these places with strangers? I groaned. Maybe the time wasn't right. I knew Grey wouldn't be happy, and the book club ladies would support his side. But Jackie would understand; she had to.

I needed to take my mind off of all of this—go somewhere else—even if just mentally. Paige had chosen *Silas Marner*, and Ruby had given me her copy since she'd already read it more than once.

I grabbed the book and settled into bed under my blankets. I read the introduction first then paused when I read, "Marner can transform himself from a falsely accused guilty person, and from a bizarre, marginalized, almost lunatic weaver into someone who can give and receive love."

Turning the book over, I read the back cover—about a man, a weaver, who undergoes a major transition in his life. *Sounds like the book for me.* I kept reading, finding the author's voice interesting—omniscient writing and a didactic tone—but I recognized that was the style most classics were written in, leaving little to no guesswork for the reading audience.

It was refreshing in its own way. I didn't have to come up with my own thoughts—just read the story. The main character, Silas Marner, essentially lived in exile, where "the past becomes dreamy because its symbols have all vanished, and the present, too, is dreamy because it is linked with no memories."

My life was becoming just that. My life with my mother, my life at the condo, my life *before*, seemed another existence right now, as if it hadn't ever occurred.

* * *

The next few weeks were even busier with the upcoming holiday. I had made a deal with myself—I'd hire an accountant for my magazine to do contracts and billing, and in trade, I'd keep my father in the house and continue to care for him. I would do this for as long as it took. Like Silas Marner, I reconciled myself to putting the past in the past.

Once I sent the word out that I was hiring, I had a dozen résumés to choose from in less than twenty-four hours. I interviewed several of the applicants over the phone and met with three of them in person.

A couple of days later, I had an accountant.

Grey approved in that measure, but he wasn't too happy with the decision about my father. Every morning he showed up faithfully at the house around 7:00. He spent an hour there to make sure the morning routine went smoothly—since my father was more grouchy in the mornings.

It was nice to have Grey around, although I felt guilty about it most of the time. He was doing a lot for me, and I was basically doing nothing for him. We never did go flying, and we couldn't now because the weather was too unpredictable.

"Can I bring you anything tomorrow?" Grey asked one morning as I walked him to his Jeep. It was already after 8:00, and he had to get through the traffic to open his bookstore by 9:00.

"We're fine." I folded my arms against the morning chill.

Grey raised an eyebrow as he opened the door. "You say that every day. I can pick up what you need after work and bring it tomorrow morning."

"Jackie's coming tonight, so I'll get out then."

He tilted his head, his brown eyes studying me. "Oh? Big plans?"

"Yes," I said, smiling wide. "Grocery shopping."

"Do you want to catch a movie too?"

I let out a sigh. I was tempted, but I knew I wouldn't enjoy it. Even with Jackie over, I worried about not being home with my dad. I hadn't even been able to spend time at my condo like I thought I would. No one knew my dad's idiosyncrasies like I did now. "I don't think so."

Grey's hands moved to my waist, and he stepped close to me. His eyes flickered with something like disapproval, but he didn't argue. "We can watch something at your place, then."

I turned my face up. I enjoyed it when he was so agreeable. "All right." Even if I fell asleep after the first twenty minutes, those twenty minutes would be worth it.

"I love it when you listen to me," Grey said, leaning down.

Before I could come up with a retort, he kissed me. I didn't even care that a neighbor was driving by, probably staring.

After watching his Jeep pull out, I hurried back into the house. My father was in front of the television, a book in his lap. Grey had brought one over, but lately, I hadn't seen my father attempt to read anything.

I fixed him a plate of fruit and carried it in to him. He ate a couple of bites, then I took the plate and sat on the couch for a few minutes, watching him. He'd been grumpy this morning, but Grey's presence really did help make me more patient and, of course, less worried about my father's episodes. Not that he was getting any better. In fact, he reminded me of a young kid—demanding, prone to fits of anger, forgetting things.

But I also found if I fed him more frequently, even if he ate only a little, he seemed to do a bit better. I spent any free time browsing through online stores, trying to find nice gifts for my sister, her family, and, of course, Grey for Christmas. I bought Dad a couple of pairs of lounge pants. Then I came across a digital scrapbook website. After playing around with it for a while, I decided to scan pictures of our family over the years and create a memory book. It might take longer than Christmas to get it done, but going through my mother's albums felt healing.

Knowing more about my parents' relationship put a different light on my childhood. Their love for each other was apparent through the way my mother took care of my dad the past couple of years, and it was obvious that my father took care of my mother for much longer than that.

I just hoped what I was doing for my father matched in some small way all the things my mother had done for him.

Chapter 28

JUST MAKE IT THROUGH CHRISTMAS, I told myself as I coaxed my father into bed Christmas Eve. He didn't want me to touch him, had hardly eaten dinner, and had had an accident earlier in the day. Three strikes.

When he finally fell asleep an hour later, I turned off the light in his bedroom.

Sitting in the living room, I watched the lights on the Christmas tree twinkle. This was the first Christmas without my mom. My heart was heavy as I sat alone thinking of all of the decorations she usually put up—I had managed the tree, but that was about it.

I'd make her wassail tomorrow, but I wasn't about to attempt the various Greek cheesecakes. Thinking about my mom, I planned to convince Grey to take me to meet his mother. I hadn't brought her up since he first told me about her—but surely he visited her on Christmas, even if their relationship wasn't very strong.

I pulled a blanket over me and leaned back, closing my eyes for a moment. The previous Christmas, my dad had still known my name, my mother was still alive, and I'd been dating Karl.

What would Karl think of me now? Living at my father's and caring for him, hiring an editor and accountant, in a relationship with Grey . . . So many changes in just a couple of months.

I must have fallen asleep on the couch because I was suddenly awakened by a scraping sound. I straightened and peered past the Christmas lights to where the sound was coming from.

A large form stood near the front door, tugging on the doorknob.

"Dad?" I said, fear and surprise colliding in my chest.

He didn't acknowledge me but kicked the door.

My heart raced. Kicking was just a precursor to more violence. I had to find a way to distract him, fast, before he undid the deadbolt near the top of the door.

I turned on the lights, hoping that it would startle him out of whatever determination had set him in this frame of mind. He kept kicking at the door and pulling on the knob. I knew better than to touch him.

I switched on the television, thinking it might draw his attention, but he didn't stop thrashing the door.

"Dad!" I shouted over the pounding. I didn't think he'd be able to get out, but he was causing damage that would be hard to get fixed over Christmas. And I worried that the glass might break.

He didn't even look in the direction of the television, so I moved to the stereo and turned on one of his favorite CDs, or what used to be his favorite.

It was like he was in his own world, and no sound or thought could penetrate his mind or affect his actions. I hurried into the kitchen, looking for anything else that might distract him. Once in the kitchen, I heard a loud crack then the sound of breaking glass.

I dashed out in time to see my dad disappear through the door. "Wait, Dad!" I called out. He was striding down the front walk, wearing nothing but a T-shirt and boxers.

I grabbed a pair of shoes and shoved them on. Glass littered the front entryway from the broken beveled window in the door. The door stood askew, although it was still on its hinges. I'd have to assess the damage later. I didn't take time to grab a jacket or robe. My dad was getting farther away by the second.

"Dad!" I called as loudly as I dared and ran after him. "Stop!"

He'd turned right and was making good time down the street. I wasn't sure what time it was, but the night was completely black, so I estimated that it was between midnight and 2:00 a.m. A neighbor's indoor lights switched on; I didn't have time to notice if someone was watching us.

I caught up with him. "Come on, Dad. We need to go home," I said, keeping a generous distance. I didn't dare take his arm until I knew what mood he was in.

He kept walking, not speaking to me. I tried a different strategy. "Where are you going?"

Nothing.

"Are you cold? Let's go back to the house."

He slowed, and I hoped that meant progress.

"Come on." I touched his arm tentatively. He didn't flinch, didn't resist, so I wrapped my hand around the crook of his elbow and gently steered him around. "Let's get you warm."

He locked eyes with me beneath the streetlight. For a moment, I thought he recognized me, remembered that I was his daughter. But his eyes narrowed, and he shoved me away.

Unprepared for his quick movements, I went down with a thump. I wasn't hurt, but my eyes stung as I climbed to my feet. My father was walking away—this time in the direction of our house. Relief flowed through me. I'd just have to steer him toward our house as we neared.

The sound of sirens pierced the night, jolting through my heart. At that instant, I knew a neighbor had called the police. Anger pierced me. I had this under control, and I didn't want the cops involved.

The siren grew louder surprisingly fast, and before I'd gone another fifty yards, a car with flashing lights came around the corner. It was the worst thing the police could have done. The lights and the high-pitched siren disoriented my dad even more. He turned around, facing me, his expression spooked.

I held up my hands. "Dad, just come with me. We're going home now. I can talk to the police."

The car had pulled up near us and stopped, and two policemen were getting out. They were talking to me, asking questions, but I interrupted. "Turn off your lights. My dad has Alzheimer's. I'm just trying to get him inside the house."

The cops seemed to understand, and one of them switched off the lights.

A few neighbors stepped onto their front porches; others looked out their windows.

It took several minutes, but I was able to get my father into the house and into his bedroom, the police following every step of the way. I shook with fear and frustration. Why did someone have to call the police? It would have been much easier to get Dad inside without all the lights and sirens. And now the entire neighborhood was awake.

When I came out of my father's bedroom, one of the cops was inspecting the broken door.

"Did your father do this, ma'am?"

I nodded.

The men exchanged glances. "You're not in a safe situation," one of them said.

My throat tightened, and tears burned behind my eyes, but I refused to let them fall. I gave the police a statement, hoping to get them out of my house as quickly as possible.

One of the cops looked down at my hands. "Did he hurt you?"

I turned over my palms and noticed for the first time that they were scraped from falling onto the road. "He doesn't know what he's doing."

The officer put a hand on my shoulder. "I understand the loyalty you must have toward your father. But you have a right to be safe too."

Tears fell onto my cheeks. *Do you really understand?* I wanted to say, but instead, I said nothing.

"We can call social services for you," the other officer said.

"No," I said, forcing my voice to work. "I'll do it." *On Christmas Day.*

When they finally left, I locked my father's bedroom door then moved the recliner back in front of the busted door to keep it closed, and curled up on the couch. The neighbors had gone back inside their houses and turned off their lights. The show was over. It was almost 2:30.

I gripped my phone, ready to call someone if my father broke out of his bedroom door.

* * *

I was still holding my phone when Grey's voice woke me up a few hours later.

"What happened, Athena?" he asked.

I opened my eyes and jumped to my feet.

"Easy," he said, putting his hands on my shoulders.

Grey was here. Everything would be fine.

I wrapped my arms around his waist and melted against him. I probably looked terrible, but I didn't care. Grey was here.

"What happened?" he murmured above me.

I told him while I pressed my cheek against his warm chest.

"Are you all right?" He drew away and lifted my arms to inspect them. "Your hands—"

"They don't hurt."

Grey kissed them gently, which made them feel miraculously better. "So are you going to do it?"

I knew he was talking about getting my father into a nursing home. "It's Christmas," I said. "Don't you have family to be with? What about your mom?"

He let out a sigh. "My mom usually sleeps through the holidays, and my siblings will survive without me. I'm not leaving you here alone anymore. Not today, not tomorrow."

The enormity of what Grey was doing for me settled in. "When Jackie comes over, maybe you can go see her. I can meet her another time."

But he was already shaking his head.

"And you have a store to run," I said, meeting his gaze.

"Then maybe the guilt over my failing business will force you into action."

"Grey—"

"I'm serious." He pulled me against him. "I know this is hard to do. But it's necessary. And until you do it, I'm staying right here."

I closed my eyes and let him hold me for a moment. I pushed out all thoughts of relocating my father and his lost life. "Why are you here so early?" I asked Grey.

"I'm always here early."

"But it's Christmas. Don't you ever sleep in?"

"Not when I'd rather be with you." He kissed my neck.

I drew away. "I need a drink of juice before you kiss me."

He smiled, tugged me toward him, and kissed me anyway.

I ducked before he could kiss me a second time and hurried into the kitchen.

Grey was right behind me.

"Don't you try anything," I said.

He smiled mischievously.

"Want some juice?"

"No, just you," he said, his arms snaking around me again. I managed to get a couple of swallows in before he was kissing me again.

A banging sound made both of us freeze.

"My dad's awake," I whispered. Something deep inside me trembled, and I hoped Grey didn't notice.

"Stay here," he said. "I'll unlock his door before he breaks that one too."

"No," I said, moving out of Grey's arms. "I should go."

"Why can't you let me do it?" Grey asked, not releasing me.

"It's not that . . . He's my responsibility." I sighed. "I'm his daughter."

"I don't want to offend you, Athena," he said, "but he doesn't even know who you are. For all he remembers, I could be his son."

The words stung, but they were true.

"Let me help."

"All right," I finally said.

Chapter 29

THE DAY AFTER CHRISTMAS, JACKIE, Andrew, and I drove my father to the care center we'd settled on in Costa Mesa, right off the 73 and 55. Andrew had called in references and was confident he'd found the right place for my father. I was nervous about committing before inspecting the place, but Andrew and Jackie told me we couldn't keep putting it off. Despite the waiting list, with one of Andrew's connections, they were willing to get my father right in. Grey stayed behind at the house to repair the door—who knew he was a handyman on top of being a bookseller . . . and a cook?

My father was quiet as we drove, as if he knew he was heading for his final destination. The care center touted all sorts of amenities, from a full-time nursing staff to 24/7 snacks. Who could pass up 24/7 snacks?

When we arrived, the first thing I noticed was the fountain in the front yard, the second thing, a high gate that surrounded the property. A curved walkway led to the front entrance. We walked into the reception area. Cheerful colors greeted us, from the rust-colored carpet to pale walls and floral paintings; the place definitely had a homey feel.

A woman greeted us immediately and took us on a minitour. My father seemed calm and stayed with us as we toured the café, the craft room, and the recreation room.

His transition into his new place was smoother than I thought possible. Jackie and I kissed him good-bye after we saw him settled into a comfortable chair in his dorm-like room. There were nice touches dispersed throughout: a vase of artificial flowers—everything was plastic, even the vase (Mother would have hated that)—a couple of canvas paintings, pale yellow paint on the walls, a colorful bedspread. It wasn't home, but the hardships of the past few weeks came to mind. My father would be safe here.

As we stepped out of the room, I took another look back. Had my father's life really been reduced to a one-room existence?

It was all so surreal, and my eyes burned as we walked out of the center. Jackie blew her nose and leaned against her husband's shoulder on the way to the car.

I felt as if I'd lost both of my parents in a matter of weeks.

* * *

Jackie and Andrew dropped me off at our parents' house. Grey was still working on the front door, so I wandered the house, walking from room to room. It was like I could feel the absence of my father already. He'd been gone fewer than a couple of hours, but it already felt permanent.

Jackie and I planned to meet over the next few days to start the process of sorting everything out. Each room contained things that would be hard to part with—each item full of memories. We'd already divvied up a good portion of my mother's personal belongings, but there was an entire house to go through now. And even though neither of us wanted to buy the home, we didn't know how we could get rid of all of this stuff. We needed the sale price of the house to fund my father's care now.

But I couldn't imagine anyone else sitting in my father's favorite chair or another family sitting at the dining table we'd shared so many meals over. I sat on my parents' bed for a few minutes and wrapped my arms around my waist. They were both gone. And all that was left were *things*. And the memories that the people they knew remembered about them.

I closed my eyes and breathed out. My mother had been loved; my father had been loved. Jackie had a husband and children to surround her. I . . . I had to keep living.

"Athena?" Grey called from the front of the house.

I opened my eyes. "I have Grey," I whispered.

Leaving my parents' bedroom, I blinked in the natural light coming through the new front door.

Grey was swinging it back and forth, testing the hinges.

My heart hitched when he met my gaze. "It looks great," I said. The door was lighter in color but still contained a glass window inset.

"How are you doing?"

I lifted a shoulder. "Fine." I waved my hand at the rooms behind me. "It's just strange, you know?"

He nodded, watching me carefully, but I was holding my own pretty well.

"Plans tonight?" he asked, stepping inside the house and walking toward me.

"Yep."

"With someone I know?"

I held back a smile. "I think you know him pretty well." I grabbed his hand and pulled him toward me, firmly placing his hand on my waist.

Grey leaned down, his face inches from mine. "What do you want to do?"

"Anything." I leaned into his hug, and he held me against him. I had done it. My father was in a care center. Safe and sound. Something in my heart ached, but for now, I closed my eyes and let Grey hold me up.

That evening, we went to a movie and then had a late dinner. It was strange to be out in public, around people doing ordinary things, and not having to worry about Dad. When we walked into the theater, I found myself staring at an elderly man in the lobby. At dinner, there was a woman who looked to be my mother's age whom I kept sneaking glances at. I wondered about her life—wondered if it had been a happy one.

Grey watched me from across the restaurant table.

"Sorry," I said, meeting his gaze. "I've been so distracted . . . Our first real night out in a long time, and I can hardly carry a conversation."

"You have a lot going on."

I nodded and looked down at my half-eaten food. I was too tired to eat much more. "I think I'm finished."

"Me too," Grey said.

He signaled the waiter, and after getting our final receipt, we stood. I let out a sigh as he took my hand. We left the restaurant and climbed into the Jeep. On the drive back to the house, I rested my head against the seat back. It was after 10:00 p.m.—after my father's bedtime. I wondered how he was faring on his first night in the care center.

"He'll be fine," Grey said, squeezing my hand as if he could read my mind. Maybe it was my sighing that gave me away.

Grey gave me a very tempting kiss when he dropped me off, but I assured him I'd be fine alone in my parents' house. I'd get things packed in the next couple of days then make the official move back to my condo.

"I don't like saying good-bye to you at night," Grey said.

I nestled against him. "Then I'd better say good-bye right now." I pulled away, and he groaned when I refused to kiss him again.

I hopped out of the Jeep before he could climb out and open the door. He met me at the steps and grabbed my hand.

I stifled the urge to invite him in. "Really. I'll be fine."

"That's too bad," he said, burying his face against my neck.

"The neighbors are going to call the police again," I said.

Grey kissed my neck. "Let them."

It took a great deal of willpower to finally pull away from Grey and send him on his way. I watched him drive down the street from the doorway. My heart pounded. I had fallen hard.

Chapter 30

FOR THE FIRST TIME IN months, I awoke to absolute silence. My heart rate spiked as I wondered what my father was up to. Had he escaped again? Then I remembered. Dad wasn't here.

I climbed out of bed slowly and walked down the hall to his bedroom. The door stood open, and all was quiet within. Something in my throat caught, and I wondered what my father had thought waking up this morning. He hadn't called me by name in a long time, but I held some comfort thinking that he at least knew me on a deeper level.

Now he was completely surrounded by strangers.

I took a deep breath and walked into the kitchen. I didn't particularly like oatmeal, but I made it anyway. I sat down in my father's usual chair and ate a few bites.

Everything about the house was too quiet—so quiet that I heard the sound of the kitchen clock ticking—the old-fashioned one above the window that my mother had bought ages ago.

I sat there for a long time as the kitchen warmed with the rising sun. I listened to the clock and the birds collecting among the fruit trees in the backyard.

Today was the first day of my new life. I should have felt freedom, excitement, and peace. But I felt none of those things. I wanted to crawl back into bed and bury my face in my pillow. I wanted to turn back time. Tell my mother I was sorry. Be a better daughter to both of my parents.

But it was too late now. I rested my head on my hands, tears pooling in my eyes. It was too late for a lot of things.

* * *

By early afternoon, I hadn't accomplished a thing. I'd fixed some tea and spent most of the day on the couch in some sort of daze. I'd ignored calls from both Jackie and Grey. I didn't want to sound whiney, and Jackie and I were already planning on visiting Dad the next night anyway.

Finally, when the phone rang and I saw it was Ruby, I answered.

"Everyone is wondering how you're doing," Ruby said. I could just imagine Ruby spending the day calling each lady in the book club to update herself on everybody's news. I told her about my father's new situation, wondering how she'd react. She'd made it pretty clear at the last book club meeting that she wasn't in high favor of nursing homes.

"I'm proud of you, Athena," her motherly voice carried straight into my heart. "I know that I said a few harsh things about nursing homes, but I've since realized that places are much nicer now than they used to be. Also, there are some people who need the extra care that only a nursing home can provide."

It felt good to hear the affirmation, although I still wasn't entirely convinced that letting my father go had been the right move.

"He'll settle right in; you wait and see," she continued.

I offered the occasional "Mm-hmm," but it wasn't necessary with Ruby. She was so much like my mother in that way. I let her voice wrap around me like a blanket.

"We'll be meeting at Daisy's house for our next meeting—she's on bed rest, you know," Ruby said. "It turns out she was pregnant after all."

I tuned more fully into the conversation. "What's wrong?" Besides Daisy's age, I meant. She must be considered high risk just because of that.

"I'm not sure exactly. Apparently things were fine, and then they weren't," Ruby said, giving me no information whatsoever. "I wondered if we could ride together to Lake Forest to Daisy's?" she asked.

"Of course," I said, still wondering about Daisy.

"I don't like driving on the freeways at night anymore. And it will give us a good chance to talk."

"Yes." I was back to mumbling.

Ruby continued on about one of her neighbors and then something about her daughter-in-law.

When we hung up, I realized I was really looking forward to book club. In the few times I'd met with the ladies, they'd become my friends, women that I realized I loved and cared about. I hadn't read much of *Silas Marner* yet, but what I had read had made me really think about my life. Why had I let so much time pass without allowing myself to love? I knew it was due to fear. Silas had been focused on accumulating gold, while I had been focused on work. We were both workaholics in our own ways: Silas tried to forget his past, and I tried to not repeat mine.

It was not an excuse, at least, not any longer. The fears I had about being in a serious relationship and losing my independence had faded as I'd learned more about my parents' marriage. Yes, I was still scared, but I had allowed the possibility of *more* with Grey enter my mind. I determined that the next time I saw Grey, I'd ask him about meeting his family. I felt bad that he'd missed spending time with his family on Christmas day. It wasn't a subject I wanted to bring up over the phone. I wasn't sure how he'd react, since he had never offered, but his mother's "condition" weighed heavily in my heart. And maybe meeting his siblings would help me understand the family dynamics better.

I spent the next few hours packing my things. It was bittersweet, and the only company I had was the ticking clock. I called Grey, but it went to voice mail. I told him I'd call back in the morning and then left a similar message on Jackie's voice mail.

I packed my office things last. Having the boxes put together would force me to get out of my parents' house a lot faster. Even though it was technically Christmas vacation for most of the world, I had fallen behind enough that I needed to catch up before the New Year.

When Grey showed up early the next morning, he pulled me into a fierce hug. "I can't go a whole day without seeing you."

I smiled, but his words made me feel like crying. Why was he so good to me? "I needed some downtime."

He pulled away and studied me. "Are you feeling all right? I don't think you've ever taken downtime."

I smiled at that. "It was great while it lasted." I took a step back. "Come on, we've got work today."

We carried the boxes to his Jeep and my car, and I told him about Ruby's phone call.

"I love her," Grey declared.

"What?" The statement surprised me. "I didn't know you were so well acquainted with her."

"I'm not." Grey took a box from my arms and set it on the backseat of the Jeep. He turned to me, and I was surprised to see his expression so serious. "Because of her, I met you."

"Not exactly. I came into your store looking for a book." I held back a smile. "It was because of *me* that you met me."

"Or was it because of Karl?" he teased.

"Uh, you might be right about that," I said, reaching for his hand. I felt suddenly nervous, but I wanted to see his reaction. "So . . . now that things are getting back to normal, as far as normal can be, when do I get to meet your brother and sisters?"

Grey gazed at me for a moment, until I started to squirm. "Athena Di Jasper," he said, "I think I'm falling in love with you."

My mouth fell open as I stared at him, then my face heated up into a full blush.

"I've been waiting a long time to hear you ask about meeting my siblings," he said as if he hadn't just completely shocked my heart.

It took several seconds to gain my speech back. "Really?"

"Yep." He turned my hand over, clasping it tightly. "Now I know."

"Know what?" I asked, my voice just above a whisper.

"That you're serious about me."

I couldn't answer for a moment, and it turned out that I didn't have to. I lifted up on my toes and kissed Grey. It was really the only answer.

Chapter 31

WALKING INTO MY CONDO WAS like entering a dream. I opened the windows, letting in the cool air. On the drive over, with Grey following me, I tried to calm my nerves. Grey hadn't said, "I love you," but it was close enough.

My heart fluttered as I replayed his words over and over in my mind: *I think I'm falling in love with you.*

I had arrived at my condo first and grabbed a box so that by the time Grey arrived, I was already walking up the stairs. All the better; I needed more time to think. Even the chilly air coming through the windows didn't seem to help sharpen my focus and clarity.

All too soon, Grey had arrived, walking into my condo, filling every space with his presence. He set down the box he was carrying on the kitchen table.

"You can start unpacking, and I'll carry the rest of the boxes up," he said, his eyes piercing mine.

"All right," I choked out, still breathless—and not from walking up the steps or carrying any boxes.

When he left down the hall, I sank onto the couch and let my head drop in my hands. There were no barriers now. I'd asked to meet his family. He'd said what he'd said. My father was taken care of. No more excuses.

Deep down, I trembled. This wasn't the same panicky fear I'd had with Karl; it was something different. Like I couldn't quite breathe normally. Like I couldn't bear for Grey to leave me alone. What was wrong with me?

This is what I had feared happening—to fall for someone—and to be dependent on him. I didn't even hear Grey come back in until the door closed.

I looked up as he was crossing toward me, his eyes full of concern.

"What's wrong?" he asked as he sat next to me.

"I don't know," I whispered.

He rubbed my back. "Aren't you glad to be back in your condo?"

I nodded then shook my head. "I . . ." I looked at him, feeling helpless. "The last time I was here, I was strong and independent. I knew what I wanted all the time. I knew where I was going."

"You're still that woman," Grey said.

"No, I'm not." I leaned back against the couch and turned my head toward him. "Something's happened, and it's your fault."

The look of astonishment in his eyes made me want to laugh and cry at the same time. "What did I do?"

My heartbeat stumbled. "You made me fall in love with you."

Grey's astonishment transformed into a grin. "I didn't do it on purpose."

"I think you did," I whispered with a smile.

"I'll never admit to it," he whispered back, pulling me onto his lap. I could have stayed there forever, but even in my newly-revised condition, I was compulsive enough to want to unpack.

I finally had to send Grey home so I could get something done. But the second I heard his Jeep roar away, I wanted to call him and tell him to come back.

I bit my lip, chastising myself for acting like a hopeless teenager.

Had I really told him that I had fallen in love with him? I collapsed onto the couch with a groan. I'd definitely said it and couldn't take it back now.

* * *

My father was sitting by the fountain when Jackie and I arrived at the care center. A woman wearing a name tag that read "Lucy" sat next to him. He stared into the moving water, and I wondered what he saw there.

As we approached, he looked over and searched our faces. I wanted so badly for him to recognize us, even if it was to accuse us of dumping him in a strange place.

The aide greeted us as we sat on each side of our dad.

"How are you feeling, Dad?" Jackie asked.

He didn't answer.

"He's been real quiet today," Lucy said. "Don't you worry about it; completely natural on some days." She patted Jackie's shoulder and stood, walking to the other side of the yard to give us some privacy, yet still keeping an eye on us.

"How did you sleep?" I ventured.

Dad looked down at his hands. In them, he held his toothbrush, his grip quite firm.

"Did you brush your teeth yet?" I asked.

He nodded. At least that was something.

Jackie and I spent about twenty minutes sitting by him at the fountain. Then the aide came over. "Dinner is soon." She gently but firmly grasped my father's arm and pulled him upward. He rose without protest.

"See you in a couple of days, Dad," Jackie said, and I echoed it.

Together, we watched him shuffle away, and I was sure that Jackie's heart was as heavy as mine.

"Do you think they sedated him?" I asked when my father had disappeared inside. "He seemed really mellow."

"I don't know," Jackie said. "We'll ask about his medications at the doctor's appointment on Wednesday."

After saying good-bye to Jackie, I hurried home, bent on finishing reviewing the articles my editor had cleaned up. So far, I hadn't made many additional corrections, and I assumed that with time, I wouldn't have to double-check so much.

But as I drove home, I worried about my father. What was going on inside his mind? He seemed to be almost completely nonresponsive to Jackie and me. He had reacted more to what the aide said to him than to what his own daughters had. By the time I arrived home, the concern had blossomed.

I called Jackie, but she didn't pick up.

I went into my office and tried to push the worries away. If my dad was being so mellow, should I have watched over him longer? Was it just a medication choice? Was it me being stressed over every little thing? Had a couple of days in the care center already put an irreversible separation between us?

I tried to focus on the articles, but my mind wandered far from the topic of summer travel in Vancouver. Truthfully, what difference did staying in a four-star versus a five-star hotel really matter in the long run?

My mind felt jumbled; I decided to save the reviewing until after dinner. Maybe it would energize me—especially since I was going out with Grey.

I was ready by the time he showed up but was feeling more and more like I'd rather stay home instead of face a restaurant full of busy, happy people when my father was alone with his television.

The sight of Grey warmed the dark corners of my heart. I practically threw myself at him in a hug.

"Whoa . . . It's good to see you too," he said.

But I didn't laugh; I hung on.

"Long day?"

I simply nodded.

"How's your dad doing?" Grey asked on the way to the Jeep.

"He didn't say much," I said, tears pricking my eyes despite my resolve. I took a deep breath. I didn't need to start our date out blubbering. "The aide said it was normal."

"That sounds about right," he said.

"How can you know though? Really. How can anyone know?" I burst out. We'd reached the Jeep, and I climbed into the passenger seat, my chest heating up with discouragement.

"Athena, we can only go with what researchers have told us; we have to let that be our guide," Grey said. "The medical field has put a lot of time into studying the disease. We can only trust their conclusions."

"I know, but cold facts don't bring me any comfort," I said.

Grey grasped my hand as we pulled onto the road. We drove most of the way in silence. I was right about the restaurant. It was a busy, cheerful place, with music blaring. If I hadn't been there with Grey, I wouldn't have lasted very long in public without crying. I had to practically force myself to eat, since I didn't feel very hungry either.

Grey told me stories about the odd people who came into his bookstore, and I had to concentrate on what he said in order to not worry so much about my lonely, helpless father.

"Oh, I forgot to tell you," Grey said, detouring from his stories. "My brother, Jed, is having my family over for dinner on Sunday night, even my mom."

I stared at him, waiting for what I knew was coming.

"So I thought it would be a good time to introduce you to everyone." He winked.

My pulse quickened. "Your whole family at once?"

He smiled. "It will be less painful that way."

"Will it be painful?"

"I'll protect you," he said, his eyes twinkling.

"All right," I managed, although nervousness had crept into my stomach. We continued to talk but about nothing I could exactly remember.

I was quiet when Grey dropped me off later that night, and he seemed to take the hint that I needed some space. After he left, I decided to go to the care center. It was after visiting hours, but I thought that if I could just be closer to my father, I'd be able to figure out why I had such deep regret.

Driving over, I realized that part of what was bothering me was the book club book and the relationship Silas Marner had with the little orphan girl. He wasn't really her father, yet they had such a strong bond of love between them. Something I felt I hadn't had with my own father. Silas and the orphan girl were so close that when the girl's real father came into the picture and offered her an incredible life with a rich inheritance, she turned him down.

With my new understanding about my father's care for our family, I ached to have a lucid conversation with him. Just one. Like Silas Marner's little girl, I was choosing the man who'd raised me, who'd loved me despite all of my faults and his. But my father would never know that I had finally chosen him.

I pulled off the freeway and drove to the care center. The outside lights created a picturesque view of a cozy retirement home. The Christmas decorations were still up and made the place look bright and festive. The lights from the residents' rooms were dark, and my father was inside one of them, sleeping.

If only I could explain to my father what I'd learned and ask him questions about my mother. But that could never happen. It was all left to conjecture now. I had worn out Jackie discussing our parents, and she was obviously not as obsessed as I with finding out what had been wrong with our mother. But she had a lot of distractions and was surrounded by her kids and husband.

Despite the merriness of the holiday lights, my heart felt heavy and weighed down. My father was alone in his nonsensical world, and my mother was gone. My sister was busy, and Grey was the only thing keeping me afloat right now.

And now I'd be meeting his family—the mother he held so much apathy for and the siblings who had been there for him when no parent had.

I stayed outside the care center for over an hour, wishing I could find peace in the decision to place my father and wishing my mom were here to tell me what to do.

I'd listen to her this time.

Chapter 32

SUNDAY MORNING, I WOKE UP feeling horrible. Not sick but despondent. I went for a long walk then ate fruit and yogurt for breakfast. But still, I didn't feel any better. I read a couple of articles in a competitor's magazine and flipped through television stations, but found nothing to pull me out of my funk.

What was wrong with me? I'd be meeting Grey's family tonight, and I didn't want to show up acting like a droopy-eyed basset.

Then, in an unprecedented move, I climbed back into bed. I didn't sleep, couldn't, but somehow, with the covers nestled around me, I felt better. Problem was, the hours ticked by, and I had no desire to get up and get ready.

Only the realization that Grey would be coming in fewer than thirty minutes propelled me into action, albeit very slow action. I pulled myself together just in time. Grey arrived, and I had to refrain from hugging him too long—seeming too needy.

Being with him made me feel better, but my stomach clenched as we neared his brother's house. What would they think of me? What was his mother like?

The introductions were a whirlwind, his brother, Jed, and his family—including the gum-cracking Chelsey, who I met at the bookstore—and his two sisters, Hayley and Suzanne. Everyone was friendly, everyone was smiling, reminding me of Grey. This family had pulled together despite the odds and had formed their own support unit. It was no wonder they were so close.

"Where's Mom?" Grey asked Jed.

"She isn't feeling well," Jed said.

Grey's face flushed. "What did she say?"

I could tell his brother was trying to keep things calm and avoid Grey's question when he said, "It's probably better. You know she doesn't like large groups."

"This isn't a large group—we're her kids." Grey's tone was carefully controlled.

"I know," Jed said, glancing quickly at me.

"I shouldn't have let myself hope."

I slid my hand into Grey's, but he didn't even seem to notice I was there.

"It's all right." I hoped to get Grey to relax.

He turned toward me. "No, it's not."

"Come on, bro," Jed said. "Let's go steal food while the women aren't looking."

I followed them into the kitchen. Everyone was in there talking and laughing. Grey didn't join in. I didn't know all that was going on, but I couldn't help but wonder how he could be so perfectly understanding about my father, yet when it came to his mother, he seemed stubbornly critical?

For a moment, I caught a glimpse of a little boy who had been hurt. Eventually, when he softened and started joking around with his sisters, relief coursed through me.

We ate in the backyard, adults at one table, kids at another. Dinner was great, and although it was strange at first to be surrounded by people I didn't know, it was fun to pick out things that Grey had in common with his siblings.

He stayed with me the whole time and either held my hand or kept his arm around my shoulders, making it clear that we were together.

I helped the sisters carry dirty plates and leftover food back into the house while the kids scattered throughout the yard, jumping on the trampoline or playing on the extensive jungle gym. When I came back outside, Grey and his brother were nowhere to be seen, but I heard voices coming from the side of the house. I started to approach then stopped when I heard Jed say, "So you really like her, huh?"

"Yeah, she's great." Grey's voice.

My heart fluttered at his words. I was about to go back to the house when I heard Jed say, "She's not one of your charity girls, then?"

"Jed—"

"Just asking. I mean, her mom died right after you met her—so it makes me wonder if you got serious before or after that happened."

"Technically, *after*," Grey said.

"So how is this different from Lisa or Bethany?"

"Well, she's not schizophrenic, for one thing, and she's not in a wheel-chair." Grey said, his voice sounding strange. Was he angry? Was he joking?

All the warmth had drained from my body. Were those women his former girlfriends? And what did his brother mean by "charity girl"? I didn't want to hear any more, but I couldn't bring myself to leave either.

"She's definitely not in a wheelchair," Jed said with a laugh. "How is Bethany doing now?"

"She just got a new job . . ."

I moved back toward the house, my stomach roiling. He still kept in touch with the Bethany woman. My heart felt as if it had been split in half then slowly burned to ash. Grey had *charity girls*? Women he dated because they had problems? Because he felt sorry for them?

My face burned with embarrassment and shame. I couldn't go back inside and chat with his sisters now. I started stacking the chairs that had been around the picnic table.

Was I one of his charity girls? He'd been so kind and understanding, so *perfect* that it was unreal. I supposed it was too good to be real. I should have known.

I had let myself fall in love with someone who felt sorry for me.

My mind raced in circles as my thoughts tormented me. How many had there been? Grey was thirty-one, so he could have had quite the illustrious career rescuing women. I felt like I was in a dream world and that the children's screeches coming from the swing set belonged to another yard in another time zone.

Grey's sister Suzanne came out, and we folded the tablecloth together. She spoke, and I responded without really remembering what I said.

Before I knew it, we'd said good-bye, and Grey and I were driving home.

He was quiet on the drive, which suited me fine. I needed to be by myself to process what I'd learned, then I'd confront him. Ask him for an explanation. But no matter what it was, or how he spun it, I knew that I could never look at him the same. I could never believe his tender words or let him kiss me again.

When he pulled up to the condo complex, he said, "Sorry that my mom didn't show up. I guess I shouldn't have been surprised."

"That's fine," I said in a stiff voice. "I'm sure I can meet her another time."

He parked and turned off the engine. "You don't get it. She deliberately stayed home—she knew I wanted her to meet you. She knew this was important to me. It was just her way of saying she can't be bothered with her kids."

No, I hadn't met his mother, but I couldn't imagine any mother being that cruel. But then again, Grey was not who I thought he was. "Maybe you should just give her the benefit of the doubt. How can we know what's really going on inside her mind?" I said a bit harshly.

Grey's jaw stiffened. He obviously heard the defiance in my tone. "The only thing that goes on in her mind is her own selfish needs. If even one drop of guilt tries to creep in, she'll just take another pill and block it out."

I was at a loss—he was obviously hurting, but he pushed it onto his mother with anger. I grasped at something his brother had said. "Maybe she really *doesn't* like crowds." *You should know—she sounds like one of your charity girls!*

"Why should it matter?" Grey asked. "Mothers make sacrifices for their kids, even if it's hard on them. This was only a dinner—with her kids and grandkids. How can that be so horrible?"

"There are people who really do fear being around a lot of people," I said, showing no mercy. It didn't add up. Grey could date a schizophrenic woman, yet he couldn't have compassion for his mother's issues?

"What are you saying, Athena?" Grey said, pulling my focus back to him. "That my mother has a justifiable reason for neglecting her children?"

The word *neglect* was a strong accusation, especially coming from a man who seemed to go the extra mile for downtrodden women. "What if she does? What if she has some condition that's gone untreated?" I thought of my mother and the way my father had taken care of her, protected her. Grey's mother didn't have that. Instead of helping his own mother, Grey turned his attentions on other needy people.

"Like a mental illness?" Grey asked in a quiet voice.

"Maybe," I said.

"Whatever it is, she brought it on herself." His tone was harsh now. "We kids were abandoned by our father and were going through what she was, yet she decided she had permission to check out."

I wasn't ready to give in to his reasoning. I had my own agenda now. "Maybe it was a trigger for her—your father leaving triggered an illness."

"Mental illness isn't triggered."

I hadn't done the research, but I assumed he knew some things—with all of his girlfriends. "What about post-traumatic stress? It wouldn't be farfetched to say that your father leaving caused it in your mother."

"I can understand stress, but to completely check out of life and neglect your own children?" he said. "She wouldn't even feed us."

I reached for the door handle. This was too much. How was I supposed to understand his mother without meeting her? How was I supposed to sympathize with Grey's plight when I'd just learned about his "charity girls"?

"There must be a deep reason somewhere. I can't imagine her not loving you or your siblings," I said, my voice trembling. I had to get away. To understand who Grey really was.

He grabbed my hand before I could open the Jeep door. "Hey. Where are you going?"

"I've got some things to do tonight before I go to bed," I said, ignoring the tenderness of his voice. It was completely different when he wasn't talking about his mother. But I wouldn't be fooled.

He tugged me toward him, but I resisted. If I let him kiss me, I'd start crying. It was hard enough to contain my emotions as it was.

"Thanks for everything," I said, pulling away, hoping he didn't notice too much was amiss. I wasn't ready to talk about it.

He leaned across the space and kissed me anyway. It was gentle at first, and I planned to pull away, but as it grew more intense, I became helpless. When I finally gathered my strength, I moved away. My heart was thundering, and I was hot all over.

"I'd better go—"

His gaze bore into mine as his fingers played with my hair. When he looked at me like that, I certainly didn't feel like a charity girl, but the fact was that I doubted now. And there was also the fact that he'd dated women he felt sorry for, and that overshadowed any justification.

Another quick kiss and I climbed out of the Jeep before he could get out and open the door for me. I hurried up the stairs, closing the door of my condo firmly behind me.

I had almost invited him up to my place. If I had, I knew I wouldn't have sent him home. Taking deep breaths, I told myself that I had done the right thing. I had to keep some semblance of myself intact. I had wanted to protect him, to eradicate the hurt that had been in his eyes, to heal the wounds of his heart.

But I didn't want to be a charity.

I climbed into bed fully clothed, but the tears didn't come immediately. I replayed the conversation I'd overheard then thought of the look in Grey's eyes just before he kissed me and the way my body ignited at his touch.

Chapter 33

I FELT LOUSY WHEN I awoke in the morning. Tears had helped but hadn't resolved anything. A heavy weight pressed down on every part of my soul. Thoughts of Grey flooded my conscience: from when we first met, our first kiss, when he came to my mother's funeral, when he fixed my parents' front door. Was it all an act of some self-fulfilling service on his part?

I peeled off my clothes and pulled the covers back over me, hoping to fall asleep into nothingness. It sounded much better than reality. I faded into some sort of oblivion, but as the sun rose, turning my white blinds to pale yellow, the heavy feeling was still there.

Taking a shower didn't help. I crawled back into bed with my laptop.

I Googled *Grey Ronning*. I didn't know what I expected to find, but there wasn't much. A link to his high school senior class, a listing for his bookstore, but nothing useful after that. *What did I expect?* Articles published on the Renaissance man who went out of his way to date less-fortunate women?

I set the laptop on my bedside table and burrowed under the covers. I awoke an hour later, disoriented and grumpy. It was Monday, and I'd accomplished nothing. I had no motivation. I didn't even want to exercise. All I wanted to do was see Grey and pretend that I didn't know anything. Pretend that when he'd told me he was falling in love with me, it was true.

What was wrong with me? Pining over a man? I was Athena Di Jasper—workaholic, former caretaker of her father, and a woman who ran her own relationships. There was no excuse for missing work because of a broken heart.

I choked on a sob.

I needed to end it. Now. I would never be any guy's "charity girl."

My hand trembled as I reached for the phone. When Grey's warm voice said, "Hi, sweetheart," I almost changed my mind.

But I didn't.

His dead silence on the other end of the phone when I told him I'd overheard his brother talking about his "charity girls" told me more than his explanations that followed.

He admitted that maybe he was drawn to damsels in distress in the past, but with me, it was different. Of course he'd say that.

"Athena," he said, "my feelings are still the same about you." When I didn't say anything, he continued. "What about you? If you hadn't overheard my brother being an idiot, would you feel differently about me?"

No. I couldn't answer because I knew that it didn't matter what I'd overheard. I was still in love with him. That's why I had to hang up.

I wanted to disappear. Instead, I turned off my phone and pulled the blankets over my head.

Now my world was like my father's. Silent and lonely.

* * *

January 3

* * *

January 4

* * *

January 5

* * *

January 6

* * *

January 7

* * *

January 8

It had been three days since Grey stopped calling and leaving unanswered messages. Even he had his limit—the saint that he was. Not that I was counting the days, and maybe the hours too, because the thought of a whole day passing without hearing from him was too overwhelming to think about.

But I had survived so far without hearing from him—a whole seventy-two hours.

When my phone rang, I jolted from my thoughts. One part of me hoped it was Grey—that he hadn't given up—and that calling me again would somehow prove that our relationship really *was* different. Yet, I didn't let myself check who was calling until after the ringing had stopped. My heart sank when I saw that it had been Ruby. Tonight was book club. That meant it was Saturday and I shouldn't feel guilty for taking the day off, but I had taken every day off this week. Thank goodness I'd hired that editor and accountant.

I waited an hour then called her back, making my voice sufficiently scratchy sounding so I could pass as being sick.

"Ruby, I'm—"

She broke in. "Oh, I'm so glad you called back. I wanted to make sure you could still give me a ride. You know how I hate driving in the dark on the freeway."

I pressed my lips together, remembering that Daisy was on bed rest and I'd promised Ruby a ride.

She continued. "Can you come around 6:30? That should give us enough time to get there. I feel like it's been forever since I've seen you gals. You know, I really miss it—the holidays aren't the same without my . . . husband and son around." Her voice cut off. Then she continued, sounding a bit shaky. "You girls mean more to me than you'll ever know."

How could I pretend that I was sick after that? "6:30 is fine."

"Oh, bless you," she said then rattled on about several other things before hanging up.

I took a deep breath and stared at the phone. I was in no condition to make small talk, and driving with Ruby meant I couldn't bow out early. I hadn't left my condo for several days, except to get food and make one visit to my father. Somehow, when we'd put him in the care center, I thought I'd be visiting him every day. But I'd only been a couple of times in the past week.

I showered and pulled my hair into a smooth ponytail that was really more of a nub aided by a couple of bobby pins. When I slipped on my jeans, they hung loosely at my hips. I stepped on my scale—something I rarely did—and discovered I'd lost a few pounds. Normally I'd be happy with that, but I knew I had lost muscle from not exercising or eating much.

After applying extra make-up, I decided I'd pass for human when I picked up Ruby.

Twenty minutes later, in my car, dressed to the nines in a shimmery blue blouse and black trousers, with matching jewelry, gushing over how wonderful it was to see me, Ruby said, "Shannon, Ilana, and Victoria can't make it tonight, so I'm so glad you came. It will just be five of us at Daisy's."

I wished I could have just a few ounces of her energy and enthusiasm— just enough to get me back to feeling normal, even if that meant without Grey.

And then came the question. "How's it going with Grey?"

I opened my mouth to respond, but she rushed on. "I'll tell you, he's a real catch. I stopped in his store a few days ago, and he was as handsome as ever. Looked a little pale though, but it's probably because of all this rain we're having."

I hesitated. I wanted to ask her if he'd mentioned me, but my voice would betray me. Besides, why did I care whether he'd said anything? It wasn't like we were together anymore.

"And your father, how's he doing?" Ruby asked as if my silence hadn't bothered her.

"He's becoming more and more quiet . . . I've been to see him a few times, and it's still so hard that he doesn't recognize me."

"Oh, my dear," Ruby said. "How hard this must be. But I know you've done the best thing for him. He has professional care around the clock."

I focused on the taillights of the car in front of us. My eyes started swimming, and I blinked back any potential tears. "It's a good place— they have a lot of activities going on." *Activities that he forgets within a few hours.* That's what his life had come to. I was grateful she didn't bring up Grey for the rest of the drive. Talking about my father was hard enough.

The freeway was pretty clear for a Saturday night, and it didn't take long to get to Daisy's place in Lake Forest.

I still couldn't believe Daisy was pregnant. I tried to wrap my mind around that fact—Daisy was a career woman with two grown children. I guess lives could change unexpectedly no matter who we were. Daisy didn't seem like the type to welcome such a late pregnancy in her life. Tall and stylish, she probably hid it well and most likely would wear the latest fashions.

Just as we arrived at Daisy's house, Ruby's cell phone rang. She waved me out of the car and said she'd come in a few minutes.

Paige had just pulled up too. She climbed out of her car, carrying some sort of dessert. I decided to wait for her.

"Hi, Athena," Paige said as she reached me. "How are you doing?"

Her tone carried weight—this was not a simple *how are you.*

"Better," I said, going back in my mind to the last discussion Paige and I had shared about my mother. It seemed so long ago, and yet I recognized the progress I'd made since then—at least in regard to my mother. "I think." *Worse*, I realized when I let thoughts of Grey intrude. "Going through my mom's things has really helped me understand her . . . and forgive her."

Paige tilted her head, compassion in her eyes. "That's wonderful. And I'm sure she knows that too."

"You really think she does?"

Paige nodded, her eyes glistening. *Was she crying?* It was hard to tell in the near darkness.

"I'm hoping she'll understand why I put my father in a care center."

"You did?" Paige put a hand on my arm. "That must have been difficult, but I'm sure you did the right thing."

My own eyes watered. "I'm hoping I did. I'm still waiting for that peace to come that you talked about, but I have faith that it will."

Paige nodded slowly. "I'll keep you in my prayers."

My chest warmed, and I blinked back tears. People had told me that a dozen times over at my mother's funeral, but I'd never felt the sincerity of it until Paige.

I stalled a few minutes after Paige went inside, wondering if I should wait for Ruby. Finally, Ruby climbed out of the car, still talking on her phone, and walked to the front door. I locked up the car, but by the time I got to the apartment, Ruby had already gone inside. No matter. It gave me time to compose myself. I had almost told Paige about Grey but had decided not to.

Daisy's place was nicely decorated, just as I'd expected it to be. Across the living room, Daisy sat in a recliner, apparently not able to even stand and greet us. She smiled at me, and I realized that we all had our different challenges—there was Daisy, managing hers with a smile. And Paige and Ruby were dealing with their own altered lives. Life wasn't easy for anyone, and I looked forward to the next hour of just chatting and eating that dessert Paige had brought.

Ruby came over and hugged me—I guess she'd forgotten that she'd hugged me when I picked her up. I was fine with it though; I'd take a surrogate mother for the evening over my empty condo.

The doorbell rang, and Livvy arrived. "I'm so sorry I'm late," she said. She looked more put together than usual, but maybe I thought that because I felt such a mess inside. "I couldn't get away from home, and then the traffic . . ." Her voice faded off then she shook her head. "Crazy."

I agreed wholeheartedly. *Crazy.* I glanced at my cell phone—she was only a few minutes late—which meant that Ruby and I had been early.

"Your hair," Daisy said, drawing all of our attention back to Livvy. "It looks awesome."

It was different. Livvy blushed as we all studied her new A-line cut. I'd been so caught up in my own feelings, I hadn't noticed right away what was different.

"You like it?" Livvy asked, smoothing it as if something was out of place. She smiled shyly.

"It's great," I added to the other generous compliments.

"I was ready for a change," Livvy said, still standing just inside the door.

"Well, it was a good one," Paige said, jumping in.

Livvy moved to the couch and sat next to me, still smiling. Another change in our group. Even a haircut could be a big deal.

"So," Ruby said from her spot on the kitchen chair across the room, "you need to give us a bit of an update, young lady. An awful lot has happened since we met in December."

Daisy glanced at everyone as if she were hesitant then told us all about her pregnancy and the surprise of it. I had the feeling Daisy wasn't telling us everything. By the soft tone in her voice, I could tell she was choosing her words carefully. When Daisy talked about her new grandson Tennyson—it was hard to imagine Daisy as a *grandmother*—Ruby asked to see pictures. Daisy passed around her cell phone so we could see a picture of the tiny infant. I was never too comfortable holding other people's babies, but fortunately, pictures never made any fuss. Daisy continued as we passed her cell around. "So anyway, I'll see what the doctor says next week. Until then, I am your token bump on a log, but I sure appreciate you guys coming all the way up here tonight. I'd have hated to miss it."

"Of course, of course," Ruby said, waving a jeweled hand. "Athena was gracious enough to have picked me up on her way. It was a wonderful visit." Ruby looked right at me as if she expected me to say something.

I had reconciled myself to not saying much but just soaking in the company and dessert.

But when Ruby said, "Athena's had a big month too," I knew I couldn't be rude. That got everyone's attention, and the room was suddenly too quiet. I smiled awkwardly, hiding the pounding in my chest. My mind raced. *Just say something. These ladies won't bite.* I had narrowed my racing thoughts down to a few possible topics when Paige said, "So, *Silas Marner.*"

I wanted to hug her.

"As I said last month, I chose this one because it was short—always nice for the holidays—and because it had kind of a Christmas message. I read this the first time in high school, and I liked it then, but I found that reading it as an adult was even more powerful. Now that I have kids of my own . . ." She paused and looked over at Daisy. A look passed between them—it was clear they had become friends. "Like Silas, I've felt mistreated by some people I trusted," Paige continued in a soft voice. "Both of those things stood out to me in regard to Silas's story, and I felt like I was reading it on a different level than I had before. What did you guys think?" We all looked at each other, waiting for someone to speak. Ruby jumped in first. She talked about how she'd always loved the story and had, in fact, read it twice. She mentioned that she had a master's in English literature and then continued on about how *Silas Marner* compared to other books during that era.

I was surprised at Ruby's insights—much more interesting than my feeble ones—about love and how Silas was able to truly bond with an orphan. I couldn't even bond with my own father, and now it was too late.

Ruby looked over at Daisy, her eyebrows raised.

Daisy quickly looked down at the book in her hands, touching the cover as if stalling for time. I tried to think of what I would say—or at least how I'd say it.

"Oh, I really liked it," Daisy said.

"Well, not at first," Paige said.

Maybe Paige thought the book started out slow as well, but when I saw the glance that Daisy flicked at Paige and the smile shared between them, I realized it was something they must have discussed earlier.

Daisy continued. "But once I really gave it a chance, I was struck by the fact that some of the most horrible things that happened to Silas were actually building blocks that prepared him to be the man he was by the end of the book," Daisy said. "That was refreshing to me."

"I noticed that too," I said, surprising myself. "Up until he found Eppie, it was like he wasn't really there. I mean, it was as though he didn't even remember his life or relationships before he came to Raveloe—like they were a dream." I hesitated, but everyone seemed to be eagerly listening. "It was like he was asleep, so absorbed by his gold, caring for and seeing nothing else. And then Eppie came into his life and became everything to him—she brought all of his life lessons to a head and solidified his life. Does that make sense?"

"That's a great way to put it," Ruby said. "Solidified. Became whole."

No one spoke. It was as if they were waiting for me to answer. "The people we love have so much power," I said, my voice shaky. "I told you about my mom's life. She was an amazing person. She loved the people in her life—she gave them everything she had. I miss that . . ." I met the gazes directed at me and offered a tremulous smile. "I mean, I miss her."

"How's your dad?" Livvy asked.

Ruby pursed her lips together—she knew the answer but was letting me talk.

"I finally did it—he went into the care center right after Christmas."

Everyone stared at me then started offering a mixture of supportive comments.

"You did the right thing," Daisy said, straightening in her recliner.

"Thank you," I said, and although I wasn't entirely convinced myself, I took comfort in the assurance in her eyes.

Livvy patted my knee. "I'm sure he's being very well taken care of."

Leave it to Livvy to go straight to the heart. "He is," I said in a shaky voice.

She must have heard the tremble in my voice because her arm went around my shoulders.

And then I let it out. "He's all alone in there. I feel like I should have done more, especially with my mother gone."

"Dear Athena," Ruby interrupted. "Your mother would have done the same thing."

But I was shaking my head. "You don't know my mother."

Paige let out a sigh next to me then redirected the conversation. She was good at that. "How is he when you visit?"

"He's in his own world." Tears burned in my eyes. "I don't remember the last time he called me by name."

"It's a terrible disease," Paige said in a sympathetic voice. "But you did the right thing."

I blinked back the tears and looked at her then at the other ladies. I felt their radiating support—like a tangible thing I could scoop up and hold in my arms.

"We can trade off and visit your father with you," Ruby offered. "Maybe having some company will help you put things in perspective."

Everyone nodded in agreement.

"Thanks, everyone," I whispered.

Livvy handed me a crumpled Kleenex she'd dug from the dark recesses of her purse. I took it gingerly and pressed it below my eyelashes. "And while I'm spilling my heart, Grey and I broke up," I said. Before they could ask a million questions, I held up my hand. "Don't worry, I'm fine. It turns out he wasn't so perfect after all."

"Are they ever?" Daisy said.

Everyone laughed, and it felt good to joke about it. I could tell they wanted to hear more details, but Ruby cut in, for which I was grateful. "Livvy," she said. "We haven't heard your thoughts on the book."

Spilling my news hadn't been as bad as I thought. I'd made it through the big confessions. I was still intact. "Oh, um, I liked it," Livvy said in a vague voice. "You guys have pretty much summed up my thoughts. It was a touching story."

"It was, wasn't it?" Ruby said. "I'm very glad you chose it, Paige."

"Me too," Daisy said.

"Good. I'm glad everyone enjoyed it," Paige said. "Daisy, it's your turn to choose one now."

"Oh, really?" she said, placing her hand on her belly with a grimace. I hoped she wasn't feeling sick. "Um, well, Paige brought me some books. One of them, *The Help*, was really good. I know there was a movie, but I never saw it." She glanced around the room and pointed toward the television.

Paige grabbed the book and gave it to Daisy. "I really liked this book and the movie," she said. "I only know about the Civil Rights movement from the History Channel and movies, but I felt like this got to the heart of the situation. I had no idea what it was really like for both sides."

"I like her writing a lot," Daisy added. "And it's about some very different women, which seems like a perfect fit for us." She waved her hand in a circle to encompass all of us.

While Daisy continued on about how great it was, Paige disappeared into the kitchen and came back with a tray of dessert plates. "This is Jell-O cheesecake, lime flavor."

Paige apologized for bringing such a simple dessert. But I thought it looked delicious. I hadn't had a decent dessert since Grey's Thanksgiving pies. I pushed away the memory of him and took a bite of the cheesecake. The creamy tartness reached all the way down to my toes. "Mmm."

I wasn't sure why Paige would apologize for making such a quick recipe—even if she hadn't had time to get to the store to make anything more creative, it was delicious.

The conversation ran down, and I noticed Daisy looking tired.

Ruby and I took our leave with Ruby hugging everyone once again. "Sorry I can't walk you to the door," Daisy said.

"Bless your heart," Ruby said. "You get all the rest you need."

As we left the apartment, my heart started pounding again. I knew Ruby would ask for the details about Grey, and I didn't know if I was ready to share them.

Chapter 34

"I THINK YOU NEED TO believe Grey—put a little trust in his explanation."

"I've tried," I told Ruby, trying to keep my emotions in check. I didn't want to be blubbering while driving in freeway traffic. It seemed that everyone was coming home from San Diego or Mexico at the same time. I had forgotten about the Saturday night traffic. "I don't know if I can believe him anymore. How do I really know I'm not one of his charity girls? Besides, what happens when he runs into the next distressed woman?"

Ruby heaved a sigh, which wasn't characteristic of her. "Well, maybe you need some time apart. From what you've said, it's been a long time since you've really liked someone this much."

I've never liked someone this much, and that's why I'm still on the verge of tears over a week later.

"Consider your past and things in it that might upset Grey if he found out, like you found out something about his past. Then decide what is really important."

"I . . ." Closing my mouth, I didn't allow myself to think about all the casual dating I'd done, all the running from men who wanted more, all the avoidance of letting my emotions get involved.

"You've dated plenty, I'll bet," Ruby said. "So with Grey, being the age he is, it stands to reason that he's dated a lot too. He just happens to be attracted to women he thinks he can fix."

"That's just it," I said. "I want him to love me for me and not because I need fixing."

"I know, honey," Ruby said, patting my arm. "I think if you look inside your heart and really listen to what Grey is telling you, things might turn out differently than you expect."

"Like how?"

Ruby smiled to herself. "I'm not one to plan your future."

I laughed. Laughing made me feel better, but Ruby's words worried me. Had I been too judgmental of Grey? If any man knew the extent of my flimsy dating career, would he stick around for long? I had hardly told Grey anything about my past. At first I was afraid he'd think the old Athena was still around, but maybe there was a reason for that.

When I pulled up to Ruby's house, I was both relieved and saddened to see her go. It felt nice to share my true feelings with someone and to have them sympathize yet give me advice. Ruby squeezed my hand. "Don't worry, dear. You'll figure it out, and when you do, I can't wait to hear the good news."

Before I could protest, she opened the car door and climbed out.

I waited to pull away until she was safely inside her home.

Ten minutes after I arrived home, Ruby called. I wondered if she'd left something in the car.

"Are you busy tomorrow?" she asked.

"Um—"

"Good. You and I are going out for a girls' day. Manicures, pedicures, massages. It's my treat."

My first instinct was to say no, to tell her it was too much, besides the fact that I never did anything like that. But my heart interfered. "I'd love to."

* * *

Spending the day with Ruby was balm to my soul. We laughed, we overate, and we smelled magnificent by the time I dropped her off at her home. It wasn't only good for me, but I could also tell that it meant a lot to Ruby. It wasn't until we spent so much time together that I realized how lonely she must be. She had such a great attitude and friendly personality that it would only take the most astute to notice that there was something more beneath her cheerfulness.

Painfully, that reminded me of my mother as well. My mother had definitely been lonely the past couple of years as she'd shouldered so much of the burden of taking care of a man who deteriorated on a daily basis, but my mother had always put forward a positive attitude. It made me all the more determined to really get to know Ruby and to revel in her friendship. Perhaps Ruby could look at me as the daughter she'd never had.

When I walked into my apartment, my cell phone started ringing. Surprised to see Paige's phone number pop up, I answered.

"Athena, my boys have a play date tomorrow afternoon, so I thought I'd come with you to visit your dad."

I sat on the couch, feeling overwhelmed with her generous offer. "That would be nice," I said in a small voice.

And the week continued like that. Both Livvy and Paige came with me to the care center—it seemed more bearable to visit with someone who wasn't so connected to my father. It was also great to get to know Livvy better. She astounded me with her giving nature and the way she instinctively made sure I was comfortable at all times.

Daisy even called a couple of times to check up on me when I should have been checking up on her!

On Saturday, Ruby met me at my parents' house. Jackie would be coming over in the afternoon, after her kids' swimming lessons. One of the looming tasks hanging over my head was to get my parents' home ready to put on the market.

When the doorbell rang, I crossed the living room to answer it, pushing away the thought of how many times I'd opened that door and Grey had been on the other side.

Ruby smiled and enveloped me into her flowery scent. She looked way too dressed up to sort through belongings and organize boxes, but I didn't say anything. I doubted Ruby owned a pair of jeans, let alone a scruffy T-shirt. Like always, her hair was beautifully styled, and her jewelry matched her lavender V-neck blouse and mocha-brown slacks.

"Why don't you start with the office area," I said. "We're not throwing anything in there away yet, just boxing it all up. Later on, I'll go through the boxes and see what can be thrown out. I'm just working on the kitchen now."

I left Ruby to her work and chuckled when she started singing to herself. Her nice alto voice carried into the kitchen.

"Athena?" Ruby called out after about thirty minutes of working.

"Yes?" I said from my perch on a stool, where I was tackling a bunch of flower vases—my mother had saved every flower vase ever given to her and had stored them in a cupboard over the refrigerator.

"You should see this."

Curious, I climbed off the stool and found Ruby in the office, sitting in the swivel chair, holding a spiral notebook in her hand.

She held it up to me, and I took it. The notebook was open to a page with my mother's handwriting.

I took the notebook. My throat tightened as I read through her notes about local care centers. It was clear she'd started her own research on nursing homes in the area, but it was still hard for me to believe. She had names and locations written down. She'd even visited one by the explanation in her notes.

Tears rolled down my face, and I covered my mouth with one hand.

Ruby smiled up at me, her own eyes watery. "It looks like your mother was making plans for your father."

I couldn't speak; I could only nod.

Every part of my body felt lighter. All the worry and questioning over the past months lifted. I felt weightless and breathless at the same time. I had to lean against the desk. Ruby stood and slid an arm around my waist. "It's okay, honey," she said.

I buried my face against her shoulder and cried on her expensive blouse. Ruby rubbed my back and let me collect myself.

Joy and relief coursed through me, and something else—like a warm whisper in my mind—telling me that my mother was proud of me, that I had done the right thing, both in caring for my father and in placing him in the care center.

I blinked back the tears and lifted my head. Ruby handed me a tissue that she'd produced from somewhere.

"Thank you for finding this," I whispered.

I kept the notebook with me as I worked in the kitchen. I carried it to the bathroom as I threw away shampoo bottles and expired medications. I read it over and over, a dozen times at least. My mother had starred the care center in Costa Mesa. It seemed she'd been seriously considering it.

Why hadn't she ever mentioned it to Jackie or me?

I knew the answer. She hadn't expected to die. Like me, she'd put off the decision but was definitely doing her homework so she'd be ready when the time was right.

When Jackie showed up, I showed her the notebook.

"It must have been much harder than Mother let on," Jackie said, shaking her head slowly.

"But she was never one to complain," I said.

Jackie nodded and looked up at me. "How are you doing?"

That was a loaded question. Ruby came up behind us to meet Jackie. "Athena is still being stubborn. She won't give that boy a call."

I was surprised by Ruby's direct manner but then realized that was just Ruby. It was what endeared me to her.

Jackie laughed. "I'm so glad you're her friend. She needs someone like you."

Ruby's face brightened, and her lips pursed into a pleased expression. "Athena has been a wonderful blessing in my life. Did she tell you about our girls' day out?"

Jackie glanced at me. "No, she didn't."

I grinned. It looked like Jackie and Ruby would get along just fine. As they moved from one subject to another, I made my way back to the main bathroom so they could gossip about me freely.

The bathroom looked different with all of the personal touches out. Like it was slowly losing its personality—what had made it my home.

My heart felt heavy but comforted, and I knew I was on the road to healing.

Chapter 35

It took about two weeks to get the house ready for the market. On Saturday morning, Jackie and I watched the Goodwill truck pull out of my parents' driveway with the last of the stuff we hadn't divvied up between us and the extended family.

"I think I'm going to see Dad," I said, turning to Jackie. "Do you want to come?"

"Andrew and I are going tomorrow with the kids."

"All right," I said. "It will give him more visiting time. I'll just go by myself tonight."

On the drive over, Paige called. I told her I'd call her back as soon as I parked at the care center. Livvy had also telephoned earlier in the day. I spoke to or e-mailed the book club ladies several times a week now. Sometimes we chatted about books, other times about other things. Paige had even tried dating again. Life really did move on, despite the hardships and tragedies.

After chatting with Paige for a few minutes, I hung up and went inside the care center. My dad was in his room, his television on, but he was staring out the window at the trees.

I turned off the television and sat across from him. "How are you, Dad?"

He turned his face toward me. "Carmen?"

"No, it's your daughter Athena."

"So beautiful." A smile crossed his face; then, just as quickly, it was gone, and he was staring out the window again.

I hugged my arms around my body. Was my dad calling me beautiful, or was he thinking of my mom? Regardless, his words warmed me through. I realized the last person who'd called me beautiful was Grey.

Sitting there, across from my dad, I remembered all the times Grey had come over to help. My mother had never met him, and my father had never understood who he was. And it bothered me. Even though I'd probably never see Grey again, he had been a part of my life, and I was tired of having people disappear on me.

I took a deep breath. "Dad, I want to tell you about someone. His name is Grey Ronning, and he owns a bookstore."

My dad was the best listener, never interrupting and never looking bored. I told him about Grey and how we met, about our first date to Balboa Island and how he took me to the hospital when Mom had the car accident. I told Dad about all the times Grey came over and kept me company. And how he'd replaced the broken door.

Then I told my dad about meeting Grey's family and the problems with his mother. And how, that one time in the kitchen, Grey told me I had rescued him.

My chest expanded with new possibilities as I stared out the window at the trees my dad was watching. "Do you think it's possible that while Grey was rescuing me, I was rescuing him?"

It was the first time I'd really considered what Grey might be going through . . . and if he really loved me, what he might be feeling. *His* loss, *his* pain, *his* discouragement.

I had only focused on my hurt and my dashed hopes.

Ruby had told me to trust him. Jackie had all but told me to give him another chance, to let him back into my heart.

That was the problem though. He was still in my heart. He had never left. I had just tried to forget.

"What should I do, Dad?" I whispered.

He didn't answer, but he didn't need to. Just sitting there with all the past behind us and the future a muddled and unpredictable thing, I realized that my dad had loved fully. Despite the flaws, despite the disappointments, and despite the faded memories. He hadn't lost the capacity to love from deep inside himself. He still knew my mother, still thought of her, and no disease could take that away from him.

He didn't need to say anything to help me. "Thanks, Dad," I said, kissing his cheek. With the sun just beginning to set, casting an orange glow in the room, I left and closed the door quietly.

My heart pounded harder by the minute as I made the drive to Grey's bookstore. Closing time wasn't for an hour. I didn't know what I'd say or if there was any chance for him to accept my apology, but I had to tell him how I felt. That he was a part of my heart. Even if he ultimately rejected it.

My hands were literally shaking by the time I pulled up to the bookstore. All of the lights were on, and the sign in the window clearly read *open.* I took several deep breaths before I forced myself out of the car.

I entered the store without looking around; my eyes were only for the person standing behind the register. I took a few steps toward the counter and then realized it wasn't Grey. "Chelsey."

She looked up from her book then fiddled with her iPod, turning it down, I assumed.

I wiped my sweaty hands on my pants. "Is . . . Grey here?" My throat was suddenly scratchy, and a wave of panic swept through me. What if she knew all the details of our breakup and was laughing at me?

"No," she said, popping her gum. She adjusted something on her iPod again, looking bored.

"Is he coming back in tonight?"

"Doubt it," Chelsey said. Her expression was unreadable, and I couldn't tell what she might be thinking. "He told me to close up. Had a bunch of flowers with him when he left. Maybe he has a date or something."

I stopped breathing for a second. "All right. Thanks," I managed before awkwardly making my exit.

Inside my car, I gripped the steering wheel hard. It was too late. Why shouldn't it be? Grey had met someone else—someone he was taking flowers to. What did I expect?

I drove home, running one stop sign. "Get a hold of yourself," I said aloud. In my father's room, all things had seemed possible. The answer had been so simple. But cold reality had hit me hard in the face.

Life had moved on for Grey; he hadn't waited for me.

My eyes were blurry by the time I reached the condo. I climbed the stairs, feeling like I had just run a marathon and collapsed a mile from the finish line. I was emotionally exhausted, and I had lost the race. I didn't see the person coming around the corner of the stairwell until I bumped into him.

Something fell to the ground. "Oh, sorry," I mumbled and bent to pick it up—a bouquet of flowers. I looked up, ready to apologize.

"Grey?" I whispered. I could hardly believe it was him. But there were those same brown eyes, the same hair that fell over his forehead, the tanned arms in rolled-up sleeves. My heart slammed into my throat.

I couldn't speak—I didn't know what to say. I tried to hand over the flowers, but he didn't take them. He kept staring at me.

I smoothed back my hair, realizing I probably looked horrific. There was nothing I could do about my puffy eyes though.

"Athena, I was just looking for you," he said.

The sound of his voice made dozens of memories collide inside of me. But he wasn't mine any longer. Those memories belonged in the past. "You were looking for me?" I tried to give him the flowers again, but he shook his head.

"Those are for you."

I looked down at them, my eyes swimming. "Why?"

"Because I'm trying to get you back," he said in a soft voice.

I thought I heard a tremor in it, but I didn't dare look at him. I just stared at the flowers—a dozen red roses.

"You aren't dating s-someone else?" I asked. "Chelsey said—"

"I could never date anyone else."

"But . . ." My heart thundered. "These are for *me*?" I dared a glance at him.

"Yes," Grey said, one side of his mouth lifting into a smile.

I took a shaky breath. "You can't just give a woman flowers and expect her to come back."

"I know." He stepped closer and ran a finger along my cheek. I was definitely looking at him now. "I owe you an apology for not telling you about my past and for letting you think that you could ever be a charity girl." He grimaced. "I really messed up. You shouldn't have had to hear about my former dating habits from my brother."

His hand moved to behind my neck, and he was so close that I could feel the warmth of his body absorbing into me. "They were women who I dated a few times—but they were friends from the start and knew it was only friendship. They were nothing like you."

I'd heard all of this over the phone, but having him stand next to me and seeing the look in his eyes made me realize how earnest he was. How could I have doubted him?

He went on. "I guess I was trying to deal with my own issues with my parents—my dad for leaving me and my mom for checking out. Maybe I thought if I could help someone, then it would fix me as well."

I placed my hand on his chest; his heart was beating rapidly.

"Can you ever forgive me?" he asked.

"Can you forgive me?" I asked back. We stared at each other for a long moment.

"I love you, Athena," he whispered. "And I'll never try to fix you."

I moved my hand up to his shoulder and breathed in his nearness. "That's good," I said, "because I really like these flowers."

Grey's arms went around me, and he lifted me up against him. We kissed, and we crushed the flowers between us. Roses had never smelled so good.

The only thought that went through my mind, other than the warmth and sweetness of Grey's lips on mine, was that I couldn't wait to tell the book club ladies.

Mom's Baklava

2 C. medium chopped walnuts
⅓ C. sugar
1 Tbsp. rose water or 1 tsp. vanilla

1 lb. phyllo dough
1 lb. butter

Sugar Syrup:
1 C. sugar
½ C. water
Juice of one small lemon or 2 Tbsp. lemon juice

To make sugar syrup: Dissolve sugar in water in a saucepan. Boil for 5–10 minutes, stirring constantly. Add lemon juice and boil for 1 more minute. The syrup should be thick enough to coat a spoon. Allow to cool.

Prepare the syrup before baking the phyllo dough. Brush a 9x13 pan or larger with melted butter. Cut phyllo dough to size of pan. Put 1–2 phyllo sheets into the pan at a time. Brush with melted butter; overlap or fold the sides over when necessary. Mix the chopped nuts with the sugar. After about ⅓ of the sheets have been put into the pan, spread about ⅓ of the nuts evenly over the phyllo dough. Add 1–2 more sheets of phyllo dough and spread on more nuts. Continue until the nuts are gone. Finish layering the rest of the phyllo dough, and brush each sheet (or two) with melted butter. Cut diagonally into lozenge shapes with a sharp knife— don't cut down to the bottom of the pan—just ½ inch or so. Bake the baklava for ½ hour at 350°F, then raise to 450°F until it becomes a light golden color. Remove from the oven and quickly pour the cold syrup over the hot baklava. Leave to cool.

When cold and ready to serve, cut the pieces of pastry out again and place them on a serving dish.

The Newport Ladies Book Club: Olivia
By Julie Wright

Chapter 1

HE WASN'T COMING HOME.

The grandfather clock I'd inherited when my mom died chimed eleven times, each marking the late hour and seeming to mock me for waiting as long as I had. The candles on the dining room table had burned to stubs, white wax dripping off the collars of the candlesticks and onto the table.

I stared at the wax, pooled and dried to the shiny oak surface, and couldn't even muster the ability to care that it was likely leaving a waxy ring that would never come out of the wood without stripping, sanding, and restaining. It was all work I'd do on my own. He'd be mad, and he'd comment on how it showed my lack of . . . whatever it was I should have. And then he'd fume silently for a while longer before moving on to something else that actually interested him, something that wasn't *me*, something that wasn't our anniversary dinner sitting cold around the two flames bobbing above their almost-spent candles.

Nick hadn't even called.

Hours had gone into preparing the dinner. Hours of my life I'd never get back. Creamed peas, asparagus with that maple-mustard sauce he loved, grilled lemon garlic halibut, and fresh homemade rolls. I scraped my chair back and blew out the flames, my breath sweeping more wax down onto the table.

I flipped on the light switch and pressed my palms into my temples as I paced around the table. *When did we come to this? How did we get to uneaten anniversary dinners?* We used to be a fun couple. We used to be the couple everyone envied—the one everyone wanted to be like. He used to be the one surprising me with flowers and kissing me loudly in front of our small children just to hear them say, "Ew! Gross!"

The pendulum of the clock ticked off every moment he wasn't home as though it were personally keeping track. *What should I do?*

With a sigh, it occurred to me that the only thing to do at the moment was clear the table and throw out the food since it had been sitting out for more than four hours. I'd picked at it after the first hour, taking nibbles from the sides where it wouldn't disrupt the visual effect—as if it had mattered. At least the only dishes I'd have to wash were the serving dishes and the cooking pans. *There. That's better. Find something positive. Breathe deeply, and look for something to be glad about.*

It sounded Pollyanna but was a habit I'd picked up as a child when my mom had snuggled under a lap blanket with me and watched old classics, *Pollyanna* among them, while thunder pounded the sky and wind howled through the rafters of my childhood home. Those had been good days in years filled with good days; I'd been held in the safety of my mother's arms, warm and loved and needed. The glad things in my life seemed endless at the time, and counting them all had sounded like fun.

Mom had encouraged me to be like Pollyanna. And later she told me my personality quirk had gotten her through some rough times in her own life. She'd once called me her life preserver. What would she say if she could see me now, clearing an uneaten meal from my dining table in a home too large to feel cozy and too cold to feel homey? A forty-one-year-old woman with four kids and a husband who didn't remember the plans of a special anniversary dinner? A woman who hid the gray sneaking into her brown hair with bottles of blonde dye? A woman who could find precious little in her cold, silent house to feel glad about?

The china plate I'd been holding slammed into the wall and shattered into an explosion of porcelain, startling me enough that I jumped.

But what startled me more than the fact that I'd thrown a grossly expensive plate into my decorator wall, leaving a dent of chipped blue paint and white drywall, was the fact that the action offered real relief.

I felt better having thrown the plate.

So I threw the other one.

And smiled.

Then frowned.

"You're an idiot, Livvy," I told myself. "Who do you think is going to clean that up?"

Talking to myself was a habit I'd picked up after my mom died four years ago. My dad had died before her. I had no siblings. Mom's passing left me vacant. She'd had a blood clot that had found its way to her brain when she'd been out watering her red hibiscus. The hose was still running, pointed up at a crazy angle, caught between her arm and body, when I'd found her. The mulch had floated on top of the little pond of water, and the drenched flowers had drooped with the water weight as though they were bowing their heads in respect for the woman who would no longer care for them.

I bowed my own head now. She was no longer caring for me either.

Even at forty-one, I needed my mommy. I blinked back the sting in my eyes for the want of her arms around my shoulders.

I went to the kitchen and came back with the dust pan and a little sweeper. "The same person who made the mess is the one who's going to be cleaning it, that's who." It's one thing to talk to yourself, but I'd started answering myself two years ago when I'd realized no one else ever did.

I stayed on my tiptoes to keep from crunching the glass into the hardwood floor as I swept around and under me, running the hand broom along the edge of the open cardboard boxes and into the dust pan before I dared to actually look *inside* the two boxes—donations to the library book drive in one box and my son's fourth grade volcano project in the other. Books and volcano both had a new coating of porcelain chunks and splinters.

Perfect.

"Just perfect!"

I stood up and dumped the contents of the dust pan into the trash then pulled out the vacuum and the hose attachments so I could suck the little shards out of the boxes without cutting myself. A lot of the sand used to make Tyler's volcano look more realistic and a couple of the plastic palm trees I'd picked up at the Newport Birthday Party Supply House went the way of vacuum bags. By the time I was done, I'd scratched up a couple of the books with the end of the hose and made the volcano scene look like the remnants of a long-dead planet. I hoped the books weren't first editions.

"What's all the noise in here?" Amanda stood in the doorway of the dining room, her arms folded across the pink tank top she slept in, which completely clashed with the green flannel bottoms covered in smiling skulls. She'd been studying at her friend's house and had planned on spending the night. Her brown hair strayed from the sloppy ponytail.

"Why are you home? I thought you were staying at Cassi's." It was just as well she'd come home. It wasn't like the big anniversary plans had panned out anyway. When Amanda said she'd be at her friend's and my oldest child, Chad, had said he'd be doing a game night at a buddy's house, I'd called the in-laws to see if they'd take Tyler and Marie. I didn't ask for those kinds of favors very often from my in-laws—even if they did live only a half hour away. The in-laws were complicated in ways that made me tired.

"Cassi's brother is a creep. He and his friends ate all the good food and then wouldn't turn off their stupid games. I finished the project and just want sleep now. What are you doing?" She stepped farther into the dining room.

"I dropped a plate. I needed to clean it up."

"You could do that in the morning. You're going to wake up Dad. It's like . . . midnight."

"Dad's not home yet." I didn't bother correcting her about the time. It was only just past eleven.

Her eyes swept quickly over the table, the candles, the dinner, and the dent in the wall. In less than a glance, understanding dawned on her face. "*Dropped* the plate, huh?"

I swallowed and looked down, feeling stupid for having been caught throwing the kind of tantrum she was famous for in our family.

She laughed. "Looks like you dropped it real hard against the wall." She wandered over to me and traced her fingers over the new dents. "Looks like you dropped it real hard against the wall *twice*."

Nothing could be said to dignify my actions. Not denial or admission. So I stayed quiet, feeling the heat crawl up my neck and into my face.

"Did he at least call?" she asked, the humor gone from her voice.

I shook my head and coiled the vacuum hose.

She took a sharp intake of breath, as if she'd been about to shout something but then had changed her mind. She nodded and gave me a gentle hug. "I'm going to bed. You should too." Her whisper was barely audible. She turned and left, her feet treading softly on the stairs like she still worried she might wake up her father who wasn't home.

By the time I'd cleaned up the dinner and the tantrum, my soul felt scoured. I checked the boxes again to make certain there weren't any stray bits of plate still hanging around and inspected the top book in the library box—Barbara Kingsolver's *The Poisonwood Bible*.

The dust jacket had been scratched pretty badly from my raking the hose nozzle over it. Donating something so damaged seemed uncharitable in every way. And they'd already asked us not to use the donations as a chance to discard worn and unwanted items but instead to try our best to donate quality merchandise. It had been quality merchandise when it had been donated by one of the neighbors.

I ran a finger along the new scars of the book. Reading had once been a favorite pastime. What had happened to time that actually belonged to me?

I hefted the book out of the box, liking the weight of it in my hands. It felt like something of substance, something more than the emptiness the evening had brought me. I opened the book and began to read.

Imagine a ruin so strange it must have never happened.

I read a few pages in, right up to the sentence:

I had washed up there on the riptide of my husband's confidence and the undertow of my children's needs.

I snapped the book closed, looking at my surroundings anew with those words echoing through me. I wasn't in Africa, wasn't in any jungle more ferocious than the 405 freeway, and yet, sitting there on the floor between boxes of charity and childhood, my hands dried out from antibacterial dish soap, I felt I *had* been washed up on the riptide of my husband's confidence and the undertow of my children's needs.

The house was in perfect shape, no dust—not even on the blades of the ceiling fans—nothing out of place or amiss in the Robbins household. Nicholas didn't yell or throw tantrums. He certainly never threw dishes at a wall. But over the years, he'd become silent. The silence felt like disapproval in so many ways. I kept thinking if I did things better, worked harder, he would start talking to me again.

He'd been married before, but it had ended badly . . . with him catching her and his best friend together having breakfast in bed—*his* bed. We had dated for almost two months before he'd confessed to having an ex-wife. Along with that information came the confession that he also had two small children.

He'd expected me to walk away. Looking back, sometimes it felt that he'd told me about his past and his two children with the *intention* of me walking away. But when I was excited to meet his kids and take on this new challenge, he finally opened up.

I felt like I'd passed a test. He knew my devotion was total. If an ex and two kids didn't make me waver, nothing would.

It had worked out well enough . . . in the beginning. His kids became my kids. And then we started having *our* kids—four of our own to add to his two. We should have been a happy family of eight. But somewhere along the way, Nick had compartmentalized his life from before and his life with me, no matter how hard I tried to mesh us all into one family unit. He distanced himself from things that weren't perfect. His previous marriage had been imperfect, and he distanced himself from that life— even the kids from that life.

But I was also imperfect. Is that why he distanced himself from me? My body had filled out over the years, going from a toned size six to a softened size twelve. And I *did* throw dishes at the wall—not that he'd ever know about that because I'd never admit to it and Mandy would never rat me out. I'd pull out the spackle and paint tomorrow and fix it myself. Calling someone to fix it would require paying a bill I'd have to explain later. I stared at the newly bruised wall and hoped a repair job was possible.

But so what if it wasn't?

What if my patch-up job looked worse? Who was around to care? My undertow children were all nestled away in beds somewhere, and my riptide husband had yet to make an appearance. I scrambled to my feet— my body not reacting to my brain's commands as swiftly or as easily as it once had—dropped *The Poisonwood Bible* on the table—I'd been right about the wax leaving its mark on the table—and headed to the front door.

I needed some air.

Walking at night was not a habit of mine. I lived in an upscale area, but it was still California, and smart women didn't go walking around on their own at midnight without at least a bottle of pepper spray and a cell phone. But anger fueled the walk. Any punk kid who might try messing with me would find himself turned upside down in a dumpster.

My anger flowed from one source.

Nick.

He would excuse himself tomorrow with, "I had to work late." And that would be the last of it.

But it wouldn't be the last of it. He'd do it again. And again. And again.

What killed me was the wondering. Was it work? He was a CFO at Soft Tekk. Could that work be exciting enough to keep him hours away from his home? Was it a woman—a secretary, a coworker, a barmaid he'd met in some dark, smoke-filled place where he could watch a Lakers game without the kids running through the house making noise? Or was it worse? Was it simply the fact that he'd rather do *anything* than be with me?

He escaped our marriage every day through the convenient excuse called work. And yet his life spun a web around me that held me cocooned in place while he came back on occasion to feed on my energy.

His house. His children. His community. *My* responsibility. Riptide.

I turned toward the shops. Too bad it was the middle of the night. No comfort shopping for me. I passed a nail spa in a strip mall. No comfort manicures either—not that I ever really indulged in things like that. It was an expensive habit, and the kids were always needing something that competed for the financial attention. A few doors down from the nail spa, a blue flyer taped to the door flitted in the night breeze. In a brief moment of need, I imagined it was waving to me— asking me to stop and read whatever message it had for me and me alone.

Looking for serious readers to join the Newport Ladies Book Club.
Women only! Eating and good conversation!
Space limited. Call Ruby Crenshaw asap.

I looked up to see the sign above the shop. *Grey's Used & Rare Books.* A book club. How long had it been since I'd held a novel in my hands for the sheer pleasure of losing myself in its pages? How long had it been since I'd held any book without needing to stuff it in a box for charity or a backpack for a child or a shelf to put it away for when the riptide wanted it?

No. That wasn't fair. Calling Nick a riptide every four seconds would get me nowhere. Find something glad.

But there wasn't anything glad I could associate with Nick at that moment. Even the fact that I lived in a beautiful home and had beautiful children just made me tired—not glad at all. It reminded me of schedules and soccer games and visits to the dry cleaners and grocery shopping and school functions and Junior League meetings and volunteer work and cleaning a house that never felt like home anymore. Tired.

The breeze picked up, and the little flyer waved at me again. I pulled the blue paper from the door, feeling guilty for removing it and hoping the bookstore owner had a spare to put up. Even if I didn't have to face my minister every Sunday, I hated taking anything that wasn't mine.

Depression replaced anger for the walk home. I blinked away the sting in my eyes again, imagining him cuddling up with some flirty female who wasn't me.

But the accusation in that image wasn't fair either. Nick had once been the victim of infidelity. Cheating was something he abhorred, something that made him physically ill. Nick was the last man on the planet who would be the cheater. He didn't even cheat at Monopoly back when he'd stayed home long enough to play a game with us. And there had been no evidence of infidelity—aside from his absence.

But what did absence prove, if not infidelity? It proved he didn't care enough to be with me. Another woman or not, I'd been rejected. He didn't need or want me.

I looked down at the paper in my hand and considered it. The woman's name was Ruby. I needed something with the ability to shine in my life. A ruby was as good as anything. And for the first time since setting the table for dinner, I found something to be truly glad about. Because I was going to, for once, do the selfish thing. I was going to join a book group, read, eat, and have good conversation.

About the Author

HEATHER B. MOORE IS A two-time Best of State and Whitney Award–winning author of several novels. She lives at the base of the Rocky Mountains with her husband, four children, and one black cat. Her favorite holiday is Halloween, when she tells fortunes to all of the unfortunate children who dare to visit. Visit Heather's website at www.hbmoore.com.